Texas Blue

**Center Point
Large Print**

Texas Blue

JODI THOMAS

CENTER POINT LARGE PRINT
THORNDIKE, MAINE

This Center Point Large Print edition
is published in the year 2011 by arrangement with
Berkley Books, a member of Penguin Group (USA) Inc.

The text of this Large Print edition is unabridged.
In other aspects, this book may vary
from the original edition.
Printed in the United States of America
on permanent paper.
Set in 16-point Times New Roman type.

ISBN: 978-1-61173-089-0

Library of Congress Cataloging-in-Publication Data

Thomas, Jodi.
Texas blue : a whispering mountain novel / Jodi Thomas.
p. cm.
ISBN 978-1-61173-089-0 (library binding : alk. paper)
1. Texas—Fiction. 2. Large type books. I. Title.
PS3570.H5643T493 2011
813'.54—dc22

2011008376

Texas
Blue

ᛒᢙ CHAPTER 1 ᏟᏋ

November 19, 1875
South of Austin, Texas

Dust circled like tiny whirlwinds in the shadowy barn as a dozen Texas Rangers saddled horses and prepared to ride.

Lewton Paterson, dressed in his best white suit, moved among them, a stranger amid these heroes. As always, he felt alone no matter how many surrounded him, but tonight his solitude was almost suffocating. He told himself he was never brave and had no desire to risk his life for any cause, yet the excitement around him seemed contagious.

Rangers were just normal men, he reminded himself. They didn't even wear a uniform, only the dusty weathered clothes of men born to the wilderness. Lewton matched their height and probably most of their skills, but he wasn't one of them. He never would be.

For Lewt knew his heart. He had never been, nor would ever be, daring. In twenty-eight years he'd seen nothing worth risking his life for, nothing he loved worth dying to protect. If he hadn't found it by now, he never would. For him, life was a game and the man leaving the table with the most chips won.

"Lewt!" Duncan McMurray yelled from ten feet away. His half-wild horse stomped around the ranger and snorted as Duncan saddled the mount as casually as if they were dancing. "You decide to give up gambling and join us on our quest?"

Lewt slipped between two horses and joined his friend. "Compared to rangering, gambling seems like a peaceful profession. Where are you men headed tonight?"

"The border." Duncan pulled the cinch tight across the mare's belly before he added, "Chasing cattle rustlers. Captain McNelly says we'll cross the river tracking them down even if the army won't. Ranches have lost enough cattle to cowards who run across the border to hide."

Lewt shook his head. He'd met the tall, bone-thin Leander McNelly. He was just crazy enough to follow outlaws straight into hell, and these men—including Duncan—would ride right beside him. Duncan McMurray was a successful lawyer, like his father, by trade, but a wild kid ran in his blood. "Maybe you should sit this one out, Duncan. You're due to leave at dawn with that load of potential husbands for your cousins. No one expects you to ride with the rangers every time."

Duncan frowned as he strapped on his gear, and Lewt sensed he'd already had this argument with himself. "There's been a change of plans. The 'suitors' will have to handle matters without me. I'm needed here. One ranger less in this fight might swing the balance. Besides, I sent all three men the train tickets and reserved rooms for them at Crystal's place across from the station if they need a room tonight. If they're too dumb to figure out that they need to get off at Anderson Glen tomorrow night, hire a buggy, and drive out to Whispering Mountain, they're sure too dumb to marry my cousins. The three men coming to court the girls can consider getting there their first test."

Lewt laughed. "You don't fool me, Duncan, you hate playing matchmaker. You're running out on the job! I've always had the feeling you're half afraid of those girls."

Duncan opened his mouth to argue, then shrugged. "I grew up with them pestering me. They made my life hell wanting me to play with them, or worse, wash more than once a week. There's not a man in the state good enough for any one. My dad, being a former ranger, will understand why I have to ride tonight, but my uncle Teagen's bound to throw a fit. I could send out royalty and he'd still find fault in any man thinking of marrying his little girls." Duncan swore. "Only they're not little girls anymore. All three are well on their way to being old maids."

"How about letting me go along?" Lewt teased his friend. "I wouldn't mind a chance to marry into one of the finest families in Texas."

Duncan swung into the saddle laughing. "No offense, friend, but if I sent out someone like you

9

to the ranch, my father and uncles would take turns shooting me and they wouldn't waste but one bullet. They'd shoot me, dig it out, load up, and shoot me again."

"Come on, Duck." Lewt used Duncan's nickname as he grinned.

"Forget it, Lewt. You'd be the last man in Texas I'd send home to meet my cousins." Duncan looked down at the gambler. "One look at you and the girls would have you run off the ranch. They may be home alone without any of the McMurray men around, but don't think they're helpless."

Lewt looked down at his tailored white suit, his colorful vest, his diamond ring. He dressed exactly like what he was, a successful gambler. He knew most of the powerful men in the state capital by their first names and they trusted him to arrange high-stakes games for them where the dealing would be honest, but not one of these rich and powerful men would take him home to meet their daughters or sisters. Duncan wouldn't even let him meet his cousins. The young McMurray women, heirs to one of the biggest, richest ranches in Texas, probably wouldn't speak to him anyway. Most of the *good folks* in this state thought the government should pay a bounty on gambler pelts.

Lewt waved farewell to Duncan McMurray and the other rangers, realizing no one thought he was good enough to be in any family. If they knew his roots, they'd be positive. His pedigree was so bad he was surprised the dogcatcher didn't try to cage him. Still, it would be interesting to get an inside look at a real family.

As the rangers rode south, Lewt walked back toward Crystal's place. It was probably too late to get in on a high-stakes game, but he didn't feel sleepy. Duncan might not want to take him home to meet the family, but they were still good friends and Lewt would worry about him until he saw the dust-covered ranger step back into the bar and demand beer.

He smiled and lifted his hand to wave at the trail of vanishing riders. Some would say the backstreets of any Texas small town were as dangerous as fighting outlaws, but for Lewt, this was home. The drunks and the beggars were as much his family as the gamblers and the dealers.

If he had been allowed to go home to meet the ladies, Duncan might have been surprised. One or more of them might have found him more than tolerable. After all, he wasn't as bad a choice as Duncan seemed to think. He'd never hit a woman. A few of the ladies at Crystal's claimed he was a grand lover, and he had money stashed in half the banks in Texas. Every saloon girl he'd ever met had mooned over him, so he couldn't be bad looking.

Lewt grinned. He wouldn't have cared if Duncan's cousin was homely as sin and toothless, he might have married her just so he could have a

11

good family; he'd just insist the lights go out when he came home at night.

A family, he laughed. There was no use dreaming. It wasn't something that he'd ever have, and marrying a woman just in the hopes of getting one would be cruel.

℘ CHAPTER 2 ℞

Lewt Paterson walked into Crystal's not interested in gambling tonight, or drinking. He needed to think, and a noisy bar felt more like home than anywhere on earth. He ordered a beer and looked around for an empty table near the back. Duncan had gotten him dreaming about getting married and living a respectable life. He needed to wash such thoughts out of his head and accept reality. Wives and children didn't belong in his world, and he had no idea how to step out of it into another.

His gaze came to rest on a stranger dressed in black, sitting alone at a table with fine leather luggage piled around him. A tall man about Lewt's size with glasses perched on a nose that must have taken generations of money to breed. His clothes were expensive, but conservatively tailored, his pale skin Boston light. Boredom seemed permanently tattooed across his face.

Lewt knew without a doubt that he was looking at one of Duncan's picks to go north at dawn and court his cousins. The stranger might as well have had old money pinned all over his chest.

Lewt ordered a second beer and wound his way toward the potential bridegroom for the cousins. Duncan had said he'd picked only from the finest families and insisted they all be well educated.

The man didn't look up from his book as Lewt neared—an easterner's mistake in any western bar. Lewt only hoped the stranger would live long enough to learn.

"Pardon me, mister, but I was supposed to meet a Duncan McMurray tonight and he doesn't seem to be around. He said he would be with a gentleman in his late twenties, and you're the only man in the bar who might fit the description he gave me."

The stranger looked up. "What description was that?" he said in a bored tone.

"Tall, distinguished, obviously from a good family." Lewt smiled. Flattery worked every time. "Any chance you are a friend of Mr. McMurray?"

"I know him, but I'll not call him a friend."

The stranger had just made his second mistake. Never admit anything to any man until you knew you could trust him.

The stranger moved his book as Lewt set the drinks on the table. "McMurray never said anything about my meeting anyone tonight. In fact, I hadn't planned to set foot in this place." His pale eyes studied Lewt from flashy clothes to fancy hand-tooled boots.

Lewt had no doubt the stranger found him lacking, but he didn't care. "You did get the train ticket and the instructions?"

His question caught the man off-guard.

"Yes," he stuttered slightly. "And the room key, but I wish to inform Mr. McMurray that the room was not at all satisfactory. I'd rather sit up for the night than be subjected to such filth."

"Crystal's rooms are some of the best around, I've heard." Lewt took a seat, acting interested in the complainer's problems. He served the beer without expecting a thank-you.

"Sir, you wouldn't believe it, but the sheets were dirty." The stranger sampled a drink, then showed his distaste for the local brew before taking another swallow. "When I informed the staff I needed the linens changed, they told me it wasn't Wednesday yet. Can you imagine?"

"Horrible." Lewt offered his hand. "Harry's the name. Harry West." He'd learned a long time ago that people rarely remember common names, and he had no intention of ever seeing this fool again after tonight.

"Walter Freeport the Fourth," the stranger said. "I don't know about you, Mr. West, but I've seriously considered backing out on this visit my family seems to think might be worth my while. If conditions near the capital are so primitive, what must it be like in the mountains?"

Lewt played along. "I'm inclined to agree with

you. One has to wonder what these princesses of Texas must look like if they have to search far and wide and offer passage from anywhere to eligible men. And I've even heard that the ranch is in the hills of Texas. The word *mountain* came when they translated the place from its Indian name." He lifted two fingers at the bartender, silently ordering whiskey. "It's said the ranch is so huge, Apache still make winter camps in its hills."

Fear flashed in Walter's eyes. He took the whiskey delivered and downed it quickly. Then, somewhat calmed, he raised his eyebrow and studied Lewt's clothes. He had the look of a man tolerating someone lesser than himself.

Lewt grinned into his beer as he shoved the second whiskey in front of Walter. He was in. Accepted. It might be interesting to spend some time with the stranger. Lewt considered himself a good judge of character and had already figured out that Duncan hadn't come face-to-face with Walter or he wouldn't have sent the man a ticket. "This your first time west, Mr. Freeport?"

"And my last," Walter answered. "If I find one of the McMurray women to my liking, I'll be making it plain from the beginning that we'll live north with my family."

"Wise choice," Lewt said, thinking this fellow didn't have a chance of taking a McMurray anywhere. "The women here are beautiful, though," he added.

"Not from what I've seen. One of the girls who works here followed me to my room and offered her services. She wasn't even pretty and when she had the nerve to touch me, I was forced to slap her hard." Walter brushed at his coat as if the touch had left a stain.

Lewt gripped the mug in his hand so hard he wouldn't have been surprised to see the glass shatter. He'd like nothing better than to slam his fist into Walter Freeport the Fourth's straight little nose. The girl he'd hit was just trying to make a living. She didn't deserve to be slapped. "What happened?" Lewt finally asked.

"She crawled away." Walter smiled. "A woman who doesn't know her place is a stain on nature. I'm telling you, sir, that if I weren't a gentleman I might have kicked her to help her along the way."

Lewt watched Walter as he talked on about his philosophy, but Lewt had already made up his mind. If he had to tie Walter Freeport up in dirty sheets, this man would not be on the train at dawn. He didn't even know Duncan's cousins, but they deserved better than the likes of this man.

As the evening passed, Lewt wasn't sure when the idea crystallized into a plan, but he decided maybe he should take Walter's place. At first he thought it might be a grand joke on his friend Duncan, then he thought it could probably be a great chance to see what a real working ranch was like and to see how a real loving family acted. It might be worth the trip to see what he'd missed out on. Lewt guessed, like everything else in life, family ties weren't all they were cracked up to be. He could be nice and polite to the ladies. At least they wouldn't feel like they'd been stood up. When Duncan got back, Lewt would explain everything.

His mind made up, Lewt turned to Walter Freeport the Fourth. "Any chance you play cards?"

Walter strutted. "I do, and I must warn you I'm quite good. What say you we pass the time with a friendly game?"

Lewt grinned. No matter what he put on the table, he knew he'd be playing to help the women of Whispering Mountain out and it felt good. They might never know, but he was saving them from a horrible fate.

Six hours later, a very different Lewton Paterson stepped on the northbound train. He was dressed in conservative black from head to toe with thin wire-rim glasses on his nose. Nothing remained from his former life except the double eagle gold piece in his pocket he always carried for luck and a knife slipped between the stitching of his belt. Everything else, from his fine leather suitcases to his watch, spoke of old money and breeding.

By the time Duncan McMurray got finished fighting at the Mexican border, Lewt would be on Whispering Mountain. If he did nothing else, he'd prove to Duncan that he could be a gentleman . . . someone worth introducing to the family.

Lewt could play the gentleman. He'd learned early that men like to play cards with a man they consider an equal. He'd spent months polishing his speech and learning which fork to use on a fancy table. Now, there'd be no bets on the table. This time, he was gambling with his future.

A hope began to form in his mind. If he could pass at Whispering Mountain, maybe he could take all the money he'd saved and buy a business. Maybe he could even marry and live a life in the daylight for a change.

Lewt pushed his dreaming down. Hope was a terrible thing. It would keep you warm now and then, but when it died the cold always came back more bitter than before.

ℬ CHAPTER 3 ℛ

Duncan McMurray rode through the night surrounded by a dozen other Texas Rangers. He couldn't help but feel like he was running away from his duty to the family, but this time, more then any other as a ranger, he was needed. Finding husbands for his three cousins would have to wait.

Every man traveling with Captain Leander McNelly knew they didn't have the numbers to do what had to be done. They all knew they were riding into hell and might not be coming back. Duncan laughed to himself, thinking the rangers had always been long on courage and short on brains. When they died in the line of duty, few commented, but when they won, despite the odds, they became legends.

Since the War Between the States, bandits from across the border had been raiding cattle off ranches in Texas. At least a hundred fifty thousand head had vanished, not counting the hundreds stolen by small-time outlaws hiding out in canyons within the state. Someone had to stop them, and Captain McNelly seemed in a hurry to take on the job.

After the war, Texas fell into chaos on many fronts. Most men who came home were heartsick as well as broken in body. They'd fought for Texas thinking of it as sovereign and free to step away from the Union. The issue of slavery hadn't made them raise their guns, but it had made them put them down. Most were lucky if they came home with a horse and a weapon.

Duncan had been a kid when the war ended. He and the girls had stayed at Whispering Mountain. Teagen, the oldest and the head of the McMurray clan, was too old to enlist. He ran the ranch and supplied as many horses as he could, while Travis, Duncan's adopted father, stayed in Austin. His wounds as a ranger kept him from enlisting, and his battles were in the courts.

Tobin, the youngest of the three McMurray brothers, was torn. In the end, he couldn't fight against his wife's people. He served as sheriff in town until the war was over. He tried to keep peace in their part of Texas. He also bought a piece of land near Anderson Glen and plowed it every spring, then planted enough vegetables to feed the town through winter. Duncan and every kid at the ranch big enough to ride spent every Saturday all summer delivering food to those who couldn't come out and harvest their own.

Sage, the McMurray brothers' baby sister, had married not long before the war. Her husband, Drummond Roak, joined Terry's Rangers with his friends and fought. Few thought he'd make it home alive, but Sage never doubted. She just said that he'd promised he would. Three months after the war ended, he walked onto the ranch. He was so thin she didn't recognize him at first, but once he was home they promised never to be more than yelling distance apart.

Duncan slowed his horse to a walk and smiled. Memories of the McMurrays, his family, kept him warm. He and Teagen's girls were the oldest of the children, and it was probably time they all married and settled down. He only hoped at least one of the three men he sent north on the train would prove a match. They were all from good families, and none had a drinking or gambling problem. Boyd Sinclair already ran his family ranch, Davis Allender was well educated, and Walter Freeport the Fourth came highly recommended by a friend of his father.

Deep down Duncan knew none of them were good enough. No man ever would be. At different times in his childhood he'd hated all three girls and loved each one. Emily, just older than him, had been his best friend when they'd been about twelve. They'd ridden the ranch and built forts all one summer, but after she went away to finishing school she barely spoke to him. Rose always drove him crazy bossing him around, but he knew she'd be at his side if trouble came. And then there was Bethie. Who couldn't love Beth? Sometimes he'd just stare at her, wondering how she could have been born so beautiful. He was in love with her until the fourth grade when she started calling him Duckie instead of Duck. A nickname of Duck was hard enough to live down. Calls of Duckie from the other guys got him into a dozen fights that year and cured him of loving Bethie.

"You're getting behind, McMurray," Wyatt Platt said as he passed like a shadow in the darkness.

"Just resting my horse, Wyatt. I'll catch up," Duncan answered. His body might be heading into a fight, but tonight his mind was only on thoughts of home.

"I almost rode right into you. With that black horse you're darn near invisible." Wyatt never learned to whisper. He talked as he lived, at full volume.

Duncan laughed. "I could say the same about you, but I've been smelling you for half a mile. Did you ever think about giving the folks around you a break and taking a bath?"

"Is it spring?" the shadow beside him asked.

"My ma always sewed me into my long johns in late September and didn't cut them off me until March. She swears that's why she raised six of the healthiest kids in Tennessee."

Duncan laughed. "More likely no one with a cold would get within ten feet of you. All those brothers and sisters still alive?"

"Yeah, all except me are married and raising families."

"Did you have any trouble getting the girls married off? I got these three cousins who don't seem to take to the idea much. They're all in their twenties and some folks are commenting that they're getting pretty ripe on the vine."

"Nope," Wyatt answered. "My oldest sister was married to three different men during the war. She figured whichever one came home first was the keeper. Course, she packed up and left for Texas the day after the first one arrived just in case the other two didn't see it that way."

"He didn't mind that she'd been two-timing him with two other men?"

Wyatt laughed. "I never heard him say. He did tell me once that he was lucky he didn't have to pay for the lessons her third husband taught her about how to act under the covers. They're living down by Galveston and last I heard they had so many kids they stopped naming them and just started numbering. So, I'm guessing what she learned they're still practicing."

Duncan smiled with his friend. Wyatt was five years older and tough as thick jerky, but he never believed in giving up. He'd die fighting.

Wyatt's shadow moved on, vanishing in the night. Duncan wouldn't count him among his closest friends, but they'd cover each other in any fight. Because they both followed Captain McNelly, they were alike in the way they felt about protecting Texas.

When the rangers had been reorganized after the war, a second group called the Special Force was formed under a thirty-year-old captain named Leander McNelly. McNelly might be thin as a fence post and look half sick most of the time, but he had thirty rangers riding to his call tonight. The captain had learned by messenger that Juan Flores had stolen a herd of cattle and crossed the Rio Grande, thinking he wouldn't be pursued. The captain was determined to capture Flores even if he had to cross the Rio to do it.

Duncan wanted to be there, to fight and to be part of history in the making. He'd help the girls get married off and add lots of kids to the family tree, but Duncan had a wild streak he knew would never allow him to settle down.

They rode until the sun was high, then turned their horses out to graze while they slept a few hours. By dusk they were near the border. Thirty rangers met three companies of U.S. Cavalry camped along the river's edge.

Captain McNelly talked to the soldiers while Duncan and the others rested. They knew what was coming and they knew they needed to be ready. Duncan checked his weapons while Wyatt checked his saddle. None of the rangers talked. The time for talking was over; soon it would be time to fight.

A little after midnight McNelly gave the command. Thirty rangers swung onto their horses and stormed the Rio, heading straight across to Juan Flores's ranch, called Las Cuevas ("The Caves").

Duncan McMurray rode in the middle of the group. The river was tricky and the far side looked steep, but that didn't bother him near as much as the fact that not one cavalryman followed.

His mare took the water well. McMurray horses were raised on a ranch surrounded on two sides by water. By the time he was twelve, his uncles had taught him how to handle a horse in currents.

Before dawn the rangers would be facing down two hundred raiders. The thought made him laugh suddenly. Every ranger he knew would say the odds were about even. The only thing that really bothered Duncan was the fact that they would be fighting on Mexican soil.

Duncan kicked his horse and moved past some of the others. If he was riding into hell, he might as well have a good view.

℘ CHAPTER 4 ℘

November 20, 1875

Lewton Paterson settled into the private car Duncan had reserved for the three men traveling north. His friend had paid for the entire car, probably planning to get to know the men before they reached Whispering Mountain. Though the train car wasn't plush, it was comfortable with a stocked bar. There was a seating area for six and a game table for four as well as a few chairs by the windows for those who wanted to watch the country moving by in solitude. The car cost Duncan ten times what three seats up front in standard would have cost, but McMurray obviously wanted to impress the men.

Remembering Walter Freepost the Fourth from the saloon last night, Lewt doubted the man would have been impressed, but Lewt was. He'd spent more time riding with the horses than in seats on trains, and even a simple car like this seemed pure luxury.

I could get used to this, he thought. *Who knows, they might like me at the ranch. Maybe I could just pick the McMurray woman I like best. Maybe she wouldn't think being married to me was so bad. Every time we travel I'll insist she has the best, and, of course, I'll be right by her side.* There was a time when he'd thought the good life was eating regularly; now he wanted more, but dreaming wouldn't make it happen and he knew this journey would be no more than a dream. In real life, rich women from good families don't marry gamblers. But if he was going to dream, he planned to at least let the next few days be a good dream. At the end of the week he could go back to reality.

He recalled how peacefully Walter the Fourth had been snoring as he and the bartender from Crystal's loaded him on a train heading to California just before dawn. Lewt had changed clothes with the man, of course, and taken half of his luggage in one turn of the cards. Like most bad gamblers, Walter wouldn't accept his losses and quit. He kept offering Lewt more and more to toss into the pot. Lewt made sure that once the man sobered up somewhere in the territories, Walter would have enough money for passage back home, though he doubted Walter would have done the same for him if the cards had played out differently.

Lewt had worked three months, spending only what he had to, sleeping in borrowed bunks and eating the salty, free food on the bar, in order to save enough to buy the suit and ring he'd packed away. At the time he saw it as a symbol of wealth, but he wouldn't wear it for this trip. For the next week he'd play his part. Maybe even flirt with the ladies a little.

If Walter Freeport the Fourth was fool enough to come back to Austin, he'd never find the Harry West he'd had drinks with last night.

Lewt smiled. The ladies didn't know it, but even if they picked him as a husband, they'd be doing better than Walter. If he ever had a lady at his side, he'd treat her like a queen.

A rattling came from the platform as suitcases and feet hit the metal steps. Lewt turned to welcome the other guests for the trip and size up his competition.

A young man in his early twenties stepped in first loaded down with bags. He wasn't tall, but he had a wide smile and a good honest face. If Lewt were guessing, he'd say the young man was not more than a year out of school. Probably one of those big colleges back east.

Behind him stood a short woman who barely fit through the door. She carried a birdcage and wore a hat almost a foot high as if the feathers and bows would somehow make her taller.

"This is it, Mother," the young man said. "Isn't it nice? I'm sure we'll be comfortable here."

The little lady's cheeks dimpled with pleasure. "Lovely," she said in a sweet voice. "I'm sure I'll be fine, but I worry about coming along, Davis. It isn't right to just show up."

"It's all right," Davis said as he settled her on the small love seat across from Lewt. "I'm sure no one will mind. I've no doubt the McMurrays are as used to entertaining on a moment's notice as we are at home. When Uncle Phil wrote Duncan, he said the Allenders would always be welcome at his family ranch. Besides"—he winked—"they'll love you. Everyone does."

Lewt stood politely and introduced himself, using his own name but adding *the Third* to it, hoping that would add respectability.

Davis Allender and his mother seemed delighted to have the company. Apparently she'd been visiting friends and checking on her son when the invitation came from Duncan. There had been no time for her to write ahead and ask if she could accompany her son, and the young man didn't look like the type who would abandon his mother even to go courting.

Mrs. Allender was one of those women made of sugar, Lewt decided. She had apple round cheeks and tiny hands as white as bleached cotton. She preceded every question with "If you don't mind my asking . . ." or "If you'll be so kind to tell us . . ." When Lewt showed her kindness and respect, he won the approval of both the Allenders.

He even told her the bird was cute, when in truth he was sure it was the ugliest thing he'd ever seen. Mother Nature must have had an off day to put the strange colors of feathers together.

Before he could settle back in his chair, another man boarded. He was of medium build, but he carried himself with the confidence of a warrior preparing to face a battle. His handshake was fast, his grip tight, his speech clipped, as though he didn't want to waste a moment more than necessary with small talk.

Lewt couldn't figure out whether he liked the man, and from the way Davis Allender watched him, neither could the young man.

"I'm Boyd Sinclair," the stranger announced. "Rode half the night to make it in time for this train." He seemed to look around as if to make sure everyone was listening, then added, "I had my man load my horses. Can't wait to see how the McMurray horses measure up to my stock."

Davis grinned. "I thought we were going to meet the ladies, not the horses."

"Of course," Boyd nodded. "I'm just thinking ahead. Normally, I wouldn't travel to meet a woman, but I've heard of the Whispering Mountain stock. The trip will be worth it just to examine their lines, and if I happen to find a suitable bride, all the better."

Mrs. Allender whispered, "Oh my."

Lewt laughed, then whispered back to only her, "I do hope he's talking about the horses when he mentioned examining their lines."

The little lady blushed.

They all took their seats as the train started to roll. Mrs. Allender looked nervous, but as soon as the train leveled off in speed, her son was up walking the length of the car as if he could help move the train along faster.

Lewt decided to play the host and offered everyone a drink. Mrs. Allender took water, Davis asked if there was any hot tea, and Boyd asked for brandy.

While Lewt rummaged in the tiny pantry, young Davis leaned into the doorway and asked, "How long?"

"Before the trains it would have taken three or four days, I'm guessing, but now, we'll be there before dark." Lewt had never been this far north, but he'd heard Duncan talk about the trip when he went home. Texas had been settled from south to north. The farther up the state you went, the more western and less southern the country and the people became.

Boyd Sinclair leaned on the other side of the tiny pantry door. "I'd rather have made the trip on horseback, but Duncan informed me that the offer to stay at Whispering Mountain was only extended for this week. We arrive tonight and leave the following Saturday morning." He gave the other two men a curious look. "I got the feeling these McMurrays are none too free with invitations. Folks in San Antonio say there's only one way into their land. It's over a bridge, and twice they've burned the bridge to keep people off their land."

Davis shrugged. "Duncan asked me three months ago when I came by his office with plans for a new federal building. I'm just the junior architect on the job, but he said then that if the time was right, he'd love me to see his home and meet the family. I thought he was just being polite, but two days ago, he asked me again."

Lewt handed them both their drinks and carried his and Mrs. Allender's water back to the seating area. He asked a few questions, but gave nothing about himself away. The conversation moved from Boyd talking about himself and his adventures and Davis talking about the rich blends of architecture that made Texas unique.

Around one o'clock a porter brought a lunch of fruit and sandwiches. They all moved to the table to eat, then settled into different areas. Mrs. Allender leaned into the love seat and napped. Davis pulled out what looked like a sketchbook and took a seat by the window. Boyd propped his feet on the chair across from him and snored the afternoon away.

Lewt took the other single seat by the window and watched the land move by as he planned. He'd always believed in chances, in playing the odds. No matter how bad his life was, he'd never lost hope that someday, somehow, a chance would open up and he'd be able to make his life better.

Looking back, he realized that from where he started there wasn't anywhere but up. He'd been born to the town drunk and the woman who cleaned rooms and did laundry at a whorehouse. His father told him once that his mother was too ugly to be a whore, but even when Lewt tried, he couldn't remember what she looked like.

His first memories were of sitting in the rain waiting for his father to wake up. He'd passed out before they'd made it home, and Lewt was too little to find his way through the backstreets of New Orleans in the dark.

His mother died before he started school and his dad made an effort to stay sober enough to work. Lewt wasn't old enough to count the months, but he remembered his father bringing home the first of a string of women before summer was over. Some were kind to him, but most showed little interest. They all made him go to school, more to get him out from underfoot than anything else.

No matter what happened, Lewt always believed that somehow a chance would come. The nice women told him to call them Mother, but they still wouldn't take him with them when they left. The mean ones were usually kicked out by his dad. But, good or bad, when they left, the same thing happened; Lewt's dad stayed drunk until all the money ran out.

During those weeks, Lewt found it safer to disappear. Once a bartender caught him sleeping just inside the back door of a saloon. He was a big Swede who'd left his children back home when he'd come west. He offered Lewt a job in exchange for a cot in the kitchen and a meal.

Lewt took the job. He worked unnoticed by the drunks and women of the night who came through.

He watched and learned. While most kids his age were fishing and playing after school, Lewt was learning to read people. He learned that if he dressed up and wore clean clothes, folks treated him better. They'd give him two bits to watch their horses or run an errand. He figured out when it paid to be invisible and how to lift the change off a drunk as he helped him out the door.

After his father dropped by a few times and took the money he'd saved, Lewt learned about banks. He swore he'd never be poor again, so every town he traveled to that had a bank, Lewt opened an account.

To the rhythm of the train, he drifted to sleep thinking of what it would be like to have a home. He'd never owned anything he couldn't pack in a suitcase. He'd never belonged anywhere. New Orleans had been the first town he remembered the name of, but there had been other towns, other places before. Once he was old enough, he took the boat from New Orleans to Galveston and began to work his way around Texas.

Some towns were so lawless he slept with a gun next to his pillow. Others were so settled there wasn't room for a man like him. When he reached Austin, he found the perfect mixture.

The train pulled to a stop at Anderson Glen, rattling everyone in the car awake. Davis jumped up, collecting his bags and helping his mother. Boyd ran to help with the unloading of his horses, and Lewt stood on the platform and studied the sleepy little town.

Duncan had told him once that the town near his ranch had been little more than a trading post when he was a boy, but now, Lewt saw streets, churches, a school, businesses, and a bank. When he married one of the McMurray women, he might buy one of the hotels, or maybe a general store, and this town looked as good as any to settle in.

He checked the watch that had once belonged to Four. If the bank had been open, Lewt would have made a deposit. He liked making deposits. Tellers who wouldn't speak to him on the street would call him sir as they counted out his money. Once he had an account, he felt like he somehow belonged.

Davis walked up beside Lewt. "Any idea where we can get a buggy?"

"We could probably rent one," Lewt said, "but my guess is that rig over there is for us."

A cowhand walked toward them and tipped his hat. "Name's Sumner," he said around a cheek full of tobacco. "I'm looking for three gentlemen bound for Whispering Mountain." He was polite, but not overly friendly. "Any chance you gentlemen are two of them?"

Lewt smiled. "We are, and this sweet young lady"—he motioned toward Mrs. Allender—"is accompanying us this evening."

The cowhand didn't question, he just helped with the luggage. They moved to the end of the platform and Davis helped his mother in while Lewt and the cowhand loaded the luggage.

Sumner looked old, but he might still be in his forties. He had a slight limp, but Lewt guessed he wasn't a man who liked questions. During these days in Texas a curious stranger usually got a wooden cross for free when he departed town.

"Any idea where the third gentleman might be?" Sumner asked as he bit off another chew of tobacco.

Lewt raised his head as two men flew by on horses already at full gallop. "Yep," he said. "He just passed us. My guess is he doesn't plan to give the buggy the chance to slow him down."

One side of Sumner's mouth rose in a quick grin. "I never slow down a fool."

"What makes you think he's a fool?" Lewt wasn't arguing, only asking.

The old cowhand lifted himself onto the front bench. "He's headed the wrong direction."

Lewt laughed and climbed in.

℅ CHAPTER 5 ℃

The sky had already turned to night when Emily McMurray watched the wagon cross the bridge and roll onto Whispering Mountain Ranch. She'd been standing in the loft opening above the barn fighting the urge to ride out and dynamite the bridge. Like her papa, Teagen McMurray, she hated strangers on her land. Her adopted father had taught her well how to run the ranch, and now with him away she planned to do just that. Tall and slender, she looked like a young man in her trousers and loose shirt, with her blond hair tucked beneath her hat. The gun strapped to her leg left little doubt that she could protect what was hers.

The barn lantern glowed from behind her near the ladder, but for once, she didn't stand in its light. Em wanted to watch the men arriving without being seen.

"Strangers," she whispered. "Strangers on my land." The words tasted sour in her mouth, and she fought the urge to spit them out.

The night had an eerie feeling to it. Wind whipped from first one direction, then another as if not able to make up its mind which way to blow. Damp wisps of fog drifted in the evening sky like a dark cloud come to play in the breeze. A full moon cast milky light between the buildings that marked the ranch. Two huge barns, one for horses and one to store the collection of wagons and buggies used mostly for training teams, seemed to stand guard over the ranch. The main house with its two wings coming off the center reminded Em of a great eagle about to take flight. A bunkhouse and several smaller buildings used for storage huddled around the area, almost making the ranch headquarters look like a town settled beneath rolling hills.

The music of the ranch, from the whine of the clothesline to the clank of the well rig keeping time to the wind chimes near the mudroom door, seemed to clang off-key tonight. The only safe home she'd ever known seemed to be standing silent, waiting, preparing for a threat yet to come. Em told herself she would be ready. She had to be ready. She was the oldest. The safety of Whispering Mountain lay in her hands.

Two men on horses galloped ahead as the buggy crossed the bridge. Even in the shadows, she recognized fine horses and superior riders. Both men handled their mounts with an easy skill as they raced for the house.

When they reached the yard and dismounted, one man stood back with the horses while the other stepped onto the porch. In an odd way he reminded her of a peacock, walking tall, stretching his legs, not looking down as he moved.

She heard the one on the porch snap an order to the man with the horses, but Em couldn't make out what he said because the buggy rattled into the yard.

A tall stranger, who'd ridden in the front beside Sumner, jumped from the bench. He began helping an older lady out of the buggy. She was short and plump, with a hat the wind seemed determined to claim and a birdcage half her size. Another man joined in the effort to assist her as wind whipped at the little creature's tall feathers and bows.

Em studied the shadowy figures. She hadn't expected a woman. Only three men had been mentioned in Duck's letter, and now there were three men and a woman. Thoughts of killing Duck crossed her mind. She'd been angry since she'd gotten his letter saying he was sending unmarried men to meet them. Her sisters Rose and Beth might be in a twitter of excitement, but Em was furious. How many times did she have to tell everyone that she never planned to marry? All she'd ever wanted was to stay on the ranch and help her papa raise the finest horses in Texas.

The thought of marriage frightened her, something she had never told anyone. If her mother knew the scars Em bore, it would break her heart. But Em had learned her lesson early, before they came to Whispering Mountain.

No man would ever touch her. She'd make sure of it.

She stared at the three men on the porch, glad that she'd talked her friend into pretending to be her for the week. Em had her hands full running the ranch. She didn't need to play hostess. She and Tamela looked alike. Teachers in school had often gotten them mixed up. Now, for one week, Tamela had agreed to play her.

The big front doors of the main house opened and women rushed out, all carrying lanterns. With Rose in the lead, lanterns circled the guests and welcomed them in. The two girls from town helping out took some of the luggage. All the men except the peacock, who'd reached the porch first, carried bags as they headed inside.

When all the guests were in, Em McMurray stood alone in the loft, staring at the house with its brightly lit windows closed tight against the wind. She wanted to be inside. She wanted to feel safe. She wanted that wonderful feeling of being home, but tonight she was an outsider. Her papa, if he were standing beside her, would probably say she picked the game, so she had no right to complain.

Only Em wasn't used to playing games, and she hated the idea that she had to lie and pretend to be someone else . . . or more precisely, have someone else pretend to be her. She hated lies and manipulation almost as much as she hated her cousin trying to marry her off. Why couldn't everyone be happy with the fact that she liked spending her days alone?

She'd been seven when her real father died and her mother ran from Chicago, fearing that her three daughters would be taken from her. They'd headed to Texas and a rancher who'd written her mother for years. Teagen McMurray started as only a customer at their family bookstore, but her mother and Teagen had ended up friends. When she showed up on his doorstep with three little ones, he'd taken them into his life and heart. For Em, she'd only had one man she thought of as her father, and that was her papa, Teagen McMurray.

He'd taught her to ride and handle a gun. He'd also taught her to love the ranch. More than any of the children raised here, Em belonged to this place. She planned to live her life here and, when she died, she would be buried on Whispering Mountain.

Slowly, she collected her lantern and moved down the stairs. Sumner was unhitching the buggy when she reached the ground. As always, he simply nodded to her. He'd been on the ranch for ten years, and the last few, when she'd taken over more for her papa so he and her mother could travel to doctors up north with her little brother, Sumner had followed orders from her, but he'd never been very friendly. He might do his job, but that didn't mean he had to like it. She had a feeling that if she asked, he'd tell her a woman's place was in the kitchen, not trying to run a ranch.

She'd once thought of asking her papa to fire him, but in truth she preferred Sumner and his cold polite manner to the cowhands who tried to be overly friendly, paying her compliments she knew they didn't believe, or worse, acting like they would court her if she gave them half a chance. Em knew they wanted the ranch, not her, even if not one of them would ever admit such a thing.

"Miss?" Sumner stopped her before she reached the door.

"Yes?" She turned to face him.

"There's a man who came in with the gentleman's horses. He says he's to be the only one who touches or feeds the animals and he's to sleep near them. Is that the way it's going to be, miss? I'm not so sure Mr. McMurray would want some stranger sleeping in the barn."

"You're right," she answered, "but the gentleman and his wrangler are our guests. If he wants to sleep next to his horses, have the stall next to the animals cleaned out. It might not say much of the way his employer treats his groom, but it says volumes of what he thinks of his horses."

"Yes, miss." Sumner turned away.

"I'll ask one of the girls from town to see that he gets his meals if he doesn't want to leave the barn to eat."

"Fair enough," Sumner said. Like everyone else on the ranch, he knew the game she and Tamela were playing by switching places. A few thought it was a lark, but Sumner hadn't said a word. She guessed in his old Texas Ranger mind a person should be what they are and nothing more or less.

"Miss," he added before she could leave. "The fellow didn't seem all that friendly when he passed by."

"Fair enough," she answered. In truth she didn't plan on being friendly at all. "They'll all be gone in a week. Don't worry about it."

Em walked across the yard, her light making a small circle at her feet. When she entered the house from the back, she could hear the two girls hired to help talking in the kitchen. They seemed to be arguing over which of the three bachelors was the best looking. One liked the tall man in black. He had a nice smile. The other one liked the horseman in his leathers and high boots. Then Mrs. Watson, the chaperone they had to invite for the week, said she liked the young one because he was not only by far the most handsome, he was kind to his mother and everyone knows that's the one trait every girl should look for in a husband. If he doesn't love his mother, he's not worth worn shoe leather on a hot day.

Em giggled as she removed her gun belt and hung it on a high peg in the mudroom.

Rose ended the discussion by popping her head into the kitchen and telling everyone to hurry up with the food. When she spotted Em by the back door, she closed the distance between them. "We've got an extra guest. One brought his mother."

Em smiled. If there were a crown for the perfect hostess, Rose would be wearing it. She was an organizer and a planner who worried about every detail. "I noticed a woman get out of the wagon. There's room in the barn if you want to put her there."

"Don't be ridiculous." Rose was two years younger than Em but considered herself far wiser. "We have a major crisis on our hands."

"She can sleep down here in Jamie's bed where I was going to sleep. I'll bunk in with Tamela. She won't mind." Tamela had agreed to make Rose and

42

Beth a few new dresses while she was playing her part as Emily McMurray. In exchange, Em promised to buy several dresses from her friend's little shop. As a two-time widow, Tamela needed the money. She had no interest in the men coming to court, however. She'd already told the girls she had her eye on the new blacksmith in town for Christmas.

Rose shook her head. "We can't have two Emilys wandering the same hall, and you know anyone who sleeps in the room off the kitchen can hear whenever anyone takes the stairs. Little Mrs. Allender strikes me as the nosy type. She'll be watching to see who is coming and going." Rose looked long-suffering. "To top it all, she brought a bird. We'll be lucky if we make the week without one of Bethie's cats eating it."

"How about putting the bird in with Reverend and Mrs. Watson? The way she drinks and he snores, they won't notice a bird."

"No, that won't work. We've got to think of her and the safety of that bird. If she's downstairs, she's bound to leave her door open and it will be an invitation for the cats to murder."

"Well, I don't care what you do with the bird, but I'm not bunking in the barn." Em wished she'd followed her instinct and really burned the bridge.

"What about the little room next to Papa's study? It used to be a bedroom before Mama turned it into a sewing room. You could sleep there with the bird. That door is always kept closed, and we'll cover the cage at night. You won't even know it's there. The men will be upstairs. All you have to do is wait until they go to bed, then slip in from the kitchen. No one will notice you."

"I'll feel like a burglar in my own house."

"It's only for a week. Six nights really."

Em knew the only other choices were the bunkhouse or the barn, and she couldn't go to either. Uncle Travis's place down by the river would have been fine, but she wasn't sure she could stay down there all alone. She almost wanted to laugh. She was running one of the biggest ranches in Texas and she was not only afraid of the dark, she was afraid of being alone. "All right. I'll take the sewing room. Where are the men?"

"Everyone's in the dining room. Reverend Watson insisted on making a toast with the only two bottles of wine we have in the house. Everyone may all be asleep before he finishes talking, so I slipped out, claiming I had to check on the food. You could go around to the front and slip in the sewing room now if you like. I'm sure the reverend will want to pray for a while after the toast. I'll bring you a plate when no one is looking."

"Fair enough, but tap lightly, I'll keep the door locked."

Rose nodded and was gone before Em had a chance to change her mind. She circled through the mudroom, where all the family who worked the ranch cleaned up before entering the house. Years ago when her papa and his brothers were boys, they stripped in the yard and washed by the well, but now the mudroom had been enlarged and offered a curtain for privacy if needed and a huge bathtub if desired.

There, with cold water, she washed, then collected clean clothes and a nightgown. She walked around to the front door, careful to avoid the windows off the dining room.

Once in the sewing room between her father's study and the dining room, Emily closed all the shutters and drapes, lit a lamp, pulled off her clothes, and slipped into a white nightgown. It was the only time during the day that she felt like a woman. Soft lace brushed her chin and toes.

Rose tapped on her door a moment later, bringing her food. When she entered, she whispered, "Are you sure you'll be all right in here? There's not even a fireplace."

"I'm fine. I'll keep the door locked and be gone at first light. There are a half dozen quilts in the corner to keep me warm. I doubt anyone will be up before I leave. If they see me in the house, I'll simply say I was hired to work with the horses and I came to talk to you or Emily about ranch business. Everyone knows to keep quiet and not give me away."

"Of course"—Rose nodded—"but try to be invisible as much as possible and keep that hair tucked under your hat. With luck no one will even notice you're not a boy."

Em frowned at the insult. True, she wasn't as rounded as either of her sisters, but she didn't think she looked like a boy, not if anyone took the time to look.

Setting her plate down on the sewing table, she asked, "How are the men? Don't tell me they're as bad as the last batch Duck brought home or I'll have to shoot the lot of them to save you a week of torture."

"No. They're fine," Rose answered. "Very good in fact. The horseman named Boyd Sinclair only talks about himself, but I think that's because he's nervous. I thought that you might like him until his comment that McMurray horses were almost as fine as his stock."

Em took a bite of potatoes to keep from swearing.

Rose continued, "The younger one, Davis Allender, is very polite, and his mother seems sweet. The tall one, Lewton Paterson, is quiet."

"Shy?" Em asked, surprised.

"No," Rose corrected. "Not shy, more of a watcher. I get the feeling he's taking measure of everything around him. I wouldn't have been surprised if he'd turned over the plate to check the markings. I'm not sure I like him. Maybe he's unsure of himself or maybe he's just trying too hard. I feel like he weighs every word before he speaks."

"You've always been a good judge of people, Rose. Trust that judgment now."

"I will." She moved to the door. "Hope you can get some sleep. If I remember right, Mama could pretty much hear everything going on in the old part of the house from this room. Maybe that's why she made it her sewing room."

"Maybe so." Em locked the door behind her sister and settled down to her meal. She could hear voices from the dining room and it didn't take long to distinguish every person.

The air in the room was still, but grew colder. Em collected three quilts from a corner and curled up in her mother's soft chair. This was the room the girls would come to at night when the house was quiet. Their mother would be working late if Papa wasn't home. They'd each grab a quilt and sit around her chair. She'd read to them, or, better yet, tell one of the stories from her favorite books.

Em loved growing up here. The warm memories almost erased her early days when they'd lived in Chicago. The days before Mama came to Papa. Em pulled up the footstool and decided this would make a fine bed for tonight.

"Good night, bird," she whispered.

The bird didn't answer.

Within minutes, the voices from the other room lulled her to sleep. With luck the week would pass without the strangers even noticing her. They'd be gone and she'd have peace once more.

ꙮ CHAPTER 6 ꙮ

L ewt pretended to drink his wine, but he wanted
to be stone-cold sober at all times. Too much
was riding on the outcome of this one week. He set
his glass down and took in each person around the
table. He supposed Duncan had hurt his pride when
he'd said Lewt was the last man in Texas that he'd
introduce to his cousins. At the end of this week,
the ranger would eat those words. Lewt would fit
in. He would. He'd play the part of a gentleman.
He'd watch the family. He'd learn about ranching.

The food was excellent. He had a feeling the
middle daughter of Teagen McMurray had a great
deal to do with not only the meal, but the running
of the house. She'd been the one to show each man
to his room in what she called "the old part of the
house." Rose McMurray was striking with her long
black hair and dark eyes, but he'd already guessed
she was one of those women who didn't realize
her own beauty or its effect on men. He watched
her play the hostess for the evening, making sure
everyone was served. He could almost see himself
married to her. He wouldn't have to worry about
her skills at running a house, and she'd be most
pleasant to take to bed—once they were married,
of course.

He almost laughed aloud. All this fresh air was

doing him no good. He was starting to believe in his own dreams.

The youngest of the three had introduced herself as Beth, but Lewt noticed the others called her Bethie as though she were still a child and not a woman fully grown. She had wonderful auburn hair that curled about her pretty face. Her green eyes seemed to hold laughter in their depths. Lewt found himself smiling every time she looked at him. She'd give him beautiful children, he decided, since he was imagining. He could see himself dancing with Beth, and she'd be accepted and loved by all. Beth would always be the belle of the ball.

Emily, the oldest, didn't have Beth's beauty or Rose's skills at running everything, but she did have a shy charm about her. Rose said that Emily loved horses. If he chose her, his house would be quiet and probably peaceful. Who knows, they might even build a summer place on the ranch so she could be near the horses she loved. She was also taller than her sisters, and he thought she'd look grand on his arm as they walked through downtown Austin.

As he watched Emily, he noticed she didn't look up at Boyd when he talked of horses. Either she wasn't as interested in horses as her sister thought, or she wasn't interested in Boyd. The latter Lewt found more possible.

Lewt smiled to himself. Who knew, maybe he could outcharm both Boyd and Davis, and then he'd pick which girl would suit him best. He'd pay her compliments and carry her around on a pillow all week and by Thursday or Friday, they'd be making a trip to town to talk to the preacher. Or, if Reverend Watson hadn't turned in his license when he retired, maybe he'd do the honors in this very room. Lewt guessed her family would want a big wedding that would take weeks to plan, but he'd insist he couldn't wait and he was sure she'd go along. When the train headed back to Austin next Saturday, one of these ladies would be his wife before anyone had time to look into his past.

Lewt laughed to himself. If dreams were gold, he was getting richer by the minute.

If he were married, his bride and he would stay at a nice, respectable hotel, or maybe with her uncle, the judge, until he found a suitable house. Then he'd . . .

"Mr. Paterson, would you like a slice of cake?"

Lewt stared at Rose for a moment. He'd been so lost in his plan, he'd forgotten about the others. "Yes, thank you, Miss McMurray."

"Please," Rose said loud enough for everyone at the table to hear. "We'll get very confused if you spend the entire week calling all three of us by Miss McMurray. Don't you think it would be all right to go by our first names?"

"I don't know about that," Mrs. Watson said, playing her part as chaperone, but the others agreed that as long as the *Miss* remained, it would be proper to switch to first names. They were already introducing themselves all over again before Mrs. Watson could get in another objection.

Davis's mother, Mrs. Allender, giggled and declared, "Now we have a party. Much better than a formal dinner."

Rose smiled down at Lewt as she handed him a slice of cake. "I'm Miss Rose," she said just to him. "Just plain Rose."

"Lewton, but friends call me Lewt, and there is nothing about you, sweet Miss Rose, that is plain." She was the one, he decided as he watched her move on to the next guest. She'd be everything he'd want in a wife.

Beth leaned across the table and offered her hand. "Please, Lewt, call me Beth."

Lewt took her small hand in his. The view from her not-so-modest neckline when she leaned over was just low enough to be interesting. "I will," he said, thinking he might as well say *I do* right now. He had no idea what love was, but this was probably as close as he'd ever get to it. Her skin was creamy smooth and her eyes the color of summer green. Miss Beth was the one.

Then shy Emily took his hand. She was polite and charming, but not overly friendly. She'd make him earn her love, and he liked a challenge. She was the kind of woman a man would never want to raise his voice around. She'd be a treasure to have at his side.

Hell, he thought, *I might as well become Mormon and marry all three of them.* The problem wasn't going to be figuring out which one he wanted. The problem was trying to determine which one to leave behind. It crossed his mind that maybe all women outside saloons were like this. No wonder their fathers and brothers and even cousins watched them so carefully.

Lewt sat back and tried to enjoy the cake but found himself jealous whenever Boyd or Davis even looked at any of the Misses McMurray. By the time the men went up the stairs to their three rooms and the women circled through the kitchen to a staircase leading to the new wing of the house, Lewt decided he'd go mad this week. The only two women he didn't want tonight were Mrs. Watson, the drunken chaperone who sported a mustache thicker than most men could manage, and Mrs. Allender, who was so wide it would take two men to get their arms around the lady.

Reverend Watson said that everyone could sleep in tomorrow morning because of the late night, but anyone interested could find coffee in the kitchen if they rose early, and he added that there would be a prayer service served with the biscuits. The old preacher seemed to think his role was head of the household, but none of the McMurrays appeared to feel that way. Lewt had an idea that these women were used to having their own way. The thought crossed his mind that if Walter Freeport the Fourth had slapped any one of them, he'd be shot dead before he could lower his hand.

Boyd Sinclair, since he hadn't slept the night before, planned to take the preacher's advice and sleep the clock around. Davis commented that he wanted his mother to rest, so he planned to spend the morning reading in his room.

Five hours later, Lewt was up at dawn. He didn't care if everyone else slept. He needed to get to know the ranch. From the dinner conversation he'd figured out that they all loved the land, so it made sense that he learn as much as he could about how the place was run. Everything he learned, every step he took this week would help him if he ever got the chance to walk away from gambling and become a respectable businessman.

He dressed in the black suit that he'd already grown tired of and followed the smell of coffee to the kitchen.

At first he thought a lean man dressed in work clothes stood by the stove, but as she moved, he recognized the grace of a woman.

"Pardon me," he said. "I'm sorry, I thought . . ."

She turned toward him, the black hat she wore hiding most of her face in the shadowy room. "You're in the right place if you want coffee, stranger. I was just leaving."

Lewt took a step into the room, then stopped as he spotted a gun hanging low on her side. "I can come back later."

"Suit yourself. I always come in for coffee before I ride out to check the herd."

"You work here?"

The woman grinned. "My papa knew horses and he taught me. I've worked the McMurray horses for years."

Lewt moved closer and pulled a cup off the shelf. "You live here on the ranch?"

"Not that it's any of your business, stranger, but I still live with my folks."

"Oh," he said, thinking this place must be big enough to have a dozen houses tucked away in the trees or around the other side of the hills. If she rode in and wanted coffee, it made sense that she'd stop in here and not bother with the bunkhouse. For all he knew, she might even be friends with the women here. If she was and she knew ranching, she'd be a gold mine to him.

She filled his cup with what looked like coffee strong enough to pass for soup. "There's bread on the table, but breakfast usually doesn't happen for a few more hours. I'll be in the north pasture by then."

He watched her make herself at home, and he did the same. When she cut a thick slice of bread and added butter and jelly, he borrowed the knife and did the same. For a while, they ate in silence.

"I'm Lewt," he finally said. "You got a name?"

"Yep," she said between bites.

"Mind telling me?"

"Em," she said. "Folk just call me Em."

"Well, M." It was far too early to try to figure out why her parents gave her an initial for a name. "Mind if I ask you a favor?"

"You can ask." She lowered her hat, but he swore he saw her smile for a second. "I'm not partial to handing out favors to strangers."

"We're not strangers, M. We've had breakfast together."

No reaction from the woman, who didn't seem to have a friendly bone in her slender body.

"I was just wondering if I could ride out to the herd with you. I'd like to look around. You know, get to know the lay of the land. Maybe learn more about ranching."

Her head rose slightly, and he knew she was looking at his city suit and thin leather half boots.

"It's cold out there."

"I'll survive." When he'd borrowed Four's clothes, he hadn't thought he'd be doing much riding.

"Can you stay in the saddle?"

"I'll manage."

"I don't know. I like working alone. You'd just be in the way."

"I swear, I won't even talk to you." He wished he could tell her he figured he'd be nuts by noon if he had to spend the morning talking to the Watsons about the good old days or Mrs. Allender about her bird's illness. "I got to do something."

"You could help cook," Em said.

"Come on, give me a break. I know even less about cooking than I do about ranching. I may never have this chance again. I've always wondered what it would be like to work on a ranch. I'll do my best to make you a good hand for the day."

She stood as if to leave.

"How about we flip for it." He pulled the double eagle from his pocket. "Heads, you take me with you for the day. Tails, I'll never speak to you again, I swear."

She shrugged. "It'd be worth the gamble, I guess."

He flipped the coin. "Heads," he said, without looking at the coin.

She snorted. "Well, then, we'd better get going."

He followed her out the back door, wondering if he'd made a mistake. It had to be near freezing, and the material of his suit would be lucky to make it to noon without ripping.

She didn't seem to care, and he figured he could handle being cold for a few hours. In truth, the look she gave him was probably colder than any norther blowing in.

When she reached the barn, she asked Sumner to saddle him a horse, then tossed him an old work coat that had been hanging on the barn wall.

The old wool smelled like the inside of a barn, and Lewt wondered if it hadn't been the home of more than one mouse.

"You're welcome to this if you want it," she said.

He couldn't shake the feeling that she was testing him. If she was, he had no intention of failing.

Straw and who knew what else was sticking to the material of the coat in several places, but Lewt tugged it on.

When he looked up, he saw her eyes for the first time. She was tall, almost his height, with a long straight nose and light blue eyes. To his surprise, she was looking at him as if fully expecting him to refuse the coat.

"Thanks," he said, trying to button it across his chest. He had nothing to prove to this woman. He didn't even care what she thought of him, but she seemed the only one around who could teach him what he needed to know to be able to talk to the beautiful McMurray sisters. Davis was from a big farming family, so he'd know all about running an operation like this, and Boyd's love of horses had made him the leader in most of the conversations at dinner.

Lewt knew how to gamble, how to play the odds, how to stay out of bar fights, and how to collect the table money fast if a fight broke out, but he knew little about ranching. He was a fast learner, though. This woman dressed in men's clothing and wearing a gun already disliked him. If he asked her dumb questions, she didn't look like she could think much less of him.

As Sumner brought his horse up, the woman moved to her mount and swung up with easy grace.

The old man held the horse's head as Lewt tried to climb on the half-wild animal. "Give him his head," Sumner whispered. "He'll follow Miss Em's horse."

Lewt, who rarely rode, managed to climb on his mount without making a fool of himself. They were out of the barn at a speed that almost knocked him off the horse. The house was out of sight before he felt like he gained control of his mount or got into the rhythm of the run.

A mile later he smiled when he realized what joy it was to ride a fine horse. The animal moved to his slightest command. The woman a few lengths in front of him used no whip or spurs. She didn't need to. These animals were born to run. He just hoped he was born to ride, because he didn't know if he could find the ranch house if he fell off, and he had no doubt this M woman would leave him behind.

The sun rose, spreading golden across the winter land. When Lewt finally had time to look at his surroundings, he was amazed at the wild beauty of the place. He could only imagine how grand it must be in summer when everything was green.

The woman finally slowed and glanced back at him. She seemed surprised he was still there.

She didn't speak or give him any hint of where they were going. He didn't ask. He simply followed and studied his surroundings. Most of his life he'd traveled by stage or train, but the dirt trails and rails passed no view as grand as this one. They crossed streams, slowed to a walk along wooded paths, and ran full-out in pastures.

When they came over a ridge, he spotted a herd of the most beautiful horses he'd ever seen. She didn't move as she studied the remuda. He finally had time to maneuver up to her side.

"They're grand," he said, more to himself than her.

She nodded, smiling now. "I know."

"M, promise you won't leave me out here. No matter what stupid thing I do or say, just make me that one promise. I don't think I could find my way back."

She pushed her hat back a few inches. "I won't," she said. "I'm surprised you stayed up with me as poorly as you ride. Mind if I give you a few pointers?"

"Blast away," he said, liking her directness. She recognized ignorance and was willing to help. He'd finally found one good quality in this woman named M.

Five minutes later, when she'd corrected almost everything he did from the way he sat in the saddle to the way he didn't use his knees to control the horse, Lewt felt pretty much like the village idiot.

"I guess I should thank you," he said.

"I didn't do it for you. I did it for the horse. I couldn't care less how you ride, but you're probably irritating the horse."

"Oh." Lewt wasn't sure whether to be grateful or feel insulted, but he had a feeling if he didn't correct everything he was doing wrong, he'd be given the lecture again . . . for the sake of the horse, of course.

They walked among the animals, and he watched as this strange woman touched each horse as if these were her friends. Now and then, she climbed down and walked among them with a saddlebag of tools and medicines over her shoulder. After a while, she let him carry the bag, and he felt like in some small way he was helping.

She'd stop and check hooves or study a cut to make sure it wasn't infected. Each time she patted the animal as if silently saying hello and then good-bye.

"Do you think they'd let me pat them?"

"If they like you, they might. Stand still and give them a chance to come up and smell you first."

Lewt froze. The first two mares who came near snorted as if blowing the smell of him out of their nose, but the third one stayed close, bumping his shoulder with her head.

Lewt raised his hand slowly and brushed her neck. When he laughed, the mare shook her head, splashing mane in his face, but she didn't run away.

Lewt glanced at M.

"You've made a friend," the woman said. She smiled at him and Lewt smiled back, proud of himself.

After a time, they collected their mounts and walked away from the herd.

Lewt knew he had to be honest with this woman. He had a feeling she'd settle for nothing less. "I've never ridden a horse like this one," he said, patting the horse's neck as they walked. "In fact, I've never owned a horse. I've only rented one now and then from the livery."

"Then what are you doing out here? Why do you want to see the herd if you can't tell a broken-down livery animal from a McMurray-bred?"

"I'm thinking that one day I might marry a woman like one of the McMurray girls. I've been saving my money; who knows, I might even buy a ranch. A small one, of course, nothing like this one. If I'm ever to get a word in at dinner, I've got to talk about horses, and I can't do that without knowing something."

"So you want to follow me and ask questions?" She stepped across a stream and stopped to let her horse have a drink. "What's in it for me?"

Lewt thought a second. "I'll pay you for your time. Fifty dollars if you'll help me."

"Help you marry the girls?"

"No, help me learn about horses. Let me ride out with you every morning and answer my questions. That's all. I'll take care of getting one of the Misses McMurray to fall in love with me." He almost laughed at his own boldness, but it felt good to tell someone of his hopes. "It shouldn't be all that hard.

My competition is a boy and a bore."

M laughed. "Which one of the girls you planning on walking down the aisle?"

Lewt shrugged. He could tell she thought him a joke and was probably just amusing herself. He felt like a barn mouse being batted around by a cat. "It doesn't matter who I marry. Will you help me?"

"All right, on one condition. You help me work the stock, not just watch. If I have to stop and answer questions, you'll need to make sure I don't get behind in my work."

He couldn't tell if she was being honest or just wanted to torture him for a while. "Fair enough. Where do we start?"

"We ride," she said swinging back into the saddle.

While he stood admiring the way her trousers tightened over her body, she took off at a full gallop.

He forced his already stiffening muscles to work as he climbed on his horse and tried to catch her. This was more the reality of his life. Here he was, chasing after a woman who wanted to torture him. Courting one of the McMurray girls was a long shot. Even staying alive till dark looked like a gamble.

ᖇᖇ CHAPTER 7 ᖇᖇ

The Rio Grande

After struggling to get a few horses up the bluff near the water, McNelly ordered the men to move in on foot. The Las Cuevas Ranch was only three miles from the river, and they needed the cover of night more than they'd need horses.

Duncan was tired, but excitement pumped in his blood like the pounding of war drums. He believed all the way to his bones that he was doing something that would make life safer for Texans, and if he lived the day, he'd have a grand story to tell. Only attacking on foot had its problems. How could they herd the cattle if the raiders turned them over? Or, if the rangers ran into Juan Flores, who was said to have two hundred men who stayed at his ranch, how could the rangers retreat? But logic and determination rarely held hands in the captain's mind. He saw the fight coming, and all other parts of the plan didn't seem to matter.

They moved over the land like shadows, silencing sentries before the men could fire a warning. Almost within sight of the ranch, they encountered a group of Flores's men, maybe thirty or forty, well armed and on horseback.

The rangers spread out and stood ground, waiting

for orders. Duncan knew if the rangers ran, they'd be cut down before they could reach the river. Their only chance was to stand and fight. McNelly marched them to within a hundred yards of the outlaws before he shouted orders demanding a quick retreat.

While the rangers took cover, the outlaws hesitated, suspecting an ambush. It must have looked obvious that only a few rangers had come forward, hoping to have the outlaws chase them. Just beyond they figured McNelly's full force waited.

As the cattle rustlers tried to decide whether to follow, the rangers took cover and began to fire.

Duncan laughed as the outlaws ran, thinking there were far more rangers than thirty.

When the shooting stopped, Duncan leaned back against a rock he'd used for protection and smiled. Maybe he would live another day. He half wished Lewt Paterson was with him. Though Duncan wasn't convinced Lewt didn't sometimes step over the line, they'd formed a solid friendship. He admired the way the gambler took life as it came. The only flaw he saw in Lewt was that the man had nothing he loved, nothing he'd fight for, nothing he wouldn't risk in a card game. It was hard for a man to be a hero when he didn't care about the outcome, but if Lewt were there right now, he'd be taking bets on how the night would come out. Duncan had a feeling the rangers didn't have the odds to win.

A few hours passed with only a few shots echoing

in the night. With the sun would come the attacks from Flores's men. Again and again they advanced, only to be held by thirty tired Texans. The captain sent a call for help, and thirty cavalrymen crossed the Rio and fought the day but returned at dusk, saying McNelly's quest was hopeless.

Duncan was so tired he could feel his heart pound when all was still. Part of him wanted to go back with the cavalry, but he knew he'd stay. He'd gone two nights without sleep and his mind began to play tricks on him. When he closed his eyes, he could almost believe he was back at Whispering Mountain. When the firing started up, he was sure he was in hell.

A Mexican spokesman carefully approached with a white flag flying. He told McNelly and his men to leave Mexico.

The captain said he would only leave with the stolen cattle. McNelly wanted this to be the end of the cattle wars.

The small delegation sent to stop the fighting left to deliver McNelly's demands. Duncan heard one man say, *"Los Diablos Tejanos."* He'd been called the name before. It meant "the Texas Devils."

Duncan settled in to try to get a few hours' sleep. He knew, without a doubt, that there was one helluva fight coming.

ℰ❦ CHAPTER 8 ❦℈

By midmorning Em decided the tall man following her every step must be the dumbest greenhorn alive. He barely knew which end of a horse to feed. He fell several times in the damp pasture because of his slippery shoes. He frightened his own mount once by yelling, and she had to go round up his horse.

If he hadn't been so funny, she might have given up pushing him. The man was a walking train wreck, and the idea that he thought he might marry one of the McMurray women made her laugh. At this rate she'd be dead of old age before he learned enough to even talk ranching and make sense. But she had to give him credit. He never stopped trying.

By midafternoon she admitted that Lewt was strong and determined. He took in advice like a sponge takes on water. He didn't seem to mind that his suit was torn by bushes in several places and his shoes were ruined. Once she showed him how to do something, he worked at it until he mastered any chore. He might not know horses, but he had a hunger to learn. She had a feeling that whatever he did for a living, he was good at it. She'd tried asking him twice, but he didn't give her an answer. She figured he must be out of a job. That might explain his determination to find a rich wife.

As they rode back toward the house, she noticed that his leg was bleeding an inch above his knee. He hadn't said a word about being hurt. She thought of several times he'd tumbled during the day. Once off his horse when he'd roped his first wild colt, once in the stream when he lost his footing, and once to his knees when he lifted a horse out of the mud. The city slicker who'd had coffee at dawn with her now looked worse than a drifter down on his luck.

"You're bleeding, Lewt," she snapped, angry that she hadn't noticed.

"Don't worry about it," he said. "The stock comes first, remember."

She fought down a smile. "Yes, of course, but you're bleeding on the horse."

He looked too tired to catch her joke. "I'll wash it off when we get to the barn."

"It might get infected," she snapped, sounding angrier than she'd meant to.

"There's nothing I can do about it until I get back, so I refuse to think about it. Another hour and we'll be back. Even you will have to stop at sundown."

She pointed to a stand of trees a few hundred yards up the hill. "There's a little place up there. I'm guessing we'll find something to at least wrap it there."

As he had all day, he didn't argue. He simply followed her to the cabin her uncle Drummond and aunt Sage stayed in when they were at the ranch and not in their house in town or on the road helping others. Sage had built a reputation as one of the finest doctors in the county. She ran a clinic in Anderson Glen and Drum served as sheriff. Their place on the ranch was small but offered them the privacy they seemed to always crave. Strange, she thought of her aunt and uncle as newlyweds even though they'd been married for years.

When Lewt climbed off his horse, Em didn't miss how he favored the leg. Either he was an idiot for not mentioning he was hurt, or he had more grit to him than she'd guessed.

The door was unlocked and the tiny two-room place was neat and organized, as Em guessed it would be. She had no trouble finding bandages and the smelly black ointment Sage always put on cuts.

"I'm not a nurse, but this will keep the infection down. Take off your trousers," she said as she lined up what she needed on the table.

"Not a chance." He winked, making her laugh. "You've finally given an order I don't plan on following."

"Look, mister, if you don't have four legs and eat grass, I'm not interested in you. Do we have that clear?"

He shrugged. "So this is no love nest you tricked me into, planning to get me in bed and take advantage of me?"

"Lewt, the only way you'll be laid out in that bed is after I shoot you for wasting my time. Now strip off those trousers." She tossed her hat on the table and let her thick blond braid fall down her back.

"The lady has sunshine hair," he said softly. "I never would have guessed."

She looked over her shoulder. "What's so unusual about blond hair?"

"Nothing. I just figured your hair would be short like a man's."

"Don't worry about my hair. We need to take care of that cut." She fought the urge to tell him not to look at her. Men, with their stares, made her uncomfortable. She laughed. Men, period, made her uncomfortable.

He tugged off his shoes, then unbuckled his belt. "If you take advantage of me, I want my fifty dollars back."

She smiled. No one had ever talked to her so boldly about such a thing. She liked the honesty between them.

He lowered his trousers. Blood dripped from the gash above his knee.

She was shocked he wore no long johns underneath his trousers. Any man in this country would have on his wools until spring. His shirttail covered his private parts, but his leg was bare.

"What are you staring at?" he asked. "Is it that bad?"

Em swallowed. "No. Your leg is just so hairy."

"Well, I can't help that. You've been doctoring hairy legs all day. Just pretend I'm a horse and get on with it."

Em pulled a chair out and sat as she began wiping off blood. "When we get back to the house I think this will need a few stitches."

"Will you do them?" he said in almost a whisper. "I don't want anyone to know I'm hurt."

"All right." She didn't want to ask him why. It was no concern of hers. If he did manage to get one of her sisters interested in him, then they'd probably never mention the day they'd spent together. For a moment, she let herself wonder which sister would even look twice at such a man, then decided neither of them would. He wasn't the kind of man who'd fit on a ranch no matter how much he learned.

She pushed the gash closed and wrapped it as tight as she could. As she worked, he put his hand on her shoulder so that he stood steady. She endured the touch until she tied off the bandage, and then she said cold as ice, "I'm finished. Remove your hand, sir."

He pulled away immediately. "I'm sorry," he said. "I was only bracing. I meant you no harm."

She looked up at him. "I'm aware of that. It's the only reason you're still alive. I don't like to be touched."

He pulled his trousers over the bandage. "I get the point. It won't happen again."

She stood and cleaned up the mess they'd made while he finished dressing. The silence seemed to stretch miles between them. He opened the door and waited for her to walk out, then slowly climbed on his horse and waited for her to do the same.

Em didn't want to explain anything to this stranger. She didn't want to talk about what had happened in the cabin. Her life was no concern of his, and his silence shouldn't matter to her in the least. Maybe this cold way to end the day was for the best. The last thing she needed in this world was a greenhorn for a friend.

She mounted and began the journey home, this time letting the horses pick the way. Em told herself it was because the mounts were tired, but she knew they still had the heart to race home. She slowed because of the stranger by her side. She didn't want to cause him any more pain than necessary.

Finally, she realized she might have caused pain with her words, but she couldn't bring herself to take them back. As they reached the barn, she said, "Sumner will help me dress that cut. We've got a corner next to the tack room that's clean. You don't have to worry about the old guy saying a word about your injury; he barely talks to anyone, including me."

Lewt's words were no more than a whisper. "You said you would stitch it."

She acted like she hadn't heard.

He followed her in, handed the reins to the cowhand who'd already taken her horse, and followed her to the small area that looked like it might be used to store supplies for the bunkhouse and the cowhands. Far too much time would be lost

71

if the hands had to ride into town every time they needed a blanket or shirt.

She talked with Sumner while he tugged off his ruined trousers, now soaked in blood. This time he sat on a bench, too tired to argue with her.

Em lit a lantern for better light, unwrapped the bandage, and cleaned the wound properly. By the time she finished, Sumner was by her side with an armload of supplies.

"Want me to do it, Miss Em?" he asked.

"No," she answered as she met Lewt's stare. "I'm the reason he got hurt. I'll do it."

When she pushed the needle through his skin, she expected Lewt to yell or swear. She'd patched up her share of cowhands and learned to turn a deaf ear to their language when they were hurting, but Lewt didn't say a word. He jerked a bit, then seemed to set his jaw against the pain.

Em finished as fast as she could, pulling the flesh together and lathering it with ointment. As she wrapped the wound, she said the first words she'd said to him for over an hour. "It'll heal fine." Her fingers slid over the tight muscle of his leg as she wrapped the bandage.

He nodded as she tied the knot. "Thanks."

She stood. "Sumner will help pull you a clean set of clothes from the store. There's boots behind you on the shelf. Most are well used, but they'll do better than those." She glanced at his ruined half boots. "Pull a pair that fit. They're good clothes for this part of the country and far more durable than that suit you had on. If you go out riding again, they'll serve you far better."

"I can pay . . ."

"It's not necessary. Despite all the questions, you put in a good day's work. I figure you earned them." She turned her back and waited on the other side of the tack room while he dressed. She told herself she'd just touched a man where no proper lady ever would, but it had been necessary. He needed doctoring. He didn't belong out here. Though not invited by her, he was a guest. She should have taken better care of him. Some of the things they'd done today could have waited, but she'd pushed.

When he stepped up beside her, she was shocked at the change in him. If she didn't know better she'd think he usually wore western clothes and never a suit. The heavy wool trousers fit his long legs well, and the shirt made his shoulders look broader than the black suit jacket had.

"Thanks for all you taught me today," he said. "I'll see you at dawn tomorrow morning."

"You want to go again?"

"Of course. Unless you've changed your mind about letting me tag along."

"I haven't," she said, then added, "I can use the fifty dollars."

He turned and placed the worn coat on the nail beside the door. Though his back was to her and his voice low, she had no trouble hearing his words.

"I really am sorry about touching your shoulder. I meant you no harm."

"I know," she whispered back. She wouldn't . . . couldn't talk about what had happened between them. It would mean explaining something that had happened many years ago, and she never planned to talk about that with anyone. Not ever. She forced her thoughts to the present. "If the cut bleeds, have Sumner look at it in the morning."

Without a word, they walked toward the house. Em could see the lamps being lit.

"Despite everything, M," he said softly, without looking at her, "I liked riding with you today. I think I felt more alive today then I have in years."

"Fresh air," she said.

"And honest company," he added.

Em swallowed. How could he think she'd been honest? Didn't he know she'd just taken him along to show him up?

She waited on the porch as he stepped inside. She didn't want to go in. It was almost time for supper, but she wouldn't be joining her sisters tonight. She'd wash up, then go back to the barn until Rose put a light in the mudroom, and then she'd circle the house so that no one would see her entering the sewing room.

Em had a feeling when she finally closed her eyes tonight she'd have trouble sleeping. Her head seemed too full.

℘ CHAPTER 9 ℘

Lewt washed up on what looked like a closed-in porch, then joined the others for dinner. The meal was excellent, the conversation lively, but he found himself holding back. Part of him wasn't ready to share with strangers all that had happened to him today. Rose seemed pleased that he'd wanted to take a look at the ranch, but Bethie said she missed him terrible. Lewt didn't know that he believed either one of them.

He hadn't lied to M. In a strange way he'd felt more alive today than he could ever remember feeling. He liked breathing air that wasn't polluted with cigar smoke and cheap perfume. He liked feeling like he was doing some good even though it was hard work. Tomorrow he'd probably be lucky if he could get out of bed.

If he was going to list his likes, he'd have to add liking being with M. She played no games, never flirted with him or tried to manipulate him. He knew she didn't like him and within a few minutes he'd figured out that if he tried to impress her, she'd probably send him back to the barn. So for the most part, he just tried his best and kept his mouth closed.

Half the time he felt like a bumbling idiot around her, and the other half she was reminding him that his feelings were accurate. He didn't know how to pretend with her, how to play games. About the time he decided she was more man than he'd ever be, she'd pulled away from his touch. He'd seen the hurt flash in her eyes for a second. All he'd done was touch her shoulder. Her reaction was that of a wounded animal. He'd give a rich pot to know what had made her react so.

"How was your day?" Rose asked as she passed him a basket of bread.

"What?" Lewt had heard the words, but he couldn't climb out of his thoughts long enough to think of an answer.

Rose smiled. "When Sumner told me you rode out to check the herd, I was surprised. Exhausting, isn't it?"

"Very." He smiled at the beautiful lady, silently thanking her for erasing the awkwardness. "You do have a beautiful ranch, Miss Rose."

"Thank you, Lewt. I sometimes forget what a wonderful place this is, and then I leave for a few days and remember. When Emily and I were away at school we used to lie in bed every night and take turns describing details of the ranch and laughing about all the things we'd do when we got home. Those were the two loneliest years of my life. If it hadn't been for my sister, I'm not sure I would have survived. Every break, when we'd come home all excited and leave crying, my mother felt our homesickness. When it was Bethie's turn to go, the thought of her having to go alone broke our hearts. Mama talked my papa into letting her have tutors come in. He said any finishing Bethie needed could be taught by us."

She patted his arm. "Now don't you think our little sister's education was lacking. She speaks French and can write poems as fine as the old masters, in my opinion. And, thanks to private tutors, she can play the piano so beautifully the angels cry with joy."

Lewt smiled and tried to follow Rose's soft voice, but his mind was wondering, thinking about how he'd worked with M to doctor a few of the stock, then later how he'd watched her long fingers slide over the cotton of the bandage across his leg. His touch might frighten her half to death, but her touch certainly didn't have that effect on him.

"Lewt, you must try one of these buttermilk biscuits. Bethie made them, you know. She's a grand cook, though her art and sewing take up much of her time."

He took a biscuit and tried to keep his mind on the conversation as Rose continued to praise her sister. It crossed his mind that maybe Rose was building up Bethie a little too much.

Lewt looked down the table as Beth laughed at something Davis said. Maybe the green-eyed beauty had told her sister she was interested in him. *That's it,* he reasoned. There was a chance the impossible might just happen.

The reverend had made a rule that the seating changed every night, so Lewt knew he'd be sitting next to either Beth or Emily tomorrow night. Beth might be interested in him, but he planned to take his time and visit with each of the girls. It was only fair.

He smiled at Rose and tried to think of something to say. She was truly lovely, and black-haired women had always been his favorite. Her dark eyes seemed those of a very old soul. If he married Rose, they'd have long talks in the evening and she'd worry about him as all caring wives do.

But as he looked into her dark eyes, he remembered the blue eyes he'd seen this afternoon and how frightened they'd looked. He could think of nothing to say but, "A woman with an initial for a name showed me around today. Do you know her?"

Rose looked confused for a moment, then laughed. "You mean Em. *E-m*. She's taking care of the horses while Papa is away."

"Em," he said. "Short for Emily?"

"I guess," Rose said before taking a bite, then adding when she finally swallowed, "Maybe they started calling her Em so they wouldn't get her confused with our Emily. Two Emilys on the ranch could be confusing."

Lewt had spent his life reading people, and he had no trouble realizing that if Rose wasn't lying, she was definitely leaving something out. He didn't want to push it. After all, Em was just someone he needed to reach a goal. As soon as he figured out enough to bluff his way through a conversation about the ranch, he'd never see the tall woman who dressed like a man again.

He gave Rose his full attention. "I hope I didn't miss anything today while I was out riding."

She smiled sweetly. "Oh, you did. We planned a party for Friday night. Beth is so kind, she never wants to leave anyone out, so we'll have the house full of people. She's even thought of organizing a small band so we can dance. If Beth is in the room, everyone always has a grand time."

Back to singing Beth's praises. Lewt was starting to wonder if something wasn't wrong with the girl if her big sister had to keep pointing out her good side.

"And"—Rose beamed—"this afternoon, we all gathered round the piano and sang songs. You should have heard Mrs. Allender. She has a voice angels would envy. Boyd joined us for a few minutes, then spotted a book on horse breeding he hadn't read. We didn't see him for the rest of the afternoon." Rose giggled. "Just between you and me, I'll bet he was sitting just outside the door listening."

"Did Davis and Emily join in any of the singing?"

"Davis did, but Emily said she'd be our audience while she sewed."

Lewt leaned back. Apparently, he'd missed nothing. He would have had a hard time not looking bored, and the only songs he knew were not proper for anywhere but saloons. This act of being a gentleman wasn't as easy as he thought.

Rose tugged at his sleeve. "Tomorrow, if it doesn't rain, we're going riding and plan to have a picnic on the summit of the hill the Apache named Whispering Mountain. Did you know there is a legend that my ancestors used to believe that says if a man sleeps on the summit of Whispering Mountain, he'll dream his future? My papa tells a story about how his father climbed to the summit when he was just married and settling here. He dreamed his death in a battle beside a mission. He spent the next twelve years of his life building the ranch and preparing his three sons to take over when he died."

"I've heard that story." Lewt smiled. "Duncan talks about how three little boys, his father one of them, took over and held the ranch against raiders."

"My papa was twelve when his father was killed at the Battle of Goliad. Teagen McMurray had to become a man the day they learned his father was dead. My mama, when she met him years later, said he was hard as granite. She was a widow with three tiny girls who saw his heart from the first. Even today when she looks at him, anyone can see the love in her eyes."

Lewt lowered his voice. "So Teagen McMurray isn't your real father?"

"He's our real papa and he'd shoot anyone who questioned it. Our 'real father' lived in Chicago and was given to drink. I don't remember much about him except that he liked to yell at my mother. When he died of pneumonia one winter, Mama brought us here. She married Teagen and we became a family. Sometimes Papa grumbles and complains that it took us too long to get here. He says he was lonely for a long time waiting for us to come."

Lewt felt an ache deep down, as if a wound had bruised his heart. He didn't know Teagen, the head of the McMurrays, but he knew what the man meant. When he'd been a boy he used to dream that he belonged someplace else, with other people. He'd dream that somewhere there was another world where people cared if he was warm or had food. Once in a while he'd almost believe that if he stepped sideways or jumped around a corner that world would be waiting for him, welcoming and warm.

Only it never appeared, and survival left little time for dreams.

He smiled down at Rose as she handed him a slice of pie. He had to marry one of these women. They knew how to build that comfortable loving world he'd never known. He told himself he wasn't using them. Whichever one he married, he'd be good to. Better than good, he'd be caring. He'd never make her sorry she'd married him. Somehow, he'd figure out how to be the kind of man who'd marry a lady.

As they left the dining room, shy Emily took his

arm. "We thought we'd all play cards tonight, Mr. Paterson. Do you play cards?"

The day's exhaustion vanished as he said, "Now and then."

Playing cards with this group was like fishing with a shotgun. Lewt offered to deal and as he did, he took control of the game.

First, he let Boyd Sinclair win. The rancher puffed up and informed the girls that they were no match for him. Lewt resented his superior attitude, but the ladies seemed to think it funny.

When Lewt shuffled again he tossed Boyd the winning hand, but to Lewt's surprise, Boyd folded. The girls consoled him once again.

Lewt frowned. Apparently he didn't understand the rancher as well as he thought he did.

Halfway through the evening he dealt a few hands where Beth won. She giggled with delight. Everyone, including Boyd, congratulated her on her brilliant play.

As the night aged and they all enjoyed the card game, Lewt found himself enjoying the game he was playing. He could tell a great deal about a man by how he acted when he was winning and, more important, how he acted when he lost. In life everyone wins and loses. The man who doesn't handle himself well at losing usually can't handle himself much better at winning.

Davis Allender rarely won a hand, but he never complained. In fact, he cheered the others on.

By the end of the evening all three women were giggling and showing him their hands, and then he'd advise them. Boyd fought to win most of the time, but Davis walked away from the evening the real winner.

When the women said their good nights, Beth kissed Davis on the cheek for helping her. Lewt would have thought he'd be jealous, but to his surprise, he wasn't. Beth was beautiful, but he had two others to pick from, and if she liked Davis, he didn't mind.

The young man had kind eyes and a gentle way. He'd make the youngest McMurray woman a fine husband.

Lewt climbed the stairs to his room and collapsed. His leg still hurt, and hiding the fact through dinner and the card game had cost him energy he didn't have. He was a man who needed little sleep, but this time he planned to take the night.

When he rolled over an hour before dawn, the throbbing in his leg finally woke him. He stood slowly, testing his weight on the leg, then tiptoed down the back stairs to the kitchen and stirred up the fire in the stove. A gentle rain tapping against the windows washed away any sound he made. He guessed it would be a while before the others woke. He planned to soak the bloody bandage off in a hot bath.

He found all he needed in the room they called the mudroom. Towels, a medicine box, a big tub, and lye soap. While the water heated, he lit one lamp in the kitchen and another in the mudroom. Then he put on a pot of coffee that would be ready before he finished his bath.

When he lowered his aching body into the tub, he couldn't help but let out a deep sigh. Every muscle had been strained while working with the herd.

The water felt wonderful, and the slow rain outside settled his nerves. Lewt closed his eyes and drifted off to sleep.

෨ CHAPTER 10 ඥ

Sometime in the night Duncan McMurray woke to the news that the cavalry wouldn't be coming to help them. They received orders that if McNelly and his band had attacked the Mexicans on Mexican soil, the U.S. Army was not to render him any assistance.

Thirty rangers outside their jurisdiction. Thirty rangers against a mounted force of two hundred. The captain's bluff wouldn't last much longer, and they didn't have their horses to outrun bullets this time.

Duncan counted his bullets and waited. This cloudy November day seemed as good as any to die. He heard firing now and then but kept his head low, waiting. He had no ammo to waste, no food for the past two days and little water.

Through the blackness, a bullet came out of nowhere and hit him in the leg as if the gods of battle just wanted to kick him while he was down. It sliced through the muscle just below his knee like a freight train on fire. Duncan swore and tied his leg with his dirty bandanna so he wouldn't lose too much blood, but within an hour blood had pooled in a foot-wide circle by his leg and was soaking into the soil.

"You all right, Duncan?" Wyatt shouted from fifty feet away.

Duncan could feel the pain of the wound all the way to his scalp, but he yelled back, "Fine."

"Good, I'm moving in some for a better possession. You got enough cover?"

Duncan glanced at the hollow he'd made beneath the rock. "I'm digging in," he answered. With trouble calling, he lowered his body into the hole at least far enough to not be seen easily by someone riding past. "I'll be all right."

He felt like he was getting weaker, but calling out for help would pull another out of the fight and they needed every man standing his ground. "If the shooting starts, I may move back some." He knew he'd need a head start to the Rio if they retreated. With his leg he'd be lucky to walk, much less run to the river. "Once the fighting starts, don't worry about me. I'll catch up to you on the other side of the Rio if we have to make a run for it."

"Sounds like a good plan." Wyatt moved away.

Near dawn Duncan began to run a fever, and

blood continued to drip from the soaked bandanna just below his knee. Now and then, if he remained perfectly still, he could almost feel a cool hand touch his brow. If he were home, the girls would take care of him. Emily would fret over him like she did a sick horse. Rose would boss him around, demanding he eat right, and Bethie would sing to him and pat his hand. They'd apologize for all the things they'd done to him and forgive him for all the things he'd done to them.

He and the girls might always fight and they'd been adopted into the McMurray clan just like he had, but Duncan considered them blood and he knew they felt the same way about him. If they knew he was in trouble they'd probably all three be riding like the wind to his aid. If something did happen to him, he knew without a doubt they'd see that his body made it home.

Duncan could almost hear them, and he felt a kind of peace knowing that he'd be buried on the side of a hill where for the rest of eternity he could look out over the ranch.

He slowly slipped into sleep, no longer concerned about the battle beyond the rock. No longer worrying about the fight.

As the sun touched the western horizon, Captain McNelly demanded that the cattle and the thieves who stole them be handed over to the rangers. He planned to stand his ground. No negotiations.

McNelly gave the bandits one hour to comply,

and as darkness fell, the rangers prepared to fire.

All except one. As the cold wind howled, Duncan McMurray turned his back to the world and into the crevice beneath the rock and vanished as he drifted between life and death.

ஐ CHAPTER 11 ℭ

Em left the sewing room with blankets folded neatly in the corner and made her way through the sleeping house to the kitchen. In a few minutes it would be dawn and her long day would begin. With the rain, she planned to make a quick journey for mail and supplies, then work in the barn. She doubted Lewton Paterson would want to join her there. It had been interesting having him tag along yesterday, but she didn't want company today. The man made her nervous. She'd taken risks she shouldn't have, and it seemed he'd been the one who always paid.

When she stepped into the large kitchen, she was surprised to find coffee already made. Rose usually woke early to start the bread, but not quite this early. Maybe, if her sister was up, they could have a few minutes to talk before anyone else crowded around. The only thing wrong with Em's great plan to avoid the potential bridegrooms lay in the fact that she had to miss most of her time with her sisters. They'd developed a habit, these weeks alone, of each listing everything they did each day. Em found it interesting and she knew that when each finished describing her day, none would have traded with the other.

After pouring herself a cup of coffee, she walked toward the only other light in the house. It glowed from the mudroom.

When she saw Lewt in the tub, surprise almost made her drop her coffee cup. He hadn't bothered to draw the drape over the corner. Maybe he hadn't even noticed it tucked away beside the windows.

His arms were over the sides, his knees out of the water, and his head propped against a towel at his shoulder. The low lamp offered little light. He was so still he could have been a painting. Even the soapy water seemed to belong more to a canvas than to life.

Em took a step closer. He looked younger asleep, she thought. The hardness in his jaw that said he'd fight the world alone if he had to was gone. Even though she'd spent the day with him, she knew less about him than about the other two men who'd invaded their quiet life.

When she'd met with her sisters late last night, they'd both learned far more about Boyd and Davis than she'd learned about Lewt Paterson. He'd said he was from the east but had not named a town. She heard no eastern accent in his voice. Yet looking at him now, it was easy to see that the man spent little time in the sun. Except for his face and hands, his body looked lean and pale. His wet brown hair appeared almost black in the light.

Em wished, for the hundredth time, that Duncan had sent them more information about the men he'd picked to meet them. He'd said they were all three from good families. If so, Lewt's family must rarely venture outside.

Duncan had written that they were all three well off financially. Maybe Lewt came from a family of bankers who never did anything but sit around and count their money. That would explain the blisters and tiny cuts he'd gotten yesterday from a day's work.

She could see the line of blisters along his open palm. He was a man not used to working for a living. Part of her thought less of him for it. Part of her admired his willingness to try. He'd obviously stepped into a foreign world yesterday, and he'd done so at a run.

Backing slowly into the kitchen, she pulled out a skillet and began making eggs, hoping the noise would wake him up. She wasn't sure she was brave enough to wake a man in a bathtub. It would probably embarrass them both to death.

About the time she'd set the table for two and the eggs were ready, he appeared in the doorway between the mudroom and the kitchen. His hair was combed back and still looked damp, but he was dressed all the way down to the borrowed worn work boots he wore.

"Oh," she said, as if surprised to see him. "I came in through the front. I didn't know anyone was up."

"I was just washing up." He watched her carefully, showing no sign of having been asleep.

He must be an early riser. A strange habit for a man who didn't work, she thought.

"No suit today?" Em couldn't help but notice he was wearing the same clothes she'd given him last night. She noticed a bloodstain just above one knee. His wound had bled a little after she'd stitched it.

"Are you still going to allow me to ride with you today?" He walked almost within reaching distance from her and stopped.

She poured him a cup of coffee and handed it to him before she answered. "If you're up for it. I guess you can tag along."

"I am," he answered, as if she couldn't see the damage the day before had done to him.

"Do you want me to check the cut?"

"It's fine. Don't worry about it. I've already put a fresh dressing on the wound. The bleeding has stopped, thanks to your excellent stitching." He glanced at the skillet she was holding. "I wouldn't mind sharing those eggs, if you're offering."

She smiled. "I am. I guessed you'd be up early again, so I made enough for two."

"How thoughtful," he said, pulling out his own chair and taking a seat.

She shrugged. "I just didn't want you passing out on me if you insisted on tagging along." She

90

dumped half the eggs on his plate. "And don't get any ideas that I'm waiting on you in here. You're doing the dishes."

"You got it, boss. What do we do today?"

Em watched him slice off two thick pieces of bread and drop one on her plate. This guy must come from the strangest rich family in the world. They did no work, they stayed out of the sun, and they ate breakfast like field hands.

"I thought I'd go into town and pick up some supplies." She shoveled in her eggs, fearing he'd eat her share if she didn't. "If you come along, you could pick up clothes that fit your taste better."

He looked up and smiled. "We taking the buggy?"

"No, there's a back path through the hills. It'll take half the time."

Glancing out the window, he said the obvious. "It's raining, you know."

"I know. Work on a ranch doesn't stop no matter what the weather. You afraid you'll shrink if you get wet? You can back out. I'm sure there'll be plenty going on here to keep you busy."

"No," he said. "This place seems to have a tendency to break into song. I'm going with you."

His comment made her wonder how bad a job her sisters were doing at entertaining him if he'd rather climb back on a horse in the rain with her.

Before she could ask, the bedroom door, off the kitchen, opened and little Mrs. Allender waddled out. She was in her robe and had funny little rag bows tied all over her head. "I didn't mean to interrupt, but I thought I smelled coffee."

Em and Lewt both stood as she came closer. Lewt pulled out her chair as Em got her a cup of coffee.

"Thank you, dear," Mrs. Allender said. "You must be Em. The girls told me yesterday that there was a woman running the ranch while the McMurray men were away. I must say, I admire a woman who makes her own way. When my Jessie was alive he used to say that he couldn't manage the house and I couldn't run the farm, but together we could do anything. He must have been right, because he bought more land every year and I had another baby. After thirty years we owned a good-sized corner of Mississippi."

"And you had a house full of children?" Em asked.

Mrs. Allender sipped her coffee, then shook her head. "For a while we did, but then my three oldest boys died in Andersonville prison during the war. Davis only has one brother left, but I'm blessed with five daughters. During the war, they dressed like you are now and did what had to be done."

"You must be very proud of them," Em said as she put her hand on the old woman's arm.

"Oh, I am. My children are my true wealth in this world. They all want to take up farming like their parents and grandparents, but my Davis, he wants to be an architect. He's says Austin is growing.

It's the place he belongs. It's his chance to leave a mark."

Em found the sweet little woman interesting, but the first hint of dawn shone through the windows. "We have to go," she said. "The rain seems to be letting up and I've a full day of work planned. It was a pleasure to meet you."

Mrs. Allender bid them good-bye as Em almost pulled Lewt out of the warm kitchen and into the rain.

"It's not letting up," he grumbled as he pulled on the dirty slicker she handed him. "If anything, it's worse."

She stepped off the porch and yelled back at him, "Then stay here and sing."

"Not a chance," he said as he followed her, splashing mud with each step.

In the shadowy light of the barn, he saddled his own horse. Sumner showed up about the time he finished and offered his hand. "Morning, stranger. Glad you're up for another day. Thought Miss Em might have killed you yesterday."

Lewt took the man's hand, then felt something slimy spread from the old man's palm to his.

When he frowned the old man laughed. "Don't blame me, son. Miss Em said you'd need some of that for your hands. Rub it in good and it'll help keep those blisters from getting infected."

Lewt wondered how she'd even noticed, but he didn't say anything when he met her at the door. A few of the ranch hands watched them, but none said a word to her or him.

She swung up and watched him climb into the saddle more slowly. "If I take you with me across the pass, I have to blindfold you."

"You're kidding." He looked like his morning had just gone from bad to worse.

She pulled out a red bandanna. "It's this or you don't go. No one outside the family and a few trusted friends is allowed to know the back way into Whispering Mountain."

He looked like he might swear, but instead he took the handkerchief and tied it around his eyes.

"Don't worry. I'll lead you safely through."

He grabbed the saddle horn and waited, telling himself he trusted her. After all she wouldn't waste oil on his hands if she was planning to let him fall off the first ledge they came to.

Em made a slight clicking sound that started both horses moving.

She had no idea what he was up to, but he seemed willing to do whatever was necessary in order to get it. They rode behind the house and began to climb. She'd been taught how to slice through the hills to the town without leaving a path an intruder could follow. There were points along the journey where she knew to stop to make sure she wasn't being tailed. The state wasn't as wild as it had been, but the family still kept the path secret. If rustlers would steal cattle, they'd steal horses as well.

Lewt had been right about the rain. It did seem to be falling harder, and the trip took more time than usual because she had to move slower across slippery rocks. Lewt didn't say a word. Without a hat, she was surprised he wasn't half drowned by the time they reached the summit and began the trip down. She might not know who the man was or what he was up to, but he wasn't a complainer. That was one thing she liked about Lewt.

When they reached a wooded area at the corner of town, Em told him he could take off the blindfold. She handed him the reins to his horse and noticed Lewt hadn't shaved. A dark shadow of the beginnings of a beard made him look far more like an outlaw than a man from a good family.

"You all right?" she asked as she watched him wipe his eyes with the wet bandanna.

"Do you care?" he answered.

"Not really." She laughed. "But I might get my pay docked for killing one of the guests."

He glared at her. "I'm all right. Don't worry about me."

"I won't." She turned to cross a stream and never looked back to see if he followed.

When they reached the road, he pulled even with her.

Within a few hundred yards, buildings began to block the wind. Em pointed to the train station. "I've got business. I'll meet you at the station in an hour. You can leave your horse in the covered area over by the livery. They never bother McMurray horses. The town square is just beyond. You'll find several stores there. You might even talk the tailor into making you another black suit."

He didn't smile when she looked over at him. Em told herself she didn't care. She had banking to do, a list of supplies to pick up from Tamela's mother, and a stop at the post office to make. She had no time to babysit him.

Her first stop was the post office, where the postman's wife told her to be careful. A couple of no-good drifters had been robbing folks outside town. The woman said they were probably two of a dozen or so trail tramps who wintered in town waiting for spring and the cattle drives to start. Most of their types made money in the spring and summer and then found odd jobs come fall. Those who didn't work either budgeted their money or looked for work on the other side of the law.

Touching her Colt strapped to her leg, Em felt like she could handle any trouble that came along. Over their mother's protests, Papa had taught all three of the girls to handle a gun.

She stopped by the sheriff's office to see if any of the deputies had heard from her uncle Drummond. When he was in town serving as sheriff, the wrong type never hung around long, but he always went with his wife, Sage, when she made her rounds doctoring the sick.

The deputy, who looked like he'd been sleeping

in the back, said he hadn't heard from anyone. He also told her not to worry about the drifters. He'd run a few of them out of town last night.

Em moved on to the bank and then to Tamela's mother's dress shop. She'd never figured out how Tamela could be so shy and quiet and her mother such a chatterbox. On second thought, Em was surprised Tamela got enough practice in to learn to talk.

When she finally broke free, she ran toward the train station.

Ten minutes later she was furious. It had taken her a little longer to do her errands than she thought, but Lewton should have been waiting for her. She'd paced the platform twice and he was nowhere in sight. For two bits she'd leave him behind and let him find his own way home.

At least the rain had stopped, or, more precisely, decided to hang in the air like thick fog. It occurred to her that this tagalong stranger might have gotten lost. After all, the town had a dozen stores, three cafés, and several saloons. They even had three hotels. With her luck one of the drifters had spotted him as an easy target and conked him on the head. He was probably lying in an ally half dead, and somehow Duncan and the others would blame her.

Another ten minutes passed and Em began planning ways to kill this son of a wealthy family.

A tall stranger stepped on the platform. His high-topped boots stomped along the planks, drawing

Em's attention. He was dressed in dark brown from his well-made Stetson to his lined leather riding coat. When his open coat flapped in the wind, it revealed a tan vest beneath the same color as his gloves.

He reminded her of someone.

When he was within five feet of Em, he raised his head and tapped his hat with two fingers in salute.

Em froze. "Lewt?"

He frowned. "You said buy something appropriate. Doesn't this pass muster?" He removed his hat and made a low bow, reminding her of what a buccaneer might have looked like a few hundred years ago.

She looked him up and down. The difference between Lewt in a city suit and this man was astonishing. "You'll do," she snapped, angry that she should care what he wore. He was still dumb as a rock about work and near worthless on a horse. "We need to be getting back. We've wasted half the day already."

He didn't argue but simply followed her to the horses. A sack hung off his saddle horn. She didn't ask what was in the bag as they headed home. More clothes, she guessed.

"You going to stay mad at me all day?" he asked as he swung into the saddle.

"You were late."

He didn't apologize; he just thought about it, then said, "So you are going to stay mad."

"You're not planning to say you're sorry."

He smiled. "Would it help?"

"No."

"Then I might as well save my breath."

When they reached the trees at the edge of town, she told him to put on the blindfold again.

He passed her his hat while he tied on the red bandanna, then leaned over and reached out for his hat. His hand bumped her arm.

"Sorry," he said as he found the hat. "I didn't know your arm was there."

"Forget it," she said, reaching for his reins. "We've wasted enough time."

Before she could turn the horses, a shadow of a man moved out from behind one of the trees. He was dressed in the ragged clothes of a down-on-his-luck cowhand. "Interesting game you two are playing," he said, looking up at them with bloodshot eyes. "You wouldn't be kidnapping this man, would you, kid?"

Em saw the gun in the stranger's hand and froze. If she spoke, he'd know she was a woman. Maybe it was better for her if he thought she was a young man. Her braid was hidden beneath her hat, and the slicker covered her body. Unfortunately it also kept her Colt out of easy reach.

She felt, more than saw, Lewt nudge his horse forward, blocking most of the drifter's view of her. Moving only her eyes, she risked a quick glance at Lewt. He'd pulled off the blindfold as if he thought he could face the man down with a stare.

She almost yelled for him to get back. He wasn't armed. But then she saw his face.

His features were hard and unyielding almost as if he were the one stalking prey, but his words came calm, casual. "We're just testing my skills at direction, friend, but I appreciate the concern. We didn't mean to disturb your sleep."

"I'm not your friend," the man shouted. He wavered from side to side as if still drunk on last night's whiskey.

To Em's surprise, Lewton Paterson smiled and said, "You don't want to be my enemy, sir."

The man looked as confused as Emily felt. Was Lewt threatening him or advising him? If Lewt wasn't going to be frightened, a robbery might not work unless the man before them was a cold killer. She could see the man stagger, unsure what to do next. He pushed the gun high as if to make sure Lewt saw it.

Lewt said casually, "Put down the weapon before someone gets hurt."

For a second, the barrel lowered a few inches, and then the drifter changed his mind and waved it.

"I think I'll take the horse before I go," the stranger said, trying to keep his voice steady. "When the deputy told me to leave town last night, he didn't seem to care that I was walking."

"I don't think I can give her up." Lewt patted his mount. "The horse is not mine to give."

"Get off that horse or I'll shoot you off it."

Em fought down a scream. No wonder Lewt's family never came out in the daytime. They were too dumb to survive in the real world.

Just as she reached for his arm, she heard Lewt say, "All right. Don't say I didn't warn you."

Lewt stood in the saddle and pulled one foot from the stirrup. "I was really hoping we could be friends. It's always so much better for one of us."

What happened next was a blur to Em. Lewt seemed to make a great show of swinging his leg over the horse. The tail of his coat flew in the air like a huge bat wing. As he leaned, his free hand moved down the side of his leg, still in the stirrup. A heartbeat later, a knife flew through the air and landed in the robber's hand.

The stranger yelled in pain as he dropped the gun he'd been pointing at them.

Lewt's new boots hit the ground. In two steps he was in front of the robber. He picked up the bumbling bandit's gun with one hand and retrieved his knife with the other.

The outlaw screamed as the blade pulled back through his flesh and his knees buckled beneath him. He cupped his bleeding hand in his unharmed palm. "Look what you did!" he wailed. "It went all the way through." He cried and babbled on about how bad it hurt. Blood filled his unharmed hand and was dripping in the dirt.

Lewt jerked the bandanna hanging loosely around his neck and began wrapping the wound.

"Sorry about that, but I did warn you."

The stranger looked like he might pass out. He glared, glassy-eyed, at Lewt as if he could no longer understand the language.

"Come on. We'll get you to a doctor." Lewt helped the robber onto his horse, climbed up behind him, and looked at Em for guidance. "Lead the way," he snapped, as if waking her with a slap. "There must be a doctor in town."

Em jerked into action. She kicked the horse and rushed toward a big white house at the edge of town. There, her aunt had run a small clinic for almost twenty years; Em knew the shortcut and she took it as fast as she thought Lewt could manage.

Five minutes later they were in the doctor's office. The nurse, Bonnie Faye, started to greet Em when she hit the door but reconsidered when she saw the blood on the man who followed her in. She began barking orders to all, including the doctor. This was an emergency, and emergencies were Bonnie Faye's specialty.

Dr. Hutchison was an old man who usually helped Aunt Sage out only occasionally, but with Sage gone, he took over in the office. He'd seen enough to no longer be curious. He simply directed them into the inner office, cleaned the entry and exit wounds, put three stitches in the palm and four on the back of the robber's hand without bothering with any painkiller, and wrapped the wound.

The robber screamed awhile and then cried.

Em watched as Lewt stepped to the doorway and talked softly to the nurse. The city slicker probably couldn't take the sight of blood, even if he was the one who caused the bleeding. All she could figure out was the guy must have some luck because he didn't look like the kind of man who'd have skill with a knife.

"You were lucky, Barnaby," the doc said as he tied off the bandage. "In a few weeks you'll be good as new if you keep that hand clean."

The disheartened outlaw nodded. "It don't matter none. The deputy is going to shoot me as soon as he realizes I'm in town. He told me to get out and never come back." He raised his head enough to stare at Lewt. "You're probably going to turn me in for attempted robbery."

"No," Lewt said simply. "I see it as just a misunderstanding between friends."

"We're not actually in town, Barnaby. Town line is at the road."

Lewt nodded at Bonnie and moved closer to the bandit. "You'll have to work off the doctor's fee. The nurse says it'll take you two weeks, but you can sleep in their barn and she'll feed you two meals a day as long as you put in a good day's work."

The tall nurse stepped inside. "I agreed to this, Barnaby, on two conditions. You don't step foot off the property or take a drink until the bill is paid."

Em raised an eyebrow. She'd heard her aunt make several such deals to men who couldn't pay. Usually if they stayed sober a few weeks they looked good enough to find a job in town or at one of the ranches around. This time she wondered if Bonnie or Lewt had thought of the plan.

Before the nurse could get chatty and give her away, Em stormed past Lewt and said, "We'd better be going. We've still got a day's work to do."

He raised an eyebrow but followed.

When they were at their horses, she twirled toward him so suddenly the man almost slammed into her. "Want to tell me what happened back there in the trees? Like for one, where did that knife come from?"

"Look, Em, can we just forget it happened? What was I supposed to do? I couldn't very well kill a man for being down on his luck. I didn't think he would have fired that old gun, but I wasn't sure. From the looks of it, I'd say the weapon was as likely to go off in his hand as at us."

"I was thinking of killing him for trying to steal a horse," Em cut in, "but you? You wound him and then help him. I swear, the man could have shot us both and you worried about his cut."

Lewt took a long breath. "Can we just act like it never happened? The guy was too thin and hungry and desperate to be able to kill us. Even if he'd got off a shot, the odds were he wouldn't have hit us."

She glared at him. Who was this man who worried about hurting a robber? A nut, she decided. A rich, from a good family, nut.

To her surprise, he pulled out his watch and checked the time. Now he was worried about the time. Not an hour ago when she was waiting for him, but now when they'd already wasted half the day.

"I know we're on your time schedule, Em, but do you think we could stop in at one of those cafés in town and have a meal before you try to work me to death again? I'm starving." He hesitated, and added, "I'll buy."

She opened her mouth to say no, then reconsidered. It was almost noon. They'd never make it back to the ranch in time for lunch, and the two eggs she'd had at dawn seemed a far memory. "All right. You've already wasted an hour knifing and doctoring a bandit, we might as well take time to eat."

They turned around and rode back into town. Lewt stopped at the first café and waited for her to swing down.

She walked in ahead of him and took the table in the corner, placing her back to the door. He circled around and took the chair facing her. When the waitress passed, he ordered two of the specials with coffee.

Emily kept her head low and her hat on.

"You eat here often?" Lewt asked.

"Never," she answered. "How'd you know what to order?"

"If there's no board and no menu, they always

have a special. If you never eat here, no one is likely to recognize you. This kind of place tends to have the same folks every day."

"If I keep my hat and coat on, they'll think I'm a man."

Lewt laughed. "If you keep them on, *I'll* think you're a man."

"I don't care what you think."

"I know," he said softly. "I think that's why you're so much fun to be around. No matter what I do or how hard I try, you're still not going to like me, right?"

"Right," she answered.

"So I guess there's little chance you'll help me figure out which one of the McMurray sisters to marry?"

"Right."

The waitress sloshed their coffee on the table as she slammed the cups down and rushed past.

Lewt tried again. "Come on, Em. Can't we be friends?"

She couldn't help but smile. "The last friend of yours has a half dozen stitches in his hand."

Lewt shoved his hat back and smiled at her. "You're right. I guess I'm a dangerous man to know."

"Why do you want to marry one of the girls, anyway? There must be a hundred girls in any big city you could marry."

"I need a wife," he said simply. "A good wife."

After a few moments he leaned on the table and

whispered, "I've got to have a lady from a good family. I need to get married right away."

She met his gaze. "In a family way, are you?"

He laughed. "Something like that."

Em decided she liked this strange man who must have been raised by rich moles and who could throw a knife better than anyone she'd ever seen. "I'll help you learn ranching, but that's all. You'll have to court the girls all by yourself."

"Fair enough."

℘ CHAPTER 12 ℘

Lewt used his own handkerchief to cover his eyes for the ride back, thinking that riding through the mountains blindfolded was about the dumbest idea he'd ever heard.

He spent most of the time asking questions about the ranch, the land, and the history of the family. Now and then he asked a question about one of the McMurray girls, but Em never gave him anything that would help. In fact, she seemed to know less about them than he'd observed. She sounded surprised when he said Beth was unsure of herself and he wondered why Rose worried herself sick trying to make everyone happy.

They came back through the far north pasture. When Em told him to pull his blindfold off, the sight before him almost took his breath away.

Horses for as far up the hill as he could see. He guessed a hundred, maybe more, and all beautiful.

He knew this was a working ranch that had raised horses for fifty years, but watching them graze and run across the land made him think they were living wild.

"They're really something," Lewt whispered.

"That they are. The first McMurray came to this land with a dozen. There are cattle down by the river and we grow wheat and corn on land on the other side of that hill, but here, in the heart of the ranch, we care for the horses."

The weather was sunny after the rain, leaving the air feeling frosty. Lewt waited for her orders, but for a few minutes she just watched the animals as if they were hers.

Finally, she turned to him, all business. "There's a storm coming in. I can feel it in the air. We ride the borders of the ranch until dark."

His body had taken a beating on the horse yesterday, but this morning when he'd climbed back on for more torture, he'd found the ride easier. Thanks to her constant shouting, he'd learned to distribute his weight more evenly and control the animal with far less effort. She'd told him it was probably far more comfortable for the horse, but to his surprise it was also more comfortable for him. His new heavy twill trousers and boots protected his legs, and the gloves buffered the blisters on his palms.

When she shot off toward the west, he was only a few lengths behind. They rode what she called *the border,* as though Whispering Mountain were its own country. They looked for breaks in the fence or places where the animals might get themselves in trouble. They stopped three times to mend a fence and once to check out tracks. She told him that once in a while big cats would come down from far back in the hills looking for food in winter.

Lewt didn't like to think about what one of the mountain lions could do to a newborn horse. He was starting to understand why she cared so much for the beautiful animals and why she wore a gun to keep them safe.

When he bumped her for the third time as he straightened the fence, he stopped suddenly and dropped the pole he'd been holding.

"What are you doing? We don't have it in place yet." She straightened, angry at their wasted effort.

"I've had enough," he said simply. "Every time I accidentally touch you, I feel you freeze in panic or bristle like a porcupine. Em, I'm not going to attack you or hurt you. Even if I thought about it you'd shoot me, so why would I even try?"

"We need to get this fence fixed."

"We need to get this settled between us." Neither of them moved. "Hit me, Em. Hit me hard. Get some of that anger out. I don't know if you're mad at all men or just me, but I'm here. I'm your target."

"I don't want to hit you." She straightened.

"Yes, you do. I got a feeling you want to hit every man in the world, so you might as well start with me." He widened his stance. "Hit me. We're not finishing this fence until you get this out of your system, and I seem to be the only male near enough for you to hate."

She glared at him, raised her hand, and slapped his shoulder.

He didn't budge. "Hit me hard!"

All the anger she'd stored since she was a child huddled in a corner of her parents' bedroom exploded, and she swung hard into his shoulder.

He staggered a half step backward and waited for another blow.

Memories of the way her real father had hurt her mother came rolling back. She'd watched him attack her and bed her. She'd heard her mother choke down screams so she wouldn't wake her daughters. But Em had been awake. She'd witnessed it all.

Suddenly, she was slamming her fist against Lewt's chest as if he were somehow to blame. He made no effort to block a single blow. The wall of his chest was solid against her assault and she guessed she must be planting bruises, but she didn't stop.

Finally a sob broke from her throat, and she would have collapsed if he hadn't held her up. She gulped down tears as rage settled inside her, no longer burning.

"It's all right, Em," he finally whispered. "I don't know if I'll be here beyond this week or if we'll ever see each other again, but I want you to know and believe that I'm never going to hurt you. If I come too close you can pound on me again, but don't be afraid of me." He looked down at her. "Em, never be afraid of me again."

She straightened and pulled away. "Why'd you let me do that to you? It must have hurt."

"I don't know. Half the time I look at you, I get the feeling you're fighting to keep from clobbering me." He studied her, wondering if she was even aware of how she watched every step when he was near. "You all right now?"

"I'm all right," she answered. He offered his hand, and she took it for a moment. "Thank you," she whispered as they turned back to the fence.

"You're welcome," he whispered back, already tackling the job at hand.

The sun was melting in the west when they rode into the huge barn. A north wind had been whipping up all afternoon, and he was thankful once again for his new coat and gloves. They unsaddled their horses, brushed them down, and filled the feeders.

When he reached to put his coat back on, Em stopped him. "Come over here." She walked toward the tack room. "You've got blood on that new vest."

"Forget it," he said as he followed.

She shook her head. "No way. If you're going courting, you need to look your best. What will the fine ladies say if they see blood?"

He grinned at her. "You do care. Helping me out just a little, are you, Em?"

She shrugged. "I figure you need all the help you can get."

"Not really. You should see the other two guys. One's little more than a boy, and he's a mama's boy at that. The other is a pompous ass. I'll be surprised if he's still around at dinner tonight. The only thing good about that reverend visiting is that he keeps Boyd from constantly bragging. I figure with me staying away a few days, the ladies will have had enough of them and be waiting to spend some time with me."

Reaching for a rag and a bar of soap, she began working on the blood spilled near the third button of his vest. She stood so close all he would have had to do was lean forward a few inches to kiss her cheek. The idea that he was even thinking about such a thing shocked him.

Em wasn't the kind of woman he wanted. In truth, she wasn't much of a woman at all. She rode like a man, talked like a man—hell, half the day she swore like a man. She wasn't like the girls he'd known in saloons, but she wasn't the soft female he wanted for a wife.

But right here, right now, with her only inches away, she certainly didn't smell like a man. Her small kindness touched him in an odd way.

Lewt laughed. He'd been around horses so long today he was starting to act like one. Smelling out for a mate didn't seem like a good plan.

"What are you laughing at?" she asked.

"You don't want to know," he answered.

"I wouldn't have asked if I didn't."

Her bluer-than-blue eyes reminded him of fragile Wedgwood china. "I was thinking I'd like to say thanks for helping by kissing you on the cheek."

"Don't even think about it or I'll—"

He took a step back. "Don't worry. I wouldn't. Between your attitude and your looks I wouldn't imagine many men would."

He saw the hurt in her eyes and wished he could take his words back before the echo of them settled in the barn. He hadn't meant to hurt her. He'd taken her insults all day without a word, but when he'd tossed one back, he felt lower than slime in a dirty horse trough.

"I'm sorry," he said, fighting the urge to touch her and brush away the pain he'd caused.

"Forget it." She turned her back to him. "Go do your courting and stop bothering me."

He tried to think of something else to say but was afraid he'd only cause more damage. This tough woman who did a man's work all day wasn't quite as hardened as she wanted everyone to believe. Somehow, if it took him the rest of the week he had here, he'd make it up to her.

"Where do you eat supper, Em?" It occurred to him that she couldn't join the hands in the bunkhouse, and she couldn't join the McMurrays.

"Do you ride home first?" She'd said she lived at home, but he'd never thought to ask how close home was.

"I'll eat in the kitchen with the two girls who clean," she answered. "When the weather's bad like this, I can bunk in with them."

He knew he'd be prying if he asked more, but he was glad she didn't eat alone. "Well," he said. "Enjoy your dinner."

Lewt grabbed his hat and coat and walked toward the house. The temperature had dropped with the sun, but he barely felt it. He went in the front door of the big ranch house and met the others in the huge living area they called the great room. They were all having a drink before the meal. Boyd, still wearing his riding clothes, seemed to be in the middle of a story about how he'd fought off horse thieves a few years ago. All the others circled around him and listened to every word, but Lewt didn't buy all the details of the rancher's story.

Lewt poured himself a glass of water and joined them. The subject moved from horse thieves to being scarred as a child to who knows what else. Lewt stopped paying attention. Davis nodded at him when he entered and the ladies smiled at him when he caught their eye, but not one of them made a comment about where he'd been or what he'd done all day. No one noticed his new clothes even after he'd taken his time making sure he was dressed appropriately for a change.

Lewt decided he was a six-foot invisible man standing in the center of the room. When he moved in to dinner, it didn't get much better. The place cards for the evening put him between Mrs. Watson, the chaperone, and Mrs. Allender, Davis's mother. Both ladies had the habit of talking to him at the same time.

After turning his head back and forth a dozen times trying to keep up with both their conversations, he finally just looked down at his food and ate. They didn't seem to mind; they both kept talking.

Mrs. Allender was a dear whose only topic of conversation seemed to be her children and grandchildren. Mrs. Watson's speech slowed with each glass of wine and her laugh grew louder. For the most part Lewt had no idea what she was laughing at . . . the volume just hit him at hurricane force every now and then.

Rose circled the table a few times and asked if he needed anything, but she didn't put her hand on his shoulder while she talked as she did when she stopped behind Boyd and Davis.

When the meal was finished and the others moved in to sing around the piano, Lewt slipped out onto the porch. He didn't care if he froze; he needed silence.

He had it for about a minute before he realized someone else was on the long porch.

Em. She sat sideways in a cushioned porch swing, her long legs filling the seat.

Lewt walked up, stared down at her boots on the cushion, and waited.

With a grumble, she moved her feet and sat up straight.

He didn't bother to speak to her. He just sat down in the swing next to her and began to rock back and forth.

She ignored him, as if hoping he'd go away without noticing her, for as long as she could, then finally turned to him and said, "How's the courting doing?"

Lewt chewed up the first dozen words he thought of saying and finally said, "When I came here, I thought I might have a hard time picking the girl I wanted. When I saw them, I figured it would be almost impossible to pick out which one was the prettiest. They were all grand. No matter which one I chose, any would make me a grand wife."

"So," Em cut in. "What's your problem, cowboy?"

He glared at her, thinking the *cowboy* comment was probably her idea of a joke. On the dark porch he could barely make out her face, but he didn't have to see. He knew she was laughing at him.

"The problem is—" He pushed hard, almost swinging them off the porch. When the swing settled, he finished. "It never occurred to me that they might not want me."

"Not one?"

He didn't like the way she asked. It sounded like she'd suspected the possibility all along.

He had a feeling Em was just playing him. "Oh, two of the ladies in there just love me. They won't stop talking to me. You could say they fought for my attention all through dinner."

"So, what's your problem?"

"The two were Mrs. Allender and Mrs. Watson."

Em laughed. Not just a kind laugh to show she was following his troubles, but a falling-over, holding-her-ribs laugh. She laughed so hard she shook their seat.

When she finally settled enough that they could continue swinging, he said, "You think my heartbreak is funny?"

"You're not heartbroken. You've spent more time looking at the McMurray girls' assets than you have at their eyes."

"Damn it! I'm pouring out my troubles to you and you're making fun of me. You're the one person on the ranch, apparently, who knows even less about courting than I do, and here I am telling my problem to you."

She seemed to take pity on him. "Oh, come on, you must have met many a girl. I bet you know the words to sweet-talk them. Maybe you just haven't tried. I can't believe you're giving up after two days. Turn their heads with words. You must know how."

He stared out at the night. "Not unless you count 'How much do you charge for the night?' as sweet talk. That's about all I usually say to a woman." He looked into the night, wishing he hadn't told her that.

She'd probably think he visited ladies of the night every chance he got. In truth, he rarely even bought one of the girls a drink in the saloons. He learned early from watching that those kinds of workingwomen value friends far more than customers.

He pushed the swing. "Until now I hadn't realized how very little I knew about the fairer sex."

"You're kidding. Don't tell me that family of yours never lets you out to go to dances and dinners with proper young ladies."

"My family's dead." Lewt spoke the truth before he thought to stop. Not that it mattered; the girl who took care of the horses wasn't likely to tell the group inside.

"All of them?"

"All of them," he said slowly. "They have been for a long time."

She didn't say anything for a long while. They just rocked back and forth. He thought she might get up and leave, but she stayed. She probably figured he'd go back inside, but he had no plan to as long as he could hear voices and music coming from inside. They were singing silly songs that made even less sense than the saloon songs.

Finally, he pulled a big quilt from the table against the wall. "Want to share? If we're staying out here we might as well try not to freeze."

She hesitated, then nodded. "I used to sit out here wrapped in a blanket with my father. We'd watch storms come in over the mountains."

He tossed half the quilt over her and leaned to tuck the end in at her shoulder. "I know you don't like to touch, but you're shivering. If you move closer, we might keep each other warm, and I promise to pretend I don't notice you're there."

She moved so near he could feel her shaking.

"It's all right, Em; I may have done a lot of things in my life, but I've never hurt a woman. In a funny way, despite all your yelling and bossing, you've been kinder to me than anyone here. If I didn't have to wait for the train in town until Saturday, I'd leave tonight."

"They like you well enough," she said. "Give them time to get to know you, and then they'll dislike you with grounds."

"That's very comforting." He grinned. "I've been around you for two days and you still can barely tolerate me."

"True." She moved closer still. "But I am getting used to you and now that I know I can beat you up, I do feel better around you." They both laughed, and she added, "Just promise not to call me your friend. I'm not sure I have as much blood in me as the last friend you had this morning."

He lifted his arm and held the blanket around one shoulder as her other shoulder slid against the warmth of his side. "You got a deal."

"Where'd you learn to throw a knife like that?" She pushed at his shoulder as if it were a pillow.

"Church," he said, remembering the year he'd

spent at a mission when his mother seemed to have forgotten he existed. She'd dropped him off there one morning in early spring to go to work and not picked him up for eleven months. The nuns made him work around the place and go to school every morning and mass every afternoon, but they never found the knife he'd had on him when he'd entered. More because of nothing else to do than for self-defense, he spent all his alone time practicing tossing the old knife. By the time he could afford a good blade, he was deadly accurate.

To this day, when he was feeling lonely or down, he'd practice with a knife. In a way it was as comforting as sitting silently with an old friend.

"Church," Em mumbled, as if she didn't believe him but was too tired to question.

Slowly, they both relaxed. They talked about the storm coming in and watched winter lightning flash along the top of the hill line. Neither asked personal questions, maybe because neither wanted to answer any.

Finally, about the time the music stopped and the lights in the main room were turned low, Lewt shifted so that Em could settle her head more comfortably on his shoulder. He could tell from her steady breathing that she was sound asleep, and to his surprise he had no desire to go inside.

When she settled against his side, her hand reached out and found his. She held on tight, even in sleep. Lewt thought it was the strangest, most tender thing he'd ever known a woman to do.

He didn't pull his hand away. In his entire life he couldn't remember one time anyone had ever held his hand. He rocked slowly and kissed the top of her head just before he drifted into sleep.

℘ CHAPTER 13 ℧

At the border

About the time the U.S. Cavalry finished breakfast, they heard a racket and felt the earth rumble as only a herd of cattle can make it do when they're running at full speed. The soldiers saddled up and moved closer to the Rio. At first all they saw was cattle, and then as the sun rose, they saw the rangers climbing down to where their horses had been left, mounting up, and herding the stolen cattle back onto Texas soil.

McNelly rode in the lead of the tired, dirty band. He smiled broadly beneath his beard and mustache. His bluff had paid off. The ranchers across the border claimed they didn't have the bandits, but they returned the cattle.

As the rangers reached Texas, they circled out, allowing the cavalry to herd.

One soldier stepped up to hold McNelly's horse while the captain of the rangers stepped down.

"You left a horse on the other side of the river, sir," the private announced.

McNelly glanced back. "That's Duncan McMurray's horse. Damn devil won't let anyone ride her but Duncan, and, to tell the truth, I don't think there's one of my men who have enough strength left to try."

"Where is McMurray?"

"He'll be along," the captain said, as if voicing his words would make it so. "He's a third-generation ranger. If he's alive, he'll make it back to Texas."

Wyatt moved up beside McNelly. "You want me to take a few men and go back to look for him?"

McNelly shook his head. "It'd take a hundred men to go after him now. They've figured out we were bluffing. Any Texan on that side of the Rio is probably already dead. Duncan's smart. My guess is he's found somewhere to hide and decided to wait it out until dark. Get some grub and some sleep. By the time you wake up, he'll be here ready to eat some supper."

Wyatt watched the river all day, hoping Duncan would somehow show up. In the dark before a sliver of moon appeared, he swam the river one last time and tried to bring Duncan's mare back. The Mexicans had left her tied, probably hoping she'd lose some of her fight when she got hungry enough.

The mare let Wyatt close enough to pull her saddle and untie the bridle, and then she bolted into the night as if she had somewhere to be and was late.

Wyatt swam back across the river thinking that at least the horse was alive, even if Duncan McMurray hadn't made it.

ᔕ CHAPTER 14 ᔐ

Lewt rolled over, opened one eye, and realized it was after dawn. He'd probably missed whatever torture Em had planned for him today. To his surprise, he felt strangely sorry for not meeting her at dawn.

The others had asked about his day, but the ladies didn't seem overly interested and the men were probably happy he wasn't around. He could probably fall over dead and the only one who would miss him would be Em. Oh, and Mrs. Allender would worry that her bird might catch whatever killed him.

Sometime, long after midnight, he'd carried Em inside and left her on an old worn couch in the big room downstairs. He had no idea where the woman slept and wasn't about to ask anyone. Knowing Em, she'd be up and in the saddle before anyone else woke.

She was one tough woman, but asleep last night she seemed so fragile. He'd remembered the way she'd looked when he'd gripped her shoulder to steady himself as she'd doctored his cut. For a moment fear and panic had flooded those haunting eyes. He never wanted to see that look again. The memory of how broken she'd appeared after he'd demanded she hit him flashed through his mind. He didn't care if she hated every man on earth; he didn't want her to hate *him*. He found it impossible to believe that no man outside her family had ever won her trust.

He guessed part of the reason she'd never married was that she was taller than most men and so slender she barely had any shape to her. Then, to decrease her chances more, she lived out here in the middle of nowhere and worked all day alone. Her final handicap in the race to the altar would be her shyness. She did a good job of hiding it with her cold brisk manner, but he'd glimpsed her hesitance around men. She never let anyone close enough to hurt her.

She wasn't homely or even plain. She just did nothing to make herself attractive. After seeing women painted up most of his life, the contrast was refreshing, he finally reasoned.

He dressed in one of the new cotton shirts and heavy wool trousers he'd bought and went down to the kitchen, deciding that Em wasn't his problem. In a few days he'd be gone and it wasn't likely their paths would ever cross again. Yet when he noticed a few slight bruises on his shoulder, he was glad he'd broken through to her, if only a bit.

Mrs. Allender and Rose were sitting at the big

round table in the kitchen. They appeared to be drinking tea and talking as the smell of cinnamon filled the room.

"Morning, Lewton." Rose jumped to her feet. "May I get you some coffee?"

"Please, sit down." He smiled back at her, liking the way she greeted him. "I can help myself. If you don't mind me joining you two sweet ladies this beautiful morning." He was laying it on a little thick, but he'd decided last night that he'd give this courting thing one more try. He'd never walked away from a game until all the cards had been played, and he'd had the dream of a home and family too long to let it die. If all the saloon girls liked him, surely one of these ladies would see something worth taking home.

Rose handed him a cup and let him pour his own coffee while she watched, as if ready to step in if he made a mistake. She barely reached his shoulder, and he decided that if he could win her heart, he'd call her Little Darling.

He leaned down to smell the warm cinnamon air coming from beneath the cover of a white towel.

She wiggled one finger at him, silently telling him to leave her baking alone. "Later," she whispered. "I promise."

The thought crossed his mind to lift Rose off her feet and kiss her right here, right now, but Mrs. Allender would probably have a heart attack, and he wasn't all that sure Rose would welcome his advances. She was nice, and friendly, but not all that friendly.

Mrs. Allender broke the mood by saying, "Join us. By the time you finish that cup of coffee, the breakfast rolls should be cool."

"You two seemed deep in planning. Maybe I should leave?"

"Oh, no." Rose followed him to the table and took her seat when he held out her chair. "We were just thinking about what we'd like to do today. Finally, it looks like we are going to have a sunny day. It's a little cold and damp to have a picnic, but we could ride out to where the men do the spring branding. There's a fire pit out there and rocks that would work as chairs. We could have lunch there and then ride up to the summit. The view is grand this time of year. Sometimes I think you can see for a hundred miles."

"Sounds like a good plan," Lewt said, thinking at least there wouldn't be any singing. He also felt a little more comfortable on a horse than he had when he'd arrived, thanks to Em.

"I won't be going, of course." Mrs. Allender shook her head. "Reverend and Mrs. Watson told me that if the group plans an outing anywhere a buggy can't go, they'll stay at home as well. The three of us could probably all use a nap. You young people are keeping us up too late."

"I think we'll manage without babysitters," he said, winking at Rose.

She looked down, not returning his smile. He wondered if he'd been a little bold. "That is if I'm invited, Miss Rose."

Those dark beautiful eyes met his. "Of course you're invited; you're our guest. We'd love to have you come along."

Lewt might have thought her invitation a little more *inviting* if she'd said *she'd* like him to come along.

They talked of little things for a while, and the table slowly filled.

First Boyd arrived and shouted with the excitement of getting to ride after two days of being in the house. For all his talk of loving horses, Em had told Lewt that he'd never come to the barn to check on his animals. Since the night they'd played cards, Lewt had the feeling Boyd Sinclair was playing more than one game.

Next came the other two sisters. Bethie didn't seem very excited about the picnic, and Emily complained that she feared she might not finish her sewing. Lewt couldn't help but wonder if either of the girls was aware of how they'd hurt Rose's feelings by dashing her plan.

He watched her carefully. She didn't say a word. Didn't defend the plan. She just packed a lunch for them all. He wasn't sure if Rose didn't care what her sisters said, or if she was just sure that, in the end, they'd give in and follow her suggestions. It was a good plan. After all, they'd been cooped up in the house all day thanks to the rain. *Except for me,* Lewt thought; he'd been out riding with Em.

As soon as he finished breakfast, Lewt said he'd go out to the barn and help get the horses ready. Davis was still eating breakfast, so he didn't offer to help, but Boyd asked Lewt to tell his wrangler to have both his horses ready to ride in ten minutes. He was explaining to the women that he never made up his mind which to ride before he saw their moods.

Lewt walked toward the barn, wondering if any other man worried about his horse's mood. In truth he'd volunteered to help with the horses only because he thought he might run into Em, but as he'd guessed earlier, Sumner told him Em had left a little after dawn.

"You have any idea where she went today?" Lewt asked the old man, who seemed to be in charge of the activities around the barn and corrals.

"Nope. I gave up trying to keep up with Miss Em twenty years ago. She rides over this ranch. That's all I know. If I was guessing, I'd say she'll be looking for tracks from that big cat. One of the men reported seeing a horse with fresh slashes, but no real damage. If the cat gets too close to the herd, they might stomp him. An animal like that hunts for the weakest, the one alone."

"Anyone ever ride with her?" Lewt didn't like the idea that she was alone.

"Nope." Sumner bit off a plug of tobacco. "Before

you, I never seen her ride with any man except her dad."

"Where is he?" Lewt asked as he saddled his horse.

"Ain't here," Sumner answered. He moved beside Lewt and strapped a rifle in a leather scabbard onto his saddle. "Miss Em told me if the group went out, one of you men should be armed. You know how to use a gun?"

"I do," Lewt said. "But I don't like them much. Too much noise."

Sumner frowned at him as if disgusted with his answer and walked off.

"Thanks for the visit," Lewt yelled.

"Anytime," Sumner yelled back. "Want to help me saddle the other horses?"

"Why not?" Lewt shrugged, surprised at how much he wished he'd ridden out at dawn and not hung around to go with the others. A picnic didn't sound near as exciting as hunting a mountain lion.

Boyd's horse wrangler appeared and worked with the Sinclair animals. He walked both horses, saddled and ready, out of the barn without saying a word to Lewt or Sumner.

The old man mumbled. "Now that's fine horseflesh. Bred for speed, but my guess is they wouldn't hold up a day working cattle."

"Really." Lewt walked the rest of the horses out with Sumner.

Sumner nodded. "They're high-strung too. That

bay reminds me of a cousin I had. One too many inbreedings in my family, I guess. He'd be just as normal as me and you and then for no reason at all, he'd fire up and start beating on whoever was closest to him."

"What happened to him?"

"He was accidentally left home alone."

"And?" Lewt asked.

"He beat himself to death." The old man waited a few steps, then smiled a toothless grin at Lewt.

Lewt burst out laughing about the time the ladies came out on the porch.

"What's so funny?" Beth asked.

"Nothing," Lewt answered. "Sumner was just talking about his family." He held her spirited black mare as Beth climbed into the saddle.

Rose was up before anyone could assist her, but Emily let Davis help her into the saddle. All three girls must have been born to ride, but apparently Emily had missed a few lessons. Lewt tied a pack to both his horse and Rose's while Beth looked like she'd strapped on a roll of blankets behind her saddle. They were ready.

Boyd took a few minutes to pick which mount he wanted, then led the group as if wanting to show off his horse. He yelled at his wrangler to give the other horse a good run before taking him back to the barn.

The man frowned, as always, then took off in the opposite direction from the group.

130

Davis stayed close to Emily because she said her mount was acting up a bit. Beth stayed close to Davis as they all circled the corrals and rode toward open range.

Within a hundred yards Rose caught up to Lewt and slowed her horse enough to stay by his side.

"We've missed you being with us during the days, Lewton," she said, smiling. "I hope Em showed you the ranch."

"She did." He thought he might as well ask a few questions. "Are you two friends?"

Rose was too busy pulling on her gloves to answer for a moment, then said, "We used to be very close. Now, she's busy with the horses."

"The last night we're here"—Lewt began choosing his words carefully—"we might want to invite her to the party. I'd bet she'd like talking with Boyd about his horses."

"I'll do that." Rose tilted her head as if looking at him in fresh light. "You're a thoughtful man, Lewton Paterson."

He smiled, thinking he'd finally said something right. After that, they talked easily. Rose told him about coming here with her mother and sisters and how foreign everything was to what she'd known.

He told her of the train trip out from Austin and how he enjoyed watching the land drift by almost as if he were sitting still and the scenery were moving.

She described growing up on a ranch and living in a little house in town when the weather was too bad to travel back and forth to school. "It's the perfect house, really, nestled between the church and the school. My papa always called it the girls' house because he said it was far too little for a man to live in. We all use it now and then when we have to stay in town late or the weather turns bad. Or"—she grinned as if admitting a weakness—"when a house full of people gets to be too much and we just want to be alone."

She asked him about his home, but Lewt talked of the work he'd done while with Em yesterday. How could he tell her he never remembered having a home? Even now, the room he rented wasn't something anyone would call a home. His mother had a room in the basement of a whorehouse in New Orleans where she spent her days doing laundry. His father sometimes came to visit, usually when he was out of money. By the time he was three or four he remembered hearing his mother yell for his father to "take the kid" when he left. Sometimes he did, and Lewt learned that there were levels of hell.

He looked over at Rose and knew he'd never tell her about his childhood. How do you tell someone surrounded by love what it was like to be starving but have to learn early to eat only half your food and save the rest because it might be days before you ate again?

He was glad for the distraction as they skirted a pasture with yearlings running across tall grass.

The group stopped to watch, laughing and picking out which one they thought was the most beautiful.

Even if he married Rose and lived with her fifty years, she didn't need to know about his childhood. He only wished he could forget.

Boyd Sinclair finally got tired of showing off and doubled back to join Lewt and Rose. The man went on and on about how wonderful his stallion was, and Rose listened politely. Lewt even asked a few questions. At least if Boyd was talking, Rose wasn't thinking of any more questions to ask him.

Now and then, he'd glance back and spot Beth, Davis, and Emily behind them. Once in a while, when Boyd stopped talking for a few seconds, Lewt thought he heard Beth's laughter. Part of him wished he were back with them, but Miss Emily rarely had anything to say to him, and Beth only had eyes for Davis.

By the time they reached the site where the fire pit and corrals were, he'd learned a great deal about Rose and her family and more than he wanted to know about Boyd Sinclair. Lewt wouldn't have been surprised if his family had sent him north to find a bride just so he'd have someone else to talk to.

Lewt helped Rose down from her saddle, even though he knew she was perfectly able to swing down alone. She didn't seem to mind his polite touch at all. In fact, she thanked him, which he had a feeling Em would never do.

All three McMurray ladies wore riding skirts

made of heavy cloth and western boots to match their coats. The day was sunny, but still chilly, and the wind had turned from the west and now seemed to be blowing more from the north.

"Looks like someone already stacked the wood for a fire," Lewt commented as they moved to a circle of rocks and downed tree trunks around a pit. He, for one, was looking forward to a fire.

"Probably Em," Rose moved closer. "I said we'd be coming this way when I saw her."

"Did she leave before dawn?" He swore he felt like she was a ghost following him. Even today when she was nowhere near, he was still thinking about her. He wouldn't have been surprised to look up in the trees and see her watching them.

Rose smiled. "Em never leaves before dawn or stays out after sundown. She's afraid of darkness. If you ask her, she'll admit that when she was a girl someone always had to hold her hand until she went to sleep."

Lewt looked up at the tree line, wishing Em were with them. He'd thought it strange when she touched his hand in the darkness on the corner of the porch last night. Now, he knew what it meant.

She trusted him. The woman to whom no one talked, who spent her days alone, trusted him. Maybe not a great deal, but some. In a strange way he felt like she'd given him a gift.

Boyd started the fire about the time Davis and the other two ladies arrived, laughing. As always, when

Bethie was around, everyone's mood lightened.

While the fire built to a blaze, they all gathered near, telling stories that could only be learned around campfires.

While the coffee boiled, Davis told about how Gypsy wagons used to stop and camp in a wooded area by their farm. One night, he and his older brother went down to the camp to see the fortune-teller. She was a woman, dressed in black except for one red scarf tied around her waist. She read their fortunes with her head down, never meeting their eyes. All he remembered seeing was her wrinkled face and twisted hands appearing almost deformed as she worked with the strange cards. When she finished, she stood and turned her back to them. There, where hair and a scarf should have been was another face . . . the face of a young woman, who winked at them.

Beth bought into the story. "She had two faces?"

"No, one had to be fake; problem is I have no idea which one. When we asked one of the others, he said she wore a mask on the front because it would be too frightening if people knew her head was on backward."

"Maybe she's been to hell." Lewt smiled. "Like in *Dante's Inferno*, where God turns all the fortune-tellers' heads backward because they tried to see into the future."

Beth poked him. "You read that poem? The whole thing?"

"I was bored one winter. I read everything I could get my hands on."

"And it made sense to you?" Bethie made a face as if she'd tasted something sour.

"A friend told me the way to read it was to get so drunk you can barely make out the words. Then, keep reading and drinking and it all makes perfect sense." Lewt smiled as he drew laughter from them all.

Boyd paced beside the fire. "Well, I for one, wouldn't want to see into the future. It'd take all the fun out of living life." He stopped in front of Davis. "And I believe she was simply playing a prank on two gullible boys. If her head were really on backward she'd be bumping into trees."

Everyone laughed, and the conversation grew with the fire. By the time Rose pulled out sandwiches and fruit, everyone claimed to be starving. They ate, then spread out on blankets and talked as the day aged. They were all adults, all knowing their own mind, but something about being away from the house and the chaperones added a degree of openness, of honesty, that had been lacking before.

Boyd admitted that he worried about filling his father's and grandfather's shoes. Davis told of his dreams for buildings, dreams no one in Austin would probably allow him to fulfill.

Lewt could think of nothing to share, or, more exactly, nothing he wanted to share. He closed his eyes and listened. After half an hour, Rose asked him a question. When he didn't answer, they all assumed he'd gone to sleep. Part of him wanted to absorb all their memories into his mind and make them his own.

Late in the afternoon, the wind kicked up, but no one seemed to be in a hurry to leave. Rose passed out the last of the cookies.

Lewt acted like he woke when he heard the word *cookie*. They all laughed and spent time telling him about all he'd missed. Only they didn't tell their own stories, they told each other's. Suddenly Boyd's frightening story of being lost as a boy became funny when Beth repeated it, and Rose's tender story of hearing ghosts in the attic when she was little sounded very different when Davis said the same words.

When they finally noticed the drop in temperature, everyone scrambled to collect their things and horses. If the weather turned bad, the two-hour trip home might seem endless.

Boyd's animal went crazy as wind whistled through the evergreens and sent tumbleweeds dancing five feet high.

Just as Davis helped Emily onto her mount, Boyd's stallion kicked wildly, hitting Emily's horse. Her mount reared, knocking her from the saddle and beneath the horses' feet.

Everyone ran to help. Lewt and Davis reached her first and shoved horses aside as they yelled like madmen trying to get to Emily.

In what seemed like seconds, Emily's horse bolted wildly across the field. Boyd held on to his mount by the neck, but the horse was lifting him off the ground each time he pitched and bucked. Davis and Lewt pulled Emily to the safety of the rocks, knowing Boyd was on his own. If he was half the rancher he claimed, he should be able to handle it.

The men stood guard as Beth and Rose knelt beside Emily, both asking questions at once. Lewt watched Boyd lose the war with his horse. The animal kicked him a few more times, then pulled free and ran into the wind, following Emily's horse.

When Lewt turned back to the women, Emily was crying in Beth's arms as Rose stood slowly.

"How is she?" Davis asked in almost a whisper. His face was pale, but he'd acted when necessary.

"I think she may have a broken rib. She says her leg hurts, but I didn't feel any bone broken, so maybe it's just bruised. It'd take too long to get a wagon up here, but I think if one of you could hold her, we'd make it home without doing any more damage." Lewt looked at Boyd. "How about you?"

He rubbed his leg but said simply, "I'm fine."

Lewt understood. Right now bruises didn't count.

"I'll carry her," Davis offered. "How about we wrap a few blankets around her legs to buffer any jolts? I saw my dad do that to my little sister once."

"Good idea." As always, it seemed Rose tackled

the job. She wrapped two blankets around Emily, then used her belt to secure them.

Lewt watched. He didn't know what to do with a woman who was crying, but everyone else seemed to. Davis patted her hand. Beth talked softly. Even Boyd knelt down and brushed her cheek, telling her how sorry he was.

Emily seemed embarrassed by all the attention and told everyone she felt much better.

Lewt doubted anyone believed her.

Beth gave up trying to keep her hat on in the wind. Her curly hair was flying around her face. "Give me your bandanna," she ordered.

Davis did so without asking questions.

She tied her hair back out of her face and announced, "I'm riding hard and fast toward home. I'll have everything ready for you, Rose, when you get there with Emily. I'll also send one of the men with a buggy to pick up old Doctor Hutchison."

Rose nodded.

Bethie urged her horse into a run even before her foot was secured in the stirrups. All her gentle, ladylike manner was gone. She was a horsewoman who could ride as fast as the wind, and they all stood watching for a moment in amazement.

The men circled Emily and carefully lifted her onto Davis's saddle, with Rose telling them to be careful with each step. Davis climbed up behind her, talking to her softly as he turned his horse toward home at a walk.

"Boyd," Rose, the planner, said, "if you'll double up with me, we can ride beside Davis just in case something happens. Lewt, since you know the way home, would you mind putting out the fire? With this wind it might catch on the dried grass."

"Sure." Lewt saw the logic. "I'll catch up to you."

He would have liked to ride double with her all the way home, but since Boyd was the one who'd lost his horse, this plan made more sense. Besides, after the mess Boyd had made, she probably was afraid to leave the man out here alone.

Lewt decided he should feel good about how she trusted him, but he still didn't like the way Boyd's arms circled around Rose's waist when he climbed on behind her.

He decided he'd put the fire out fast and catch up to them.

But putting a fire out in a strong wind wasn't as easy as he thought.

℘ CHAPTER 15 ℃

Em watched the small gathering around a blazing fire. It never should have been that big, she thought, but Boyd Sinclair kept tossing extra wood on it like he thought there'd be a snowstorm before their afternoon was over. They were laughing and picnicking.

She waited in the trees as they spread blankets

and relaxed in the cool afternoon sun. Finally she got bored and circled around them, heading for the summit. She'd planned to check to make sure the fire was out on her way home, when they would have been long gone.

Only when she returned, no one was there but Lewt. It crossed her mind that maybe they had run off and left him, but his horse was tied twenty feet from the fire. He could have left if he'd wanted to.

Riding in, she watched him trying to shovel dirt on the blaze. The wind caught more dirt than landed on the fire. The breeze also caught him swearing at his efforts.

"Evening," she said from five feet behind him.

He jerked around and frowned. "Rose told me to make sure the fire was out. I dumped all the water I had on it, and I even went down to the creek a couple of times and refilled the canteens, but every time I get back the fire seems bigger. At this rate I'll burn the whole ranch down by nightfall."

She fought down a laugh. "Want some help?"

"Are you offering?"

"I am, but you'll have to ask me nice."

He raised an eyebrow as if suspecting a trap. "Please give me a hand?"

She turned and rode off toward the creek.

A few minutes later she found him sitting on a rock waiting. "I guess there's no need to tell you I've never camped out more than a few times in my life. You probably already figured it out."

She tossed a dripping wet blanket toward him. Swinging off her horse, she took one end of the blanket while he held the other. "Follow me," she said.

They walked on either side of the fire and lowered the blanket all at once, smothering the flames. Steam rose, creating a fog between them for a minute before she tossed him her corner and said, "Go wet it again. One more time should do it."

He used her horse as he headed to the creek.

Em took his seat on the rock and tried to figure out this strange man. Apparently his rich, now dead, mole family never let him camp out. The only places they let him go seemed to be cheap restaurants without menu boards and parlor houses where women were rented by the hour. He didn't know how to dress or ride, but he'd learned to throw a knife with deadly accuracy while attending church.

She decided someone should put Lewton under glass and study him. He was definitely some kind of freak of nature. Shaking her head, she knew she'd have to stay out here with him until the fire was out. She couldn't leave him. She'd seen headless chickens running around with more sense of direction.

He returned with the blanket dripping with cold water. They repeated their walk on either side of the fire. This time when they pulled the blanket free, the fire was low, scattered among coals.

"You really should stay here awhile to make sure it's out, or cover it with dirt." She moved to her horse, wondering if he'd try to stop her from going.

"What are you going to do?" He didn't look like he thought much of the idea of staying out here alone.

"I'm hoping to get back to the barn before dark," she said.

"Em, if I asked you to stay, would you?"

"Why?"

"Because we're friends."

"So you're asking me for a favor?"

"Yes."

She pulled her saddlebags and rifle off her horse. "I'll stay. Not because I want to be your friend or because I'm worried about you, but because one of these days I might want the favor back and you've got to swear you'll do it."

"I swear. No matter how mad I'll probably be at you when it happens, if you call in the favor, you'll have it."

They sat down on the rocks close enough to the dying fire to feel the last of its warmth. She opened her saddlebag. "Rose packed me a sandwich and some cookies when she packed the picnic. I didn't have time to eat it."

He watched her unwrap the sandwich but didn't say a word.

"You want some?"

"No thanks, you must be hungry."

"Not really. Most days I don't stop to eat lunch."

"Afraid you'll get fat?" he asked.

"No, I just don't take the time. There's always a handful of things I don't get done every day." She offered him half.

He took the sandwich slowly, as if he expected strings to come with it. When she didn't say anything, he ate.

They sat watching the smoke drift up from the dying fire for a while, and then she asked, "How'd the courting go today?"

"Better, I think." He stretched his long legs in front of him almost touching her. "I'm learning women are not near as easy to figure out as I thought."

"You mean it's simpler if you tell them what you want and they tell you how much it'll be?"

"Yes, that would be nice. Then I could save up for just the right kind of wife."

"So, Lewt, what do you want?"

"I want a good woman; you know, someone who doesn't drink or swear or yell. Someone who'll be home when I get there with a hot meal waiting. Someone who will keep the kids and will—"

"Stop right there." She laughed. "If you want kids they cost extra."

"All right. I'll take two. A boy and a girl."

"What about in the bedroom?"

"We'll have the bedroom. That's just the way it is when folks are married. She won't mind the bedroom, she might even like it, but of course she'll pretend she doesn't because I think that's what proper ladies do."

"They do?"

He swore under his breath. "I can't believe I'm even talking about this with you. If it weren't dark I don't think we'd be having this conversation. But since we are, if I could just go to the store and buy a proper wife, what do you think she'd cost?"

"Would she have to love you?"

"I don't care. It's not important. I've been living without love all my life, and from what I see, the emotion causes more pain than joy." He thought about it a minute and added, "I'd tell her I loved her if she needed to hear it. I'd want her to be happy."

Em handed him two cookies, ate two, and then gave him the last one.

He broke it in two and gave her half.

She stared down at the half, thinking that he was thoughtful even when he wasn't trying to impress anyone. He'd also told her something very strange. His rich mole family hadn't loved him.

"Do you know what it takes to make a woman happy?"

He laughed. "I thought I did. Money, a solid house, a man who comes home every night and never beats her. That should be enough to make any woman happy, don't you think?"

"I think it's a lot more than that, Lewt." She stood and picked up her gear. "We'd better be getting back."

They rode halfway back before the cloudy night grew so dark that Lewt had trouble following.

She stopped and pulled up close. "Turn your horse loose. She'll go back to the barn eventually. You'd better ride double with me or we'll be out here all night. There's a shortcut through the trees and I'm not sure you'll be able to keep up with me."

He climbed down, looped his reins over the saddle horn, and slapped his horse hard enough on the rump to send her along. Then he felt for the stirrup and climbed up behind Em. Their hats bumped, along with knees. He spooned his long leg behind hers and removed both their hats and handed them to her so she could string them over the saddle.

She stiffened as he settled in behind her.

He let out a frustrated breath. "I know you don't like it, but do you mind if I circle my arm around you? I feel like I could fall off without anything to hang on to."

"All right," she said. "I'll just pretend you're not there."

"Fair enough," he said, close to her ear.

They rode through the shadows of the trees. She'd crossed this way a hundred times in daylight, but never in darkness. Probably for fear he'd touch the wrong thing, he put one hand on the saddle horn and the other at her belt buckle. In the blackness, she laid her hand over his.

He seemed to understand. He turned his palm up and held her gloved hand tightly in his.

CHAPTER 16

As they rode through the trees, Lewt closed his eyes, then opened them, realizing he could see nothing either way. It had been so long since he'd been in the country he'd forgotten how black the night could be on a cloudy, moonless night.

He felt like since he didn't have his sight, his other senses were playing tricks on him. He was very much aware that he held a woman in his arms. She might look more like a man in the light, but in the darkness she seemed all woman. Her hair smelled slightly of honeysuckle, and once in a while the horse shifted and his arm brushed just below her breasts. He'd feel her stiffen in his arms, but she didn't say a word. She must have been as sure as he almost was that each brush was simply an accident.

This time he had no intention of lying to himself and believing that the woman liked him. She'd made it plain how she felt about him and if he did one thing wrong, she'd probably dump him off the horse and leave him out here to bump into trees until he died.

A branch brushed just above them. Em turned her head toward his shoulder for protection, and Lewt's arm went up to block the assault of dry branches. Instinctively, his other arm tightened around her as the limbs bombarded them.

A few feet later the branches disappeared as the horse moved on, but Lewt didn't loosen his hold. "You all right?" he asked.

"I'm fine," she whispered as she straightened.

The straightening did more to make him aware she was a woman than if she'd stayed still.

"Want to tell me why you're afraid of the dark?"

"No," she said. "And I'm not afraid of the dark. I just don't like it."

"Oh." He fought down a laugh.

She elbowed him hard, then said, "All right, maybe I am a little afraid, but it's none of your business."

"Got it," Lewt answered.

They talked of the day. Lewt filled her in on what had happened to Emily about the time they emerged from the trees.

Em kicked the horse and they broke into a full run.

Lewt leaned against her, pulling their bodies close so they galloped as one, but she didn't seem to notice. He knew her thoughts were now on Emily.

They didn't stop at the barn but rode to the front door. Sumner must have anticipated her action, for he was waiting to take the horse.

"She's in the great room," he said, before they could ask.

Lewt hit the ground and swung her down with one quick action. When her feet touched, she was already running into the house.

He hesitated, unsure of what to do. He knew he'd be no help to Emily; she was surrounded by people worried about her. He'd be just an intruder, watching someone else's pain.

"How is the girl?" Lewt asked Sumner. He'd figured out two days ago that very little happened on the ranch that Sumner wasn't aware of.

The old man shrugged. "When Miss Beth rode in first, she sent one of the men for the doctor in town, but Mrs. Watson came out for air about ten minutes ago and said she thought the girl was milking it a bit. Mrs. Watson seems to think the leg is bruised, but not broken, and since she can take a good breath in and out, there's little chance the rib is more than cracked."

"So she's playing up being wounded?" Lewt filled in the blanks. "What kind of woman would do that?"

Sumner laughed. "All of them, I figure, when there's two men in there already fighting over who gets to carry her around."

"Maybe I should join them."

Sumner shook his head. "You do and the poor girl is liable to be at death's door. Besides, looked to me like you had your hands already full a minute ago."

Lewt shook his head. "We were just riding double because she was worried that I might get lost in the trees. Believe me, if I wasn't a guest here, Em would have left me to get back alone. I doubt she'd notice if I stopped breathing and fell dead in front of her. She'd just step over my body and go see about the horses."

"It's dark in those trees, is it?" Sumner whispered.

"Black as a closed trunk," Lewt answered. "I would have never been able to follow her through the twists and turns."

"Strange thing about horses, they can find their way at night like that. As long as you stay on your mount, it'll follow the lead horse, and when horses are heading back to a warm barn it takes some effort to talk them into going the wrong direction." Sumner's gaze met Lewt. "You get my meaning, son?"

Lewt might not know horses, but he wasn't dumb. No matter what Em had said to him, she'd wanted him close. Now all he had to figure out was whether she liked him or simply hated night.

"I think I'll go in and check on everything." Suddenly Lewt wanted to face Em in the light. He'd always been good at reading people once he could look them in the eye.

Sumner said softly, as Lewt took the first step, "Son, if you hurt Miss Em, every man on this place will take a turn at beating you to a pulp."

Lewt turned. "None of you even talk to her. I thought you didn't like her."

"We like her just fine. She just don't like to have much to do with nothing but horses. Every man here respects her and gives her the space she wants.

If they didn't, I'd see that they were riding over the bridge heading out by dawn."

"Does Em know this?" Lewt couldn't believe she had her own army of bodyguards here.

"She don't need to know. We know and now you know."

Lewt reached the porch and turned back. "I'm not going to hurt her, I promise. I'm here to court one of the McMurray girls. That's all I'm interested in. Miss Em and I can never be more than friends, and until a minute ago, I didn't even think we were that."

He stepped inside, not wanting to disturb the bedlam going on in the main room. Shy, pale Emily had been propped up with pillows on the long couch. She looked like she was fighting hard not to cry.

Boyd stood at the end as if on guard, and Davis knelt in front of her telling her the doctor would be here soon. He kept whispering, "Hang on just a little longer," like her eyes might roll back any second and she'd be heaven-bound.

Mrs. Allender and Mrs. Watson were both there, but Lewt thought it odd that both Beth and Rose were missing. Shouldn't they be hovering over their wounded sister? Then he realized Em wasn't there either.

He moved down the hallway leading to the kitchen and found all three women standing near the mudroom whispering. They all seemed to go mute when he stepped into the kitchen.

All he'd heard of the conversation was Rose's

comment that "This has gone on long enough."

"I just came in to see if I could help in some way." Lewt said the first thing that came to mind. Emily obviously didn't need any help, and even if she did, what could he do?

He didn't miss the way Em looked at Rose before saying, "Thank you, Lewt, for the offer, but we stay with the plan."

He had a feeling the last words were meant for Rose, because he had no plan. If he could think of one right quick, it might be to try to look invisible. He wasn't needed in the great room, and he didn't seem to be wanted in the kitchen.

"Yes." Rose nodded once at Em. "We stay with the plan. It's only three more days."

"Three more days until what?" Lewt wished he hadn't asked the moment he said the words.

For a long moment the room was silent as a grave, and then Bethie smiled her sweet smile and said simply, "Until the party."

"Yes," Rose added. "We were worried that Emily might not get to be at the party if she's broken something."

Lewt stared at the three women. He knew they were all three smarter than him probably, but something had dumbed them down to about plant life level. It didn't make sense that they were in the kitchen worrying about the party when their sister and Em's friend had been hurt.

Mrs. Watson rushed in to tell them the doctor

had arrived. All the girls bumped into Lewt on their way to the great room. Before he could decide what to do, Boyd, Davis, and the reverend had been banished to the kitchen with him.

They were all complaining about how they needed to know what was going on, but Lewt didn't think that was possible in a house run by women. He kept his mouth shut, though, believing fools should always hope.

The reverend took a seat at the worktable and cut himself a slice of apple pie so hot it fell apart before he could get it to the nearest plate.

Boyd began to pace. "This is all my fault," he muttered to himself. "I should have been able to control the horse."

"It's no one's fault," Davis said. "We were all there within five feet of her. It was simply an accident."

Lewt considered telling Boyd that he was right—it was all his fault and maybe now would be a good time for him to leave. But the man looked too miserable to torment.

Boyd continued to storm. "If I hurt Emily, Rose is probably never going to speak to me again, much less marry me."

"Probably not," Lewt agreed. Both the reverend and Davis frowned at him. "I mean, if she thought it was your fault."

Davis sat down by Reverend Watson and spooned himself a few dips of the pie, offered the reverend some more, and then silently they nodded, agreeing to split it. Davis spoke his thoughts as he spooned out his share. "I hope she's fine, but I have to tell you, it sure did feel good the way Beth cried on my shoulder when we got back here. I don't mind that at all."

Lewt frowned. "Maybe we should clobber another one of the sisters so Bethie could run into your arms. We could bonk Rose on the head a few times if you think it would help your courting, Davis."

For a moment all three men looked at him as if he'd gone mad. Then they laughed.

Lewt didn't have the heart to tell them that he was only half kidding. He'd learned a great deal in the past few minutes. Apparently, Boyd had set his cap for Rose, and Davis was falling hard for the youngest, Bethie. That left him with Emily, the broken one.

Suddenly, Lewt moved to a whole new level of worry about her. As he ate half of the second pie, he worried about something else. What if Sumner was right and she was playing the injured card for attention? He didn't like the idea of anyone manipulating him, and he wasn't sure he could marry a woman, even a rich one, who acted like she was hurt when she wasn't.

Mrs. Watson came into the kitchen, took one look at the empty pie pans, and glared at her husband.

"How's the girl?" the reverend asked before she could start on him. "We've been in here praying for her speedy recovery."

Lewt tilted his head for a better look at Watson. Apparently, lying was rampant on the ranch. He needed to get back to the saloon, where he expected everyone to be making up stuff.

"The doc says she didn't break her leg, but he wants her to take it easy. No dancing at the upcoming party. As for her rib, he wrapped it and said she may have cracked a bone. There's no way of telling. He says in a week or so, she should be fine."

"Praise the Lord. Our prayers have been answered."

Mrs. Watson scowled down at the empty pie pans. "The doctor invited himself to dinner, and now I don't have enough pie to go around."

Lewt figured that in Mrs. Watson's world, broken bones and missing pie weighed about the same on the worry scale. All the men promised not to eat pie, but it didn't seem to make her any happier.

Lewt slipped from the kitchen and went back into the great room hoping to get a look at Em, but she'd already gone and the girls were all talking at once about how happy they were that Emily had survived a near-death experience.

He told Emily that he was glad she was doing well and promised to carry her around for the rest of the week.

She smiled and told him she already had two offers for the job.

An hour later they all gathered around the big table for a late dinner. Emily's adventure was told over and over, everyone adding more details that no one else observed. Rose swore she saw a snake just before the horse bolted, and everyone quickly agreed that no one, not even Boyd, could have held the horse if a snake was threateningly near.

Lewt was amazed at the way they let the rancher off the hook. He also didn't miss the moment when Bethie described how terrified she had been. Davis covered her hand, patting it gently as if reassuring a child. Lewt doubted that a woman who'd been raised on a horse ranch would terrify so easily.

Halfway through the meal, he found himself missing Em. She'd rushed back to the house when she thought her friend was hurt, and then she'd met with the sisters, but she hadn't stayed for dinner. From all he could see, Em pretty much ran the ranch by herself. The hands were her loyal army, and she and Rose were best friends, but she didn't come to dinner.

He didn't know the McMurray women well, but he knew Duncan, and none seemed like snobs. He and Duncan had been friends since the day Duncan sat for the bar to become a lawyer. He'd been twenty and wanted to celebrate that night, only the whole town was full of drovers just back from a drive. A fight had broken out in the saloon and McMurray was in the middle of it. Lewt pulled him out the back door, sobered him up in the horse trough, and sent him on his way.

The next morning, Duncan showed up to say

thanks, and they'd been friends ever since. Duncan was the kind of poker player any gambler likes. He played with the money in his pocket, never left a marker, and even if he lost, he walked away without getting mad at himself or the dealer.

So, based on what he knew, Lewt had to think that if Em wasn't at the table it was because she didn't want to be. The McMurrays didn't seem like the kind of people to leave someone out who might want to be invited.

After dinner, everyone was tired. Boyd carried Emily up to her room and everyone but Lewt followed, telling him to be careful with every other step he took.

Lewt stepped out on the porch to smoke his last thin cigar, wondering if he had enough nerve to ask Em if they could ride into town for more. He propped himself against the porch railing and thought about how different this kind of life was from his. In the saloons, he knew what most people were by the time he'd talked to them five minutes. He could tell the ones down on their luck and the ones at the end of their rope. He never cheated when he played cards, but he had folded a few times when the pot seemed like a last-chance stand to a man. He could tell who would be trouble by the time they ordered their third drink, and he could spot a con man when he walked in the door.

But Lewt wasn't sure how to read the people in this world, and he didn't like it. In three days the week could be over and he'd be headed back to where he belonged.

He glanced at the swing at the far end of the porch and smiled when he saw Em curled up in a blanket. Grounding out his cigar, he walked up to her and said simply, "Mind if I join you?"

"Suit yourself," she said.

He sat down and rocked for a while. He wasn't close enough to touch her but enjoyed knowing she was there. Finally, he whispered, "Em, do you think we could be friends? Real friends? I've come to discover lately that I don't know all that much about the fairer sex or people in general."

"I've never been friends with a man," she answered.

"I've never been friends with a woman, but I'd like to try. Picking one who already knows she can beat me up anytime she likes seems like a good choice to start with."

She didn't say anything for a while, and he guessed she was planning on reminding him about the robber he'd called his friend just before he'd tossed the knife into his hand.

She stood suddenly and began shaking out the blanket.

Before he could think of what to say, she sat back down and settled the blanket over them both. "I guess we could try. What does this being real friends entail?"

He studied her in the pale lights coming from

the house. "Well, first we try hard to be honest with each other. No pretending." When she didn't move, he added, "No subjects are out of bounds, but if you, or I, don't want to answer, we don't have to. As friends we'll respect each other's boundaries."

"Fair enough."

He decided that if this was going to work, he needed to risk losing the hand right now; otherwise, he wouldn't be following his own rules. "Why'd you have us ride double back in the trees?"

She didn't answer. He pushed so they would swing gently and waited. Strange, he thought, how the most interesting woman at the ranch wasn't one of Duncan's cousins. He admired Em, but he wasn't sure he liked her. Right now, so the week wasn't a total waste of his time, he hoped to go back to Austin with a little better understanding of women, and this one next to him seemed as good a subject to study as any.

"We didn't need to," she finally said, drawing her knees up to her chest. "Your horse would have followed mine."

"I figured that out," he offered.

"I guess I just wanted to be close to you. I don't ever plan to marry, but sometimes I wonder what it would be like to be close to a man, to see what he smells like and feels like. Most of the men here on the ranch are related to me or old enough to be my father, and I stopped going to the few socials in town years ago. I'm twenty-six years old and I've never been kissed."

"That's impossible," he said.

She shook her head. "When I was in my teens I'd cry if my mother tried to make me go to a church picnic or a dance. After I turned twenty, I think my family just assumed I'd never marry. Besides, I'm not likely to meet anyone out here, and I hate leaving Whispering Mountain."

Lewt frowned. He had no desire to kiss Em. Not that she was ugly, she was just plain. The kind of plain that makes a woman invisible to a man. Some women, just watching them move stirred a man. Others had pretty faces or big eyes that a fellow never tired of looking at. Some were top heavy or nicely rounded on the bottom. Em was none of those, but somebody had to give the girl her first kiss and he seemed to be the only one around willing to risk death to do so.

"Would you promise not to shoot me if I kissed you, Em?"

"I wasn't asking," she snapped.

"I know, but I'm offering anyway. And before you yell at me and say no, I'd like to promise that I wouldn't give or expect more than a kiss."

"No strings?"

"No strings. I'll just kiss you and then you'll know what it's like."

She was silent so long he considered the possibility that she'd fallen asleep, and then she straightened and said simply, "All right, what do I do?"

He stretched his arm over the back of the swing. "Move closer and look up at me."

She did, but he wouldn't have been surprised if she had her hand on her Colt beneath the blanket.

"Now take your hat off."

He thought he heard her swear, but she pulled the hat off and tossed it on the table where the blanket had been. He put his arm gently around her. "Relax, Em. This isn't going to hurt, you know, and when it's over you can say you've been kissed."

He leaned over and brushed his lips lightly over hers. When she didn't move, he asked, "You all right?"

She nodded. "That wasn't so bad."

"I'm not finished." He smiled an inch away from her. "Now take a deep breath and let your mouth open slightly."

This time when he touched her lips, they felt soft, ready to be kissed. He tugged her gently toward him as he let her get used to the feel of his lips on hers. When he circled his other hand at her waist, he felt her stiffen again and whispered against her mouth, "It's all right. Relax, Em. It's me, remember."

He half expected her to bolt from the swing, but she didn't. She let him taste her lips. "Feel the warmth of it moving through your body. There's something magic in a kiss."

She made a little sound of pleasure, and his hand

at her waist moved to her back. "Now, put your arms around my neck and open your mouth, Em."

He held her close as she jerked when the kiss deepened and his mouth fit over hers. There would be no more talking, he thought; from now on he'd have to show her.

He kissed her as tenderly as he guessed a woman would want her first kiss to be. Her cheeks were warm when he finally released her mouth and kissed his way across her face to whisper in her ear, "That was great, Em. Now breathe and we'll finish this kiss."

He could hear her rapid breathing, but he wanted to feel it. He tugged her closer until the rise of each breath made her breasts brush against his chest. He hadn't been prepared for how good she would taste. He wanted more, but he waited until she calmed in his arms.

"Open your mouth again," he whispered, "and this time kiss me back."

His mouth lowered over hers as his tongue plunged inside. Then, she was kissing him back. Awkward at first, but hungry, and Lewt felt like his mind was exploding. A hunger built inside him. Roughly, he pulled her onto his lap and held her so tight he feared she couldn't breathe. When she'd decided to kiss him back, he'd lost all control of this little favor he thought he was doing for her.

Finally, when they both had to come up for air, he broke the kiss but held her tightly to him. There was nothing plain about the way she kissed.

She slipped off his lap, pulled the blanket over them both, and leaned her head on his shoulder. "Thanks," she whispered. "That was nice." As her breathing returned to normal, he realized she was asleep with her hand laced in his.

Lewt rocked for a while, wondering what had just happened. He'd been kissed a thousand times. When he'd been about fifteen and had no money, the ladies in one of the bars would play a game with him. They'd all walk past him and kiss him and laugh as they teased him. Their kisses had been bold, hungry, sometimes savage.

But Em hadn't been teasing him, and she didn't pull away when the kiss got interesting. She didn't want him any more than the ladies of the night did, but what they'd just done hadn't been a game.

He lifted her up and carried her to the couch. The blankets Emily had used were still scattered around. Lewt covered Em, then knelt down and kissed her on the cheek. "See you in the morning," he whispered as he brushed a stray strand of white-gold hair away from her soft cheek. He knew that the woman he'd meet at dawn would be nothing like the woman he'd just held in his arms, but maybe, if he was lucky, he'd see this Em one more time before he had to leave.

℘ CHAPTER 17 ℘

Across the border

Duncan woke slowly one pain at a time. His mouth was so dry he thought he must have eaten the sandy dust around him in his sleep. His entire leg throbbed as if it were slow-roasting on a fire, yet the rest of his body was so cold he couldn't stop shaking. And, on top of everything, something was jabbing into his back over and over, harder with each blow.

"You dead, mister?" Each word was punctuated by another stab.

Duncan figured if the outlaws had been the ones poking, they would have just fired a round to make sure he was dead and not asked. "No," he tried to say as he rolled over and grabbed the stick. "But I'll make you wish you were."

He jerked the branch toward him so fast the pile of rags on the other end squealed and let go.

Duncan's leg was worthless. He pulled himself out from under the rock with his arms. "Who are you?" he demanded, as if he had some right to know.

The figure before him reminded him more of a character in a nightmare than a real person. She couldn't have been five feet tall. With the scraps of clothes layered all around her and her sombrero, she looked like some kind of huge, colorful mushroom. He wouldn't have been sure she was female except for the squeal, and half her face was draped in black as though she considered herself in half-mourning.

The creature grabbed back her stick and hurried a few steps away. "I'm Toledo, named for the town in Spain where I was born, and you, mister, are a dead man talking to me."

Duncan tried to sit up but couldn't. "You're not telling me anything I don't know, old woman." He stared at the pile of rags, knowing that if the wound on his leg didn't kill him in the next few hours, one of the outlaws would. If an old woman could find him, surely a lookout would. As soon as it was full light, he'd be an easy target. If he tried to move toward the border, he'd leave a wide trail of blood for anyone to follow.

"Folks don't like rangers on this side of the border, and they have good reason. You Texas devils come down here and cause nothing but trouble. You'd better vanish or they'll be using you for target practice in an hour."

Duncan tried to focus. "I don't much like being here," he said, as he spotted her cart sparkling in the first rays of dawn. The old woman was a tinker; her wares of pots and pans and brooms hung from her cart much like her clothes hung from her body. "Any chance you could help me get to the river?"

"There are guards watching the river," she

answered. "I saw them last night when I passed. They had a wild-eyed horse staked out to catch you, but he got away."

"She broke free. I knew she would."

"*Sí.*" Toledo snorted. "And she unsaddled herself also. A very wise horse you have, Ranger."

Duncan guessed his horse was halfway back to the ranch by now. He knew his only hope of staying alive now was to bargain with the woman. "I could pay you if you helped me."

She laughed. "I could just sit here and wait until you die and then take all your money. I'm too old to go helping half-dead men who sleep where they do not belong."

He swore. She was right, and from the way he felt, she wouldn't have to wait long to collect his coins. He thought of pulling his gun and demanding her help, but she didn't look like a woman who'd fall for that. Right now she could swing that stick and knock him out before he could clear leather with his Colt.

"Name your price for helping me," he said, knowing he'd have little chance surviving the day, and if he did, he'd be too weak to make it to the river, much less swim across.

"I want your word that you'll help me make a little money to tide me over the winter, but I'll not ask anything of you until you can walk."

"You're not asking me to do something illegal?"

She shook her head.

"How do you know I won't walk out and forget your problem?" The lawyer part of him wanted to make both sides clear, even though he realized it might cost him his life. He doubted that he had enough life left to be of much help to her. The sun seemed to be fading even though he could still feel its warmth on his face. If he passed out now, in the open, he had a feeling he'd wake up dead.

The woman rattled on as if he were paying attention. "Because if I help you, I'll be risking my life, and when you're well, even if I ask you to do the same, you're honor bound. I haven't figured out what, but I bet I can make use of you."

She stared at him and shifted her weight. Her skirts moved just enough for him to see the rifle at her side. "If you get away without making me a little money, I'll find you and kill you along with every relative you have. Don't doubt Toledo. I've done such a thing before and I'm more than capable of doing it again."

Duncan didn't see any choice in the matter. Either way he was probably counting his time left by hours. "All right. You have my word. If you can get me out of this mess, I'll help you, but if we don't do something fast the only way you'll be helping me is to bury me."

She poked him again with her stick. "Wake up," she ordered. "Wake up."

He rolled over, trying to ignore the pain in his leg. She helped him to his feet, and then with the stick as a crutch and the little woman holding him up on one side, they made it to the cart. While he held on to the little wagon, she pulled everything from the floor, shoved him in, and began dumping her goods on top of him.

As she worked, he looked up just as the wind caught the scarf covering one side of her face and lifted it long enough for him to see what she hid. Twisted scars rippled from her eye to her neck, reminding him of a dried-up riverbed still echoing the water's flow. The left side of her face was deformed, but not unbearable to look at. He found it surprising one so old could still be so vain.

With no care, she dropped something heavy on his leg, sending fire shooting through his entire body. He fought down a scream, but the effort cost him. As layer after layer of fabric and boxes and tools rained down on him, Duncan's mind slipped into muddy water until he heard nothing, saw nothing, felt nothing.

The old lady named Toledo was forgotten, as were the battles. In his mind he was home, lying in the cool grass, staring up at Whispering Mountain, waiting to die.

He had no idea how long he was out, but slowly his mind drifted from the peace of the dream through muddy waters where no thoughts made sense. Two people were carrying him. One had his shoulders, one his feet. From what seemed like miles away he could hear the old woman's voice yelling for them to be careful and not kill him too soon.

A moment later they dropped him, and then, like panicked children, they picked him up and begin half carrying, half dragging him again. The old woman yelled for them to hurry before someone saw them. He slipped away, welcoming the darkness this time.

He had no idea if minutes passed or days. When he opened his eyes again, he was lying on something soft. He tried to move but couldn't budge. He felt as though the last ounce of energy in his body remained in his mind, and if he struggled too hard even that would leave him.

He heard the old woman named Toledo say, "You better take care of him. If he dies I'll beat you both."

Gently, he felt someone pulling away his clothes. Warm water washed over him, and Duncan managed to open his mouth. A hand cupped the back of his head and let him take a long drink. When he finished, he let out a sigh and relaxed, trusting the hands moving over him, washing away blood and wrapping his wound.

℘ CHAPTER 18 ℭ

Em woke in a thunderstorm mood. She couldn't believe she'd let Lewt kiss her last night. No, she corrected herself. She didn't just let him kiss her, she'd almost begged him to. And then, he'd kissed her, really kissed her. It had been so much more than she thought a kiss could be.

Crossing to the mudroom, she bathed, put on her oldest clean clothes, and joined Rose, already in the kitchen. As she combed her hair by the fire, Em made up her mind that the only way to deal with what happened on the porch last night was to stay as far away from Lewt as possible. He'd be on the ranch only three more days and then he'd be gone and forget all about her and the kiss. And she'd stay here, glad things were back to normal, only she'd remember the kiss and cherish it. She might never marry, but she'd have the one perfect kiss to remember.

Braiding her hair, Em was lost in thought when Rose finished the biscuits and finally had time to join her in a cup of coffee.

As usual, Rose didn't mess around. She said what was on her mind. "We have to stop this game, Em. I almost called Tamela by her name last night. I really like these men and suddenly the game doesn't seem fair. They're all decent and honest. What are they going to think if they find out that Tamela isn't a McMurray, she's just a look-alike Emily because the real one wouldn't give up working with the horses?"

"Don't worry. We only have a few more days. After the party Friday night we will all say good-bye and I'll have Sumner drive them into town. They can spend the last night at the hotel so there is no chance they'll miss the train Saturday morning. You can say you think that would be easier on Mrs. Allender."

Rose didn't like the idea, but it did seem easier to continue the game than change it now. "Beth and I thought we'd take the men into town just to show them around. I'll stop by the hotel and ask one of the waitresses to deliver lunch to the little house. It'll be so much nicer that going into one of the crowded cafés."

Em nodded. Most of the time the family was in town they either brought their own food or had one of the hotels deliver a meal. Their papa hated what he called "eating with strangers." The girls never minded. Often Em and their mother would stay at the house while everyone else went shopping, and then they'd all ride home together talking of their day.

"Will you come with us?" Rose asked as she stood and began breakfast. The two girls from town they'd hired to help for the week never seemed to make it up for breakfast and weren't that good at cooking. So Mrs. Watson and Mrs. Allender pitched in with helping prepare lunch and dinner and left the cleanup to the girls from town. It was a schedule that worked well, only Rose had began to notice that the meal deliveries to Boyd's man in the barn seemed to take longer each time.

"I've got too much work to do here," Em answered. "I saw more mountain lion tracks yesterday. It's getting cold enough that the cats might be hunting this low. I told Sumner to make sure every man riding out had a rifle. He told me he'd already issued the order."

"I don't like the idea of one of the mountain lions being killed, but I've seen what they can do to a colt."

"If we see them, we'll fire in the air first and try to chase them back into the hills, but if they come back, we'll have to protect the herd." Em knew that deer in the mountains were not plentiful as in years past because of a bitter cold winter last year. If the cats and wolves came down, they were just doing what they do: hunting for game. Much as she hated it, she had to do what she did: protect the horses.

"Will Lewt be going with you?" Em asked, hoping to get Rose's mind off the cats.

"I don't know. I haven't seen him to ask."

"Ask what?" Lewt surprised them both. He stood in the doorway to the hall, looking all ready for winter in his wool work clothes and coat.

Rose smiled at him, her usual pleasant, not-too-friendly kind of smile Em had seen her give people on the street. "Would you like to go into town with us today, Lewton?"

"Who'll stay here with Emily?" he asked, acting concerned. "Surely she's in no condition to travel."

"Mr. and Mrs. Watson will keep her company. Mrs. Allender said she'll go along with us if we'll take the buggy and lots of blankets."

Lewt hesitated, then shook his head. "Much as I'd like to accompany you ladies, I think I'd better stay here. I promised to help Em for a few hours this morning, and then I might be able to make myself useful and visit with Miss Emily if she's not resting. She told me she liked to play card games. I'm sure we can find one we both know."

Rose was busy putting biscuits in the oven. Lewt looked at Em as if for help. She could understand his feelings. Going into town with a group sounded only slightly more fun than cleaning the barn. "Oh," she said, knowing he expected her to say something. "I forgot, you did offer to help. We'd better eat and be heading out."

Rose faced them. One of her lovely eyebrows lifted, but she didn't say anything. A few minutes later Mrs. Allender joined them for a breakfast of ham, scrambled eggs, and biscuits with gravy. The dear lady had a habit of always discussing the next meal. She liked to plan lunch while eating breakfast, and dinner while still having lunch.

Em thought she was kind of like an oral menu board. And, not surprisingly, since she raised a large family, she was quite the cook. Em had noticed Rose jotting down instructions on how to prepare a few dishes Mrs. Allender suggested.

When the little woman finished her morning questions about lunch, silence fell over the group.

Em finally made an effort to talk about work. Rose talked of town. Lewt didn't talk at all. In fact, he didn't even look in Em's direction. She had no doubt in her mind that his wanting to stay at the ranch had more to do with him not wanting to go to town than any notion that he should help her.

As he downed the last of his coffee, she motioned for them to go. He said his good-byes to the women and promised he'd check in on Emily when he got back.

Em didn't say anything. Her mind was already filled with all the things she had to do. They walked to the barn without a word, and within minutes they were both in the saddle and riding out. She took off fast, and this morning he followed like a shadow.

He'd learned a great deal, and since dawn he'd worked beside her as if they had been a team for months.

At midday, they stopped to let the horses rest and she finally turned to him. "You should have gone with the others to town. It would be a good chance to talk to the McMurray women."

"I didn't want to." He didn't look at her when he answered.

"Then you should have stayed with Emily."

"I'd be of little help there, and by now I'm sure I would have strangled Mrs. Watson. The woman reminds me of an out-of-tune wind chime set off by the slightest breeze. I've seen rivers that babbled less."

When Em didn't comment, he added, "Miss Emily

is sweet, though, too sweet. There's something about all that shyness and sewing that makes me nervous. You'd think she was getting paid, the way she works."

Em shrugged and pulled off her hat to wipe her brow as she tried not to laugh. "Then I guess you'd better stay with me. I may work you to death, but at least we'll have no shyness or sewing." She smiled. "Of course, unless I'm sewing up your hide."

He mumbled a swear, then laughed. "I'm afraid if she did the stitching on my leg, I'd have French knots and needlepointed initials."

She laughed with him. "So I guess Miss Emily is out of the running?"

"She was never really in it. When a man is looking for a mate, there has to be some attraction there."

"But she's pretty."

"I know. Beautiful, in fact, but I . . ."

He didn't finish, and Em didn't know if he had no answer or if he just didn't want to tell her.

He turned away from her and was silent for a while as he watched the horses, and then he whispered, "About last night."

"Last night is over," she said, too quickly to be casual. "Thank you for showing me what a kiss was like, but I'm in need of no more lessons. What happened last night was a mistake."

"Fine," he said between clenched teeth. "I wasn't asking for a thank-you or a repeat."

"What's the matter?" she snapped back at him.

"I thought we were going to be honest with one another."

"Nothing," he answered, moving toward his horse. "Let's get back to work."

They rode north, following a set of mountain lion tracks. Neither talked, but when Em pulled her rifle, he did the same.

For the tenth time that day, she slipped from her horse and studied the tracks. "He's close," she said.

"You can read that in a track?"

"No, I can feel it. I'd swear he is the same big cat that came down last winter. We never saw him, never even got one shot off at him, but I remember one of the men saying he was missing a few claws. The prints show that now."

"Maybe he's too old to hunt? Or maybe there are more deer up in the hills than you think?"

She looked up at him, making no effort to hide the worry in her face. "Or maybe, he's back."

They followed the cat's trail for another hour, and then the wind turned cold and Em knew it would be wise to head home.

Just as they turned, she caught a movement at the edge of the clearing.

Lewt saw it a second later. Without a word they moved closer, both rifles ready to fire.

Twenty feet into the shadows of a stand of tall pine, they recognized what lay in the grass. A colt, not three months old, tried to stand, then tumbled into the grass.

"He's hurt," Em said, as she kicked her mount and closed the distance to the young horse.

Lewt remained frozen in place as she jumped down and ran to the colt. Blood from what looked like a puncture wound dripped from his side, and he stared at her with wild, frightened eyes.

Just as she reached the animal, something moved in the trees, and she realized too late that the mountain lion must have smelled them and had moved into hiding but had not left.

Before she could pull her sidearm from the holster, she heard a rush in the brush and knew the lion was rushing toward her. Instinct allowed only a second for her to lean over the downed colt, and then the blast of a rifle whistled just above her head. One long silent moment later she heard the thundering thud of something falling in the bush between the trees.

Em looked up to see Lewt jumping from his horse, his rifle still in his hand as he ran toward her.

"Stay down!" he yelled as he passed her and crossed into the trees.

Em wanted to help the colt, but she knew what she had to do. If the mountain lion was wounded and not killed, he might still be in the brush. She ran for her rifle and chambered a round. She stood a few feet from the colt, ready to fire if needed.

The north wind was the only sound she heard besides the pounding of her own heart. She'd been an idiot to leave her rifle and run to the colt. Her papa would be furious at her for risking her life. How many times had he told her in the past to take precautions? She'd be no good to the stock if she managed to get herself killed.

A rustling came from the edge of the pines. A moment later Lewt appeared, his rifle pointing down as if at rest. "I got him," he said simply. "He's dead."

Em gulped down air. She hadn't realized she'd been holding her breath. "If we'd been a few minutes later, he would have finished the colt off."

Lewt reached her side and took the rifle from her hand.

"If you hadn't been here"—she met his gaze— "the lion might have finished me off too."

Lewt set the rifles on the cold grass as he knelt beside the horse. "Get your saddlebags and the canteen, Em; don't panic. You can thank me later; we've got to see to this horse first."

She followed orders, but as soon as she began to work on the wound, she snapped, "I wasn't panicking. I never panic. I was just so worried about the horse I forgot to take proper precautions."

He helped her doctor the wound, which didn't seem so bad once they got the blood cleared away. Over the days they'd learned to work well together, almost reading each other's thoughts. When the wound was treated, they watched the colt stand. He was too big to carry, so they watched him walk away.

"Shouldn't we do something, like take him back with us or build a pen to hold him for the night?"

"He'll be all right. He'd only hurt himself more fighting his way out of a pen. He knows where his mother went. I'll come out tomorrow and check on him." She shoved her rifle back in place and put her hat on the saddle horn so the cold air could cool her cheeks and calm her nerves.

They walked their horses, following the colt until he spotted the rest of the herd.

"I thought you didn't know how to shoot," she said, breaking the silence.

"I said I didn't like guns, not that I didn't know how to use them."

Em nodded. "You're a mystery, Mr. Lewton Paterson."

"Not really. Half the time when people ask me what I'm thinking, I'm not."

Em laughed. "All right. What are you thinking now?"

He turned toward her. "I'm thinking I'm glad the lion didn't get you because I sure as hell would like to kiss you again. Same rules as before. No strings."

Before she could think of an answer or react, he circled one arm around her and pulled her close. His mouth covered hers. The kiss was raw with a need that surprised her, and she didn't fight the feeling shooting through her body as the kiss deepened.

She'd wanted it too. One more taste. One more time to confirm just how good it had felt. One more time to remember forever what a kiss could be.

His arm was around her, holding her, but not imprisoning her. She could have jerked away if she'd wanted to, but the feel of his mouth against hers made her want more. Lifting her hands, she tugged his hat off and let her arms rest on his shoulders as her body leaned into his. There were a thousand reasons she shouldn't be kissing him, but she'd think of them all later. Right now, all she wanted was to feel alive. One hundred percent alive for the first time in her life.

Lewt felt her surrender and gentled his hold around her. The kiss deepened as his hands moved over her, gently stroking her back from her shoulder to just below her belt.

When he finally broke the kiss, he brushed her cheek with his lips and moved across her face with light kisses until he reached her ear. "I've been wanting to do that all day," he whispered. "And it was every bit as good as I thought it would be."

She let out a sigh, agreeing with him. No matter how many times she'd told herself she never planned to kiss him again, she couldn't keep from thinking that she was glad they'd had this one last time.

His hands gripped her sides just above her waist and tugged her against him as he whispered, "Don't say a word, Em. Just let me hold you for a moment. I felt like I'd been kicked in the chest when I realized something was stalking you from the trees. I knew if I fired too soon I might miss, or if I waited a second too long, it might be too late."

She cupped his face in her palms. After days of yelling at him for doing everything wrong, she said the only thing she could now. "You did it right. You saved my life."

He brushed her mouth with his words. "I'm glad." He kissed her again with a gentle kind of tenderness she never would have thought him capable of, and then he just held her tight in his arms for a long while.

Finally, she whispered, "I'm freezing."

He laughed and let her go. "Me too. We'd better get back."

For once, she let him help her up onto her horse, and she didn't miss the way he slid his hand along the length of her leg as if it were a natural thing to touch her so. To her surprise, she didn't mind. Sometime over their days together she'd learned to trust him and the truth shocked her.

℘ CHAPTER 19 ℘

Lewt felt frozen to the bone by the time they raced back to the barn, but he didn't comment. If the weather hadn't changed, he would have been happy to stand out in that north pasture and kiss Em all day long.

He'd never felt that way about a woman. In fact, since he'd been that kid the soiled doves played at driving crazy with kisses, he'd really never kissed a

181

woman at all and never with any passion. It seemed a waste of time, and most of the ladies he knew didn't have a mouth that tasted like honey inside and lips that felt all soft and hesitant like Em's did. She might be hard as a horseshoe when she was working or bossing him around, but when she was in his arms, she was all woman. She seemed to fit just right against him. Just the right height, just the right feel. She was tall and slender, but he'd felt where her hips flared and couldn't have missed her soft round breasts pressing against his chest.

He thought about telling her how she started a fire inside him . . . about how he'd like to do more than kiss her . . . about how he wanted her beneath him in bed more than he could ever remember wanting a woman.

But Lewt knew he'd never say a word to her. She'd told him his kiss had been her first. She might be near his age, but she'd been raised here on Whispering Mountain completely away from the wildness he'd known. She might not be a lady like the McMurray women, but she wasn't like anyone from his world and he'd be doing her an injustice to treat her so.

When they reached the barn, rain had started to fall. Sumner was there waiting for them. As always, he stood ready to help Em, and as always, she refused his assistance.

"I expected you in earlier," he said. "Norther's blowing in."

"We found a hurt colt in the north pasture," Em said, without looking at the old man. "Lewt shot the mountain lion that planned to have him for dinner."

Sumner looked at Lewt for the first time but didn't say a word.

"Are the others back from town?"

Sumner slowly turned away from Lewt to answer. "No, they sent word about an hour ago with the mail and medicine. They all decided to stay in town. The women at the little house, the men at the hotel."

Em nodded. "Makes sense. The ride back in a buggy wouldn't be pleasant in this weather."

Lewt stepped beside her. "You would have crossed the hills and cut the time in half, right?"

She smiled. "Not with Mrs. Allender. I had enough trouble leading you."

He lightly brushed her shoulder with his. "I'd hate to see sweet little Mrs. Allender tumbling from a horse and rolling down a hill."

"Me too." Em smiled at him and took off running to the house.

He was right behind her, barely noticing the pounding rain or mud splashing to his knees.

They hit the mudroom laughing and tossing wet coats and hats.

Light shone from the kitchen, but the mudroom was in shadows. Lewt knew without asking that Rose left a light for Em every night. Only tonight, Miss McMurray was in town. Neither the reverend nor his wife would have thought to light the lamp.

Em pulled the curtain by the bath and disappeared behind it. "Get out of those wet clothes and I'll toss you dry ones. Uncle Travis keeps a set of work clothes here. They should fit you."

He looked at the tall shelves squared into boxes, each with sets of shirts and trousers. He'd never really noticed them before, but now he knew they were a change of clothes for every McMurray. Any member of the family who'd worked hard was expected to change and clean up in the mudroom before stepping in the house. A washstand stood in each corner of the room, and he knew without testing that there would be fresh water in the pitchers.

He glanced over at her silhouette on the curtain. She was tugging off one of her boots. "What are you going to wear?"

She froze for a moment, then said, "I can wear Emily's work clothes. We're almost the same size and she rarely needs them."

He tugged his shirt off as he watched her shadow. "You're a little taller," he commented, wishing to add that she was braver and bolder and more strong willed.

"Am I?" she said as she wiggled out of her wet jeans.

He stopped moving. He even stopped breathing as he watched the shadow peel away clothes. What he'd thought was almost a man's body was very much a woman's. She was tall and lean, but she definitely had curves in all the right places. Fighting down a yell when she tugged on a shirt, he forced himself to look away.

"You about ready?" She wiggled into new trousers that washed away her shapely figure and made her look boxy again.

He poured water into the basin and splashed. "Give me one more minute."

When she pulled the curtain, he was buttoning his shirt and facing the wall. Part of him didn't want to look at her. He felt like he'd learned some grand secret and she'd have to kill him if she knew he knew.

Lewt made up his mind he'd never say anything to her, or to anyone. He wished he could forget about the body he'd seen outlined in shadow, but he knew he never would. He'd see that body in his dreams probably every night for the rest of his life.

When he turned, he kept his head down as he buckled his belt. "Any chance you'll eat dinner with us tonight, Em? I'm not sure I can handle both the Watsons alone, and Emily never has much to say. Half the time I think she's dreaming about something else and not bothering to follow the conversation."

Em laughed. "I didn't think guests could invite guests."

He frowned, guessing she was right. "Probably true, but if you don't join us then I plan to eat with you and those two giggly girls in the kitchen."

"All right. Emily and I have been friends since

we were in school. I'll ask if she'd mind if I join you all tonight. I often do when just the girls are at home." She watched him finish dressing. "Besides, if you eat with the girls, you'll be eating in the barn. They both have taken a liking to the wrangler Boyd brought along to care for his horses. Sumner tells me every night the meal in the empty stall lasts a little longer. He claims the giggles are keeping the horses up."

He looked at her. "So you'll join us?" He studied her eyes, deciding that when she wasn't mad about something, she had wonderful eyes. They reminded him of the blue Texas sky.

"I will."

Lewt smiled at her. "Thanks." Then he thought of her body and had to look down again.

She hit him in the head with a pair of rolled-up socks. While he put them on and rubbed his hair dry with a towel, she went to find Emily.

He was standing in the kitchen downing a cup of coffee when Miss Emily came in, looking flustered.

"I'm glad you're back," she said, twisting her hands together. "I've asked Em to join us for dinner, if you have no objections."

"I have none," he said, thinking he could never marry a woman who got so flustered over one guest for dinner. She was a beauty, like her sisters, but in a million years Emily McMurray would never be wild enough for him.

With less sadness than he'd thought he'd have,

Lewt realized he would be going back to Austin alone. None of Duncan's cousins were right for him. He liked them all, admired them even, but he couldn't see himself spending the rest of his life with one of them. The only woman on the ranch that he was attracted to had made it plain she never wanted to marry. The day after the big party they'd all planned, he'd ride away from Whispering Mountain and probably never return. In fact, he doubted he'd ever be welcome after Duncan figured out what he'd done.

Miss Emily gave him a smile that lasted less than a blink and turned toward the hallway. "Mr. and Mrs. Watson are in the great room having sherry before dinner. If you'll join them, I'll check on the meal. I'm afraid without Rose's or Mrs. Allender's help, the girls only managed a simple meat pie tonight."

Lewt wondered where the dueling gigglers were, but he didn't ask. He'd been told one day at breakfast that they liked to sleep in after cleaning up from the night before, but he'd guessed they had helped with the rest of the meals. Apparently not.

Looking over at the counter, he saw two meat pies cooling, bread in need of slicing, one bowl of vegetables, and another of peaches. "How about I help you carry this stuff in?" He picked up the largest bowl.

"Oh, no, Mr. Paterson. I couldn't let you."

"But you'll have to make several trips, and two

187

people could cut the time in half."

"Oh, no." Emily looked so upset, he set the bowl back on the counter.

Em's laughter came from the doorway. "Let him help or he'll drive you crazy; I should know." She walked past Emily and picked up one of the pies. "We'll all three help."

Miss Emily calmed and nodded as they marched in to dinner.

To his surprise Miss Emily seemed less at ease at the table than Em did. Em told everyone how Lewt had saved her life, and Mrs. Watson seemed very upset at the danger and very thankful at the outcome. Mr. Watson stopped the eating for a moment of thanks. Five minutes into the prayer, Lewt opened one eye and saw Em staring at him. They both spent the rest of the thanks fighting down laughter.

After dinner Lewt helped clear the table while the Watsons and Miss Emily moved to the great room, promising to set up a card game. By the time he and Em laughed their way through clearing the table, Mrs. Watson had Miss Emily settled into a comfortable chair with her sewing in her lap.

Mr. and Mrs. Watson had little interest in playing cards, leaving Em and Lewt at the game table alone. Within minutes Mr. Watson had found a book he simply had to read and Mrs. Watson was snoring in her chair, her knitting tangled in her hands like a worn fishing net.

"You two don't have to entertain me. I'm fine,"

Miss Emily said, but they both swore they were just passing time.

"What do you want to play?" Lewt asked, sensing that Em might not be as easy to fool at cards as the others had been.

"I don't know," she answered, showing little interest in the game.

"How about poker? Ever play?" He smiled, guessing she wouldn't know the game.

"All right. I'll give it a try."

He shuffled the cards. "Five card?"

"Fine. What do we play for?"

He glanced around and noticed the matches in the tin near the cold fireplace. Standing, he retrieved them and gripped two hands full. "I divide the matches, you pick which pile you want."

She touched his left hand and he released his grip, letting the matches tumble onto her side of the table. They began to play, with him doing more teaching than gambling.

An hour later, he'd let her win all the matches and Emily was dozing along with Mrs. Watson.

Em leaned across the table and whispered, "We'd better call it a night."

Lewt touched Mrs. Watson on the shoulder. She jumped, came awake enough to mumble good night, and headed up to her room.

Em woke Miss Emily more easily, and Lewt insisted on carrying her up to her room. Emily protested as he lifted her. He was as careful with her as if she'd been glass, but from the way she stiffened in his arms he knew she didn't think she needed to be carried to bed.

Em showed him Emily's room. Lewt quickly set her down and backed out of the room as Em made her comfortable. With one glance he decided Emily's room didn't seem to fit her. He'd expected quilts with detailed hand stitching and lacy things on every surface, but the room was plain; even the windows had no cover. If he didn't know better he would have thought this room belonged to someone who always woke and watched the dawn and who spent very little time there.

He could hear the Watsons talking as he passed one of the bedroom doors but didn't really care what they were saying. Soon he'd be gone and none of the people would be on his mind, except maybe Em. She'd stay in his thoughts for a long time.

In the great room he poured himself a brandy and played with the cards, as he had thousands of hours before. His mind didn't need to stay clear tonight. The other two men were gone. There was no competition and no one to court.

Not that there really was anyway. Bethie only seemed to have eyes for Davis, and Rose was no more interested in him than she seemed to be in Boyd. Lewt had been an idiot to risk the one true friendship he had in this world for a chance to court a rich woman. Duncan had been his friend for years. They'd helped each other out of a dozen scraps and covered the other's back in more than one fight. Now he'd go back to Austin without a wife and probably without a friend. Lewt had a feeling when the ranger found out what Lewt had done, at the least it would be the end of the friendship; at the worst the ranger would call him out for a fight.

Lewt shrugged, knowing if the worst happened he'd step out with an unloaded gun strapped to his hip.

He poured himself another drink. He'd honestly thought all three women would have fallen in love with him at first sight. All the saloon girls seemed to. The reality that none of them even flirted with him hurt his pride. He felt like he'd paid dearly for the lesson learned. Even the woman he'd kissed this week had told him a dozen times that she never planned to marry. He was just someone to learn something unknown with, not someone to mold a life with.

When he looked toward the door, he noticed Em leaning against the frame watching him.

"You look down," she said, without moving into the room. "Like a man who has just lost a friend."

He lifted his glass. "I thought I'd drawn the last thought of a dream I had."

"To marry a rich woman?" Her smile seemed somehow sad.

"That and to have a regular family. I never had one growing up. I thought it would be nice to have a wife to come home to. Someone to talk about the day with, but I guess that's not an option for people like me."

She watched him but didn't say a word. Maybe she figured he'd be gone soon and she had no need to know any more about him.

"I did learn a great deal this week, thanks to you, Em. I think when I get back to Austin, I'll buy a horse, a good one, and go riding. I have a feeling I'll still hear your lessons echoing in my ears."

"I learned something too," she said. "I learned what a kiss was like, and I thank you for that. I still know marriage is not for me, but at least I have a nice memory. I never dreamed the touch of a man's lips could make a warmth go all the way down my body."

He picked up the cards. "You want to play another hand?"

"For what?"

He smiled slowly. "For one last kiss."

She laughed. "One good-bye kiss."

"Fair enough." He dealt the hand without either of them taking a chair. He played it straight and won.

When she dropped her cards on the table, she stepped into his arms. His hand cupped the back of her head and held her just the way he liked to kiss her, leaning down only slightly, turning his head one way as he moved hers the other.

Tomorrow everyone would be getting ready for the party and he'd probably have to stay around, but for this one quiet moment he wanted to give her a kiss they'd both remember.

He'd meant it to be a sweet farewell kiss, but the memory of her shadow filled his mind and he pressed against the length of her. He knew this woman. Not only the taste and feel of her; he knew how she lived and felt and talked. She was as honest as the land she worked all day and the opposite of him. For one moment, as they held to each other, day and night touched. His rotten life at the bottom of society and her pure-air life on Whispering Mountain had collided, and they both knew that neither could step out of their world and into the other's.

He tugged at her oversized shirt until he freed the cotton from her waist and pushed his hand inside so that he could feel her warm skin. He'd thought she might jerk away, but she didn't.

Brushing his hand over her back, he whispered in her ear, "Thanks, darlin'," like she'd just given him a gift.

Between the night and the brandy he didn't seem capable of reason. All he wanted to do was hold her for as long as she'd let him. This woman's spirit drew him as no woman ever had. She was strong and stubborn as no woman he'd ever known, but right now, in his arms, she was sweet and warm and yielding.

When he finally ended the kiss, he couldn't let go. "You're the one thing I'll miss when I leave," he whispered against her cheek.

She rubbed her cheek against his chin. "You'll be surrounded by women in Austin."

"Not like you, Em. I've never met anyone like you."

Without another word, she circled his neck and pulled him down the few inches for another kiss. He felt the warmth of her body press against him and wanted to breathe her deep into his lungs so he'd never get the fresh smell of her or the taste of her out of his mind. His hand moved over her back and along her sides. Her skin was soft as velvet. When he brushed just beneath her breast, he heard her soft sigh of pleasure. She might never want a man, but she was a woman meant to be cherished and made love to, often.

When she pulled away to breathe, he whispered, "I don't suppose you'd consider coming to Austin with me?"

She shook her head as he noticed for the first time how pretty she was when she blushed.

"I can't," she whispered. "I've never trusted a man to get this close before. I fear I'd panic if we got any closer. In a few days you'll forget about me."

"And you'll forget about me," he teased.

"Maybe," she whispered, and he knew she was lying just as he was.

She laid her hand flat against his heart. "I thought I'd be terrified if a man ever came so close, but I like the feel of you."

He slowly unbuttoned his shirt and gently pushed her hand over his heart with no cotton to hinder her touch. "If you like the feel of me, Em, then feel me. Look at me. See me. Everything will be crazy around here and we may not be together like this again, but for tonight, know that you are with me. Not just some man you let kiss you. Not a stranger, but me."

Panic flashed in her eyes for a moment, and then she smiled. "I can feel your heart."

He thought of saying something flowery and romantic, but he wanted no more lies between them. If he left she'd never know that he wasn't the honest man he pretended to be.

He unbuttoned the rest of his shirt and watched her as she moved her fingers over his chest. Her hands were worn from hard work, but her touch was light and gentle.

"Tell me your thoughts," he asked, standing very still with his hands resting easy on her waist.

"The hair on your chest is softer than I'd thought it would be. The muscles tighter." She stopped her hand over his heart once more. "We shouldn't be doing this."

"Why? We're not children who need watching." He leaned over and kissed just below her ear. "I know you may not believe me, Em, but I've never been like this with a woman."

She raised an eyebrow and studied him. "You've never kissed a woman?"

He grinned. "I've kissed a few, but none I'd kiss again."

"You've never had a sweetheart?"

"Never."

"But you've been with women. More than one?"

He closed his eyes, wishing he could lie to her, but he wouldn't. For once in his life he'd answer honestly whatever she asked. "Yes, more than one."

He felt her body stiffen in his arms as she lifted her chin and asked, "Did you force them?"

"No, Em. I've never forced a woman. I never would. I may be a lot of things you might not think are grand, but I swear to you, I'm not that. I didn't have any feelings for them. We were just passing time."

She relaxed slightly. "I believe you. I'm glad that the one man who kissed me was you."

"With you it's far more than I expected. With each kiss, each touch, a hunger grows in me. It'll be hard saying good-bye to you, Em, but I'll do it if that's what you want."

"That's what I want," she said. "You have to become a memory."

He wanted to hold her gently in his arms all night. There were deep, dark secrets within this woman. Secrets he wasn't sure he could bear to know, but it helped realizing that somehow he'd reached her and she felt safe in his arms.

Pulling away from her, he turned down the light until the room was in shadows, guessing she wouldn't want to be in the dark. "The rain's slowed. It's too cold to sit on the porch swing tonight, but would you sit with me for a while in here? We could listen to the rain."

He touched her hand and tugged her toward the couch.

She hesitated, then followed and curled up beside him as if they were on the swing. After a while, she said, "I'm sorry you didn't find your dream here."

His arm tightened slightly over her shoulder. "Don't worry about it. I think it was an impossible dream. I thought it would be grand to have a wife and maybe kids. A home I could come to at night when I'm tired. A place where the world would seem at peace." He closed his eyes and leaned his head back against the leather couch. "It wasn't to be. Not for a man like me, I guess."

She cuddled closer. "You'll find it someday. You found me for a friend, didn't you?"

"That's true. The first day I went out with you I thought you might be trying to kill me."

"I was." She laughed, and he wasn't sure if she was joking or not.

He kissed the tip of her nose. "Should we play for another kiss?"

"It's too dark."

"Then I guess I'll have to let you win," he said, with his lips already brushing hers. She giggled and collected her winnings.

When he broke the kiss, she cuddled close to his

side as she had before. "Stay here with me tonight, Em. Sleep on my shoulder. Let me hold you."

"But it's not right."

"No one's in this part of the house. No one will know. I just want to hold you for a while."

"All right," she said. "For a while."

A few minutes later he felt her breathing slow, and he knew she was asleep. This was as near as he'd ever come to sleeping with a woman. He smiled, loving the peace of it.

In her sleep, she reached for his hand and held on tight. Lewt drifted into sleep, feeling as if all was right in the world.

Six hours later at dawn, the pounding on the door woke him to the fact that he'd guessed wrong. Something was very wrong.

ஃ CHAPTER 20 ௸

Duncan felt as if he were drifting in a nightmare of pain. Once in a while someone dripped water into his mouth, and he tried to remember to swallow. Fever raged through his veins like a freight train loaded with hot coals. Again and again small hands wiped the sweat from his face.

The fog cleared for a time, and he managed to open his eyes. He was in a room made from logs with the bark left on the wood. There was no sign of the old woman who'd helped him, but the room was warm and someone slept on the floor a few feet from his bed. She looked little more than a child, with wild hair the color of dark rich earth.

Duncan remembered someone touching him, cleaning his wound, washing him with cold water when the fever raged. He drifted back to sleep, thankful that whoever she was, she was near.

One time, deep in darkness, he thought he heard the old woman shouting orders, but he didn't know or care what she said. There was movement in the room and the sound of someone sweeping with a slow rhythm that reminded him of the sound the water makes along the Gulf Coast. Without windows he had no idea whether it was day or night.

When he woke again the door was open, and he saw that it was daylight beyond. The girl with the wild brown hair was helping him drink. She had a gentle touch and huge sad eyes. Saint's eyes, Duncan thought.

"Thanks," he whispered.

She nodded, but didn't speak.

"What's your name?"

She didn't answer, but he saw a blink of fear flash in her eyes. Somehow in her world the idea of someone asking her name meant danger.

"I'm not going to hurt you," he said in Spanish, then repeated the words in English.

She still didn't respond.

A big man with an arm that swung useless at his side banged his way into the room. He carried a load of firewood in his good arm that few men with both arms could have managed. He was dressed in work clothes but wore a gun low on his hip. After making little effort to put the wood in the bend, he dropped it in a pile and stared at the girl.

Duncan watched him with half-closed eyes for a few minutes. The big man took a step toward the girl and raised his hand as if to pat her head, but she slipped to the other side of the bed. The big hand moved again as if they were playing a game. She countered, keeping as far away from him as she could in the small room. The man laughed, but Duncan could tell from the girl's face that she wasn't enjoying the exchange. She didn't seem overly afraid of him, more bothered.

When the girl tripped over the firewood trying to stay out of his reach, he moved away as if giving her time to straighten. He stepped to the foot of Duncan's bed and looked at him.

Duncan opened his eyes, hoping the man would stop his game of stalking the girl if he knew someone was watching.

He seemed disappointed to find Duncan still alive. While the girl picked up the wood, the man moved closer to Duncan as if the girl were no more important to him than a kitten. "Don't talk to the girl." His voice was a low growl, as though at one point in his life he'd screamed until his vocal cords gave way. "If you do, you'll get her in trouble. And don't touch her. No one is allowed to touch her, not even me, though I know she's waiting for the time when I do."

Duncan nodded slowly, never taking his eyes off the big man. He'd seen outlaws with the same kind of dead eyes this guy had. Dark, cold as an open grave.

The girl moved to the fireplace and began stoking the fire as if the room were cold and not already warm. She didn't look at the man, but he glanced in her direction, keeping her in his sight.

"What's your name?" Duncan asked, not sure he liked the way the man glared at the girl.

Both men were silent as the girl hurried out of the room with a bucket.

The big man watched her go, then seemed to relax his guard when he turned back to Duncan. "Not that it's any of your business, Ranger, but my name's Ramon. I don't figure you'll be around long enough to get to know anyone, not even the girl." The big man moved a step closer. "She don't say nothing, but she knows, just like I do, that you're a corpse still breathing."

Duncan gave no reaction to Ramon's words. "My wound's not that bad. I think now the fever's gone, I might pull through this." He knew Ramon didn't care, but he wanted to keep the man talking, possibly make a friend if he could.

"It ain't that wound that will kill you, it's that ranger badge you were wearing when crazy old Toledo found you. She'll make a pretty penny turning you over, but she has to get you in good enough shape to die. Nobody wants to hang a man out of his head with fever, and if she handed over a corpse, she wouldn't get a tenth the money she'll get if you're alive and can dance at the end of a rope for a while."

"She's not turning me over," Duncan said, as if he believed his own words. "She asked if I'd do her a favor. When I do whatever she wants, she'll let me go on my way and I'm heading straight to Texas."

Ramon laughed. "Well, if I were you I'd get real worried if she asked you to step outside. Knowing Toledo, she'd even hand you a gun just to make it more interesting when the outlaws come to claim what they bought. And they will come, Ranger, mark my words."

Duncan glanced around the room. Not only his clothes seemed to be missing, so were his guns. "Any chance you'd get a message for me across the border? Let them know I'm still alive. It would be worth a double eagle to me if you could."

Ramon shook his head. "If she found out, she'd turn me out at best; at worst, she'd beat me like she beats that girl now and then. Crazy old Toledo ties the little creature up outside at the hitching post so everyone can see like it was a show we'd enjoy, then she beats her with whatever's handy until the girl passes out. Some say that when little Anna first came here she'd cry after she was beat, but I've been here six years and I've never heard her make a sound."

"Why would anyone hurt that child?" Duncan remembered how the big guy had teased her and asked, "Is she your kin?"

Ramon grinned, showing several gaps where teeth had once been. "I'm a mixture of about everything. My dad was a buffalo soldier at Fort Davis, my mother a native caught stealing food. She claimed her mother was a white woman and her dad a Mexican rancher up near Santa Fe, but I doubt it was true. She was a woman threaded together with lies."

Duncan wondered if the big man before him hadn't inherited his mother's traits.

"I tell you of my mixed blood so that you'll see how someone like me would know the value of little Anna. She's pureblood."

Ramon sat down on the chair next to the bed and leaned back as if he'd been invited to stay a spell on an evening porch. "The girl's kin to Toledo," he volunteered, without being asked. "Their blood runs all the way back to Spain. I think I heard one of the cooks say that the old witch is the girl's great-aunt. Something happened to the kid's family and they shipped her here, having no idea that Toledo would hate her own kin."

He shook his head. "The old woman don't seem to need a reason to beat the girl. Once, when Anna hadn't been here more than a few years, she tried to run away. Toledo pulled off her shirt looking for any bud of womanhood, saying she'd marry her off and the child would be someone else's worry. When she found only a child's body, she stripped the girl completely and used a whip for the first time.

"The old woman was so exhausted by the time she'd completed the job, I had to carry her inside, and then I went out and covered the child with blankets so she wouldn't freeze. Her back was covered in blood. Toledo had promised she'd beat her with the whip every time she ran away. The girl never ran again, and Toledo went back to using a stick. It makes welts, but it won't kill her."

"Why'd you care if she lived? You didn't care enough to stop the beating." Duncan had seen something in Ramon's eyes when he glared at the girl. Not caring, more like ownership.

Ramon grinned. "I'm the one who caught her when she ran. Toledo says I can have her every night if I want after she gets her monthly bleeds. The old woman wants to breed her, claims she's no more than a cow who should produce a kid a year once she's able. Toledo says she'll tie the girl to my bed at night until she fills with child, and then I can't touch her until she gives birth."

The big man puffed up. "But I don't think we'll have to tie her. I think once she gets used to me, she'll stay. I may have a worthless arm, but I'd be better for her than most around here. Once I break her from running from me, she might even take to my touch."

When Duncan raised an eyebrow, Ramon quickly

added, "I try to help her out when I can. It ain't my job to bring in the wood, but I do and I make sure she eats sometimes even when she doesn't want to. I'm the nearest she's got to a friend around the place. If it wasn't for me she'd be locked in this room every time Toledo leaves the place, but I let her out. I watch her to make sure she doesn't run, but I let her go about her day, doing her chores."

Duncan fought to keep his face free from emotion. "Why would Toledo want the girl to have children if she hates the sight of her so much?"

"I don't know. Don't care. All I want is her. Now and then I brush my hand across her accidental-like to see if she's developing up top. I'm beginning to think she won't, or if she does they'll be small, and that's all right with me. I'll still take her. I only got one hand that works, so she don't have to have much up top to satisfy me." He laughed and wiggled his eyebrows as if sharing a secret, then continued, "Toledo did say once that when the babies come she'll have a wet nurse take care of them so the girl can breed faster. She says if I keep her well rounded I'll have less duties around the place and if the girl bears three brats that live the first three years we're together, Toledo promised she'd double my salary. I'm thinking if we go to six, I'll be expecting another double."

"What kind of place is this?" Duncan had the feeling he'd landed in hell.

"Toledo's run a roadhouse for more years than

205

folks can remember." Ramon seemed to think he needed to answer the question. "In the front left side, we got drinks, food, and a poker game going most all the time. There's beds for rent upstairs, with or without a woman to serve as a bed warmer, if you know what I mean. We get all kind of travelers, mostly men running from the law and drifters looking for trouble. On the right side, Toledo has goods to trade with anyone who comes to the door. Blankets, supplies, hardtack." He rubbed his face with his one useful hand. "I figured out a long time ago that what she really sells in here is information. She goes out and collects information about who is where as she peddles her goods. If anyone wants to find someone lost, they come here."

"Why are you telling me this? You think she wants to sell something to the rangers?"

Ramon shook his head. "No. I'm just talking. With Little One running out of the room every time I walk in and Toledo only talking to me when she yells, I guess I just wanted to talk for a change. Anything I tell you don't matter. You'll be dead in a day or two anyway. Even if you thought of running and were able, she's got more guards than me about the place. You wouldn't make it out of the yard."

The big man stood and started out of the room, favoring his left leg.

"How'd you get hurt?" Duncan asked, hoping to learn more about this place.

"Wagon turned over when I was running guns. I

caught my arm in the wheel and twisted it all up. Broke my leg, but it didn't heal right." He looked at Duncan with his cold eyes. "But don't you think I can't stop you if you think of leaving." He raised his good arm. "There ain't but one way out of this room, and I'm on the other side of the door on guard. One hit with this fist and you'll be out cold. Toledo put you in the girl's room 'cause there's no escape, and she put me on guard because nothing gets past me."

"I believe you, friend," Duncan said, thinking of Lewt Paterson in Austin, who always called a troublemaker his friend a moment before he ended the problem. "Mind my asking why you stay?"

Ramon shrugged. "I got nowhere else to go. I killed four people in that wagon accident, and word got around that I was drunk when it happened. One of the men in the wagon was the ringleader's son. He let out word that if I ever came within shooting distance of him or any of his men I'd be dead, so I crossed the border and found this place."

The girl came back into the room carrying a tray of soup. She didn't look at either of them as she moved across to the stool beside the bed.

Ramon's glare followed her every step. "It ain't so bad here. I get regular meals, the work's not hard, and I got the promise of some fun coming soon when she turns into a woman." He walked to the door. "I'm locking you in. You ain't in any shape to move anyway, but remember I don't want you talking to the girl." He grinned. "Not that she'd answer you if you did. She's been slapped around enough to know that it's not her place in this world to say nothing."

Duncan heard the bolt slide closed just after Ramon stepped out of the room. He relaxed back against the pillows. In the fever of the first day, he'd thought he was safe and someone was taking care of him. Now he knew he was in a prison and the nurse was just another prisoner.

He looked at the girl Ramon had called Anna. She would one day be a beautiful woman if she lived. He'd seen women begin having children when not fully grown. By the time they'd had three or four they looked forty even though they were still in their teens. Then, year by year each baby seemed to drain more life out of them. He wondered if Anna knew the life her great-aunt had planned for her. Nights with a bull of a man. Carrying a child every year without being allowed the joy of raising it. The girl would go mad, if she wasn't already.

She stirred the soup and tasted a sip to make sure it wasn't too hot, then offered him a spoonful.

"Thank you, Anna," he whispered, not wanting his voice to reach the door in case Ramon was listening.

She fed him the soup as he fought to stay awake. Thanks to her, he was healing, but it would take at least a few days before he had the energy to walk, much less fight his way out of this place. Duncan had a feeling he didn't have that long.

They heard the door bolt rattling, and she pulled the bowl away. With a feather touch, she brushed his eyes closed and pulled the cover up. By the time the door swung open, he'd figured out that he needed to stay asleep if he wanted to stay alive.

He heard Toledo move into the room, her layers of rags swishing like willow branches as she walked. He also heard the girl move the tray away, but he couldn't hear where she went.

"Ramon!" Toledo yelled. "Have you heard a sound from our guest?"

"Nope," Ramon answered from near the door. "But I've been sitting here on guard like you told me."

Duncan felt the old woman's bony hand on his cheek and forced himself to totally relax. When she slapped him, he gave with the blow like a man out cold. He wasn't surprised when she hit him again, trying to wake him.

"He's no good to me like this, but his color is better, I guess. Lock him in here in the girl's room tonight. She can take care of him. If he's dead in the morning, tie her to the hitching post and leave her there until I wake. It's been far too long since I've taught her who her betters are. If she doesn't keep him alive, she'll be wishing she was the one who died."

Duncan heard the old woman move a few feet away and kick something. If it was the girl, she didn't make a sound. "If he dies, I'll beat you, Anna." Toledo almost giggled with excitement. "Do you understand, you worthless child?"

Ramon's laughter came from near the door. "You'll beat her anyway, and we both know it. If he dies, you'll beat her. If he lives and is traded to the outlaws, you'll beat her. I've never known you to go more than a month without beating her."

Toledo's voice moved away. "Well, if I do it's none of your business, now is it? I don't break any bones and I haven't had to strip her and use a whip in years. She learned not to run away. And you best remember that you'll not touch her until she's ready. Do you understand, Ramon, or I promise I will break the rest of your bones."

"I understand. You've told me often enough. She's not a whore and she'll not come to my bed until she's a woman and the priest has said the words over us."

Toledo laughed, as if their plan made some kind of sense in her mind. "Her children will be of mixed blood from peoples her parents wouldn't have stopped to talk to. If they knew their only child will become nothing more than a breeder to children who will always be servants and thieves, they'd curse me from their graves." Her laughter bore a touch of insanity in its joy. "They hated me, but I'll have the last laugh."

The room fell silent when the door closed. Duncan listened, not sure Anna was still in the room. The old woman didn't just hate the child, she hated Anna's parents enough to punish them through Anna. Duncan knew he could never understand that kind of hate, and he doubted Anna would either, even though she would suffer from it.

He also guessed that Ramon had lied about hearing anything because the longer Duncan was out, the longer he needed a guard at the door. On a normal night locking Anna in would be enough, but with a ranger trapped inside, Toledo must have ordered a guard. It has to be an easy assignment, one a man like Ramon would like.

He felt the bed beside him give, and he knew Anna was near. He raised his arm, fighting back the anger at what he'd just heard. She reminded him of a frightened puppy as she curled into a ball beside him with her head on his chest. He made no move for fear of frightening her. Suddenly his problems didn't seem so big. He knew, if it cost him his life, he wouldn't leave without taking her.

Through the thin sheet, he felt her silent tears falling against his heart. After a long while, he matched his steady breathing with hers and they both slept.

She wasn't afraid of him, and he guessed why. For them both, the nightmares began when they woke.

ဆာ CHAPTER 21 ର

Lewt fought the urge to cover Em's ears so she wouldn't wake, but it was too late. She was already scrambling to her feet.

"Stay here," he ordered. "I'll see who it is and then tell them I'll go looking for you." When he glanced back, he noticed that her hair had pulled free of the braid and was flying around her shoulders. "Try to tame that wild, beautiful hair of yours."

Fighting down a smile, he headed for the door, thinking that when they were alone again he'd curl his fingers in the sunlight gold of her hair.

He couldn't resist one last look. She was trying to find her boots and tuck in her shirt at the same time. There was little left of the hard woman who'd ordered him around for days.

He walked slowly to the door, making little effort to look like whoever was pounding hadn't woke him.

"What is it?" he said as he opened the door. "No one must be up to answer the door in this place. I almost killed myself tumbling down the stairs."

A tall, dust-covered ranger frowned at Lewt. "What are you doing here, Paterson?"

Lewt tried to see past the mud and hair. "Wyatt

Platt? Is that you? Hell, you look like you lost a fight with a tornado."

Wyatt pushed him aside and walked in. "I don't have time to figure out why you're opening the McMurray door. I need to speak to Teagen McMurray. It's urgent. I've been traveling two days by train and horse to get here."

"Teagen's not here. Where's Duncan? You rode out with him a week ago, didn't you?" Lewt hadn't spent a great deal of time talking to any of the other rangers, but he thought he remembered Wyatt being somewhere in the barn the last time he saw Duncan. The thin man had a way about him. He moved like he was made out of rawhide: easy, bendable, boneless. People didn't seem to notice that Wyatt Platt was in the room until the fight started. Maybe because he was thin as a board, he had the ability to blend into the woodwork.

Wyatt looked as out of place in the big house as a toad at a banquet. Lewt's words about Teagen not being home didn't seem to sink in, because the ranger looked around. Finally he shouted, "I'll talk to any McMurray. Travis or Tobin will do. I need help fast."

Em's slim frame walked from the kitchen, her hair now pulled back into one long thick braid. "I'm Emily McMurray; who are you?"

Wyatt straightened and introduced himself. The ranger actually looked nervous.

Lewt almost growled aloud. Em would probably

get in big trouble for passing herself off as a McMurray, but somehow he couldn't imagine poor injured Emily upstairs standing up to the ranger. For all he knew Emily McMurray had shoved Em out of the kitchen and told her to play like she was the family member at home.

To Lewt's surprise, Wyatt removed his hat and shifted from foot to foot before he finally continued, "I come from the border hoping I can round up some help, ma'am. Duncan is in real trouble, may be already dead. I remember him talking about a few men who work on his ranch who know the badlands across into Mexico near Adobes. He said they know that part of the country like the back of their hand and told stories about the people who hid out there."

"Haven't men already gone after Duncan?"

The ranger shook his head. "Everyone from the captain of the rangers to the army has orders that no one is to cross over, but Duncan got left behind when we made the raid, and I'm afraid if we don't go get him he might not be able to make it back alive. I figured I could come here to get a guide. Or, if none is able to ride, I'll try to go in alone. Not knowing where anything is, it won't be easy, but I'm going down there after my friend, orders or no orders. I'll bring him back, dead or alive, but I'll bring him back."

Em motioned for them to follow her to the kitchen. Lewt noticed Sumner standing in the doorway listening to every word the strange rider had said. He nodded for Sumner to follow, and the old man did.

Lewt made coffee while Em brought out bread and cheese for Wyatt. "Now slow down, Ranger, and tell us everything."

Wyatt ate a few bites, then forced himself to slow as he began to talk and eat at the same time.

Lewt would have been surprised if the man had had any food in days.

The ranger told them all that had happened. The raid led by Captain McNelly and all that had happened the first night. Wyatt said he talked to Duncan the next morning before the cattle were released and every man was fighting to get in the saddle before he was caught in the stampede. He explained that when they reached the Texas side of the river, Duncan wasn't with them, but his horse remained tied at the bank on the other side. Wyatt told how he swam the river and untied the horse. He tried to get someone to go back with him to look but everyone had orders not to cross.

He downed half a cup of hot coffee before adding, "I waited a day, hoping to see some sign of Duncan. If I'd seen him crawling toward the water I would have gone after him no matter how many guards had been placed to shoot any man stepping foot in Mexico."

Wyatt took another drink. "The next night I was still waiting. I got lucky and saw a gambler crossing far down the river from where we'd run the cattle over. He wasn't too interested in talking to me, but I got him to tell me what he knew. He said he heard there was a wounded ranger being held at a way station of a ranch that sold supplies, guns, and whiskey to whoever needed them. He wasn't sure, but he thought the place was called Three Forks. He claimed the old woman who owns it bragged that she planned to auction the Texas Ranger off like he was a prize pig. Said there were so many outlaws who hated rangers, the bidding could go pretty high and the show it would make would be good for business."

Sumner shook his head. "If that was two days ago, he's already dead."

Wyatt nodded at the old man in respect. "Maybe, maybe not. The gambler said the old lady was patching him up. She seemed to think a standing ranger might go for more than a wounded, near-dead one. The gambler laughed and told me the old woman was good, she'd draw it out as long as she could."

"Did the gambler see Duncan?" Lewt asked.

Wyatt shook his head. "No, but he did mention that several around the poker game that night laughed about how they'd like to kill a Texas Ranger real slow."

Lewt paced the kitchen. "You believe this gambler?" he asked.

Wyatt gave him an odd look. "Much as I believe

any gambler. By the way, what *are* you doing here? This is the last place I would have expected to find the likes of you."

"You know each other?" Em asked.

Wyatt nodded. "Duncan always has been one to have all level of friends. I didn't think he sent them home to visit, though."

Lewt stared at him for a moment. Right now it didn't matter much if the ranger gave him away. Lewt had far more important things to worry about. "I'm going after Duncan with you. I've heard of high-stakes games down there at a place called Three Forks. If they'll let one gambler in, they'll let me."

Wyatt shook his head. "You have no idea where this ranch is that houses both gamblers and outlaws. You'd just get yourself killed, and if Duncan does manage to get out he'd blame me for letting you go down there."

Lewt's gaze hardened. "I don't believe I'm your problem, Wyatt."

Sumner raised his head. "I know where Three Forks is, though when I was down there, it was more a trading post and whorehouse than a ranch. Twenty years ago it was a place wild as any outlaw holdup ever born. Near as I remember it was run by a woman named Toledo. Heard someone say once that she'd been a beauty until her brother burned off half of her face. I saw her once. She wore a veil."

Em frowned. "Why would a brother do that?"

Sumner shrugged. "Folks said she got pregnant without being married and embarrassed the whole family. Heard they made her drink something that caused her to lose the baby. From what I could see the scars had twisted more inside of her than the skin outside. She was as cruel a woman as I've ever met. If she has Duncan, there's no telling what she'll do."

Wyatt almost jumped out of his chair. "That's it. I heard the gambler say the witch who auctioned off secrets and people alike was named Toledo. We've got to go get him out of there."

Lewt and Sumner agreed and stood.

Em looked from one man to another as if all three had gone mad. "This is crazy. Sumner, you're too old to ride across the border, and Lewt, you'll never pass for a gambler. This sounds like a mission that would get you all killed."

Wyatt smiled. "Oh, believe me, Miss Emily, this guy will pass for a gambler, and Sumner was a legend in his day. If he's half the man he was, I'd ride with him any day."

"Great!" Em stood. "Then I'm going with you. He's my cousin."

All three men shouted no at the same time, but she'd already started packing supplies.

ဪ CHAPTER 22 ၄

Duncan closed his eyes when he saw a priest come in.

"Give him his last rites, Father," Ramon said.

"Is he that near death?" the priest asked.

"He will be," Ramon answered. "Toledo told me to have you do it before you head back to the mission."

The priest moved around Duncan, speaking Latin. He thought of trying to whisper something, but feared he might get them both killed.

"That's enough," Ramon said after a few minutes. "You'd best be on your way."

Duncan had missed his chance. He lay still, trying to hear what was going on. There seemed to be more talking beyond the door. Toledo was out probably collecting information. He'd noticed that when the old woman was away, the cooks talked and others came into the kitchen to eat and visit. Duncan tried to make out what they were saying, but he couldn't. He drifted off to sleep.

Ramon woke him when he unlocked the door, saying he had to take Anna for a walk before she started her duties in the kitchen.

He chased her until Duncan could smell the big man's sweat. Finally he grabbed her arm. The girl fought him, but he dragged her out of the room.

Duncan managed to sit up, but without clothes or a gun he knew he'd never make it beyond the door even if he was strong enough to stand.

A few minutes after Ramon and the girl had gone, he heard the lock slide open once more and two middle-aged women hurried into the room. Neither looked to be more than five feet tall, and he guessed from the sweet smells surrounding them that they were cooks.

"You see, Sarah J. I told you he was still alive," the shorter one said.

The second woman leaned close, looking ready to jump back if he snapped at her. The two of them were as out of place as bear cubs in a church. They both had red hair dusted with gray and pulled up in braids circling their heads. Not only their dress, but their talk told him they were from Ireland.

The one called Sarah J poked at Duncan with a wooden spoon. "He looks more dead than alive, if you ask me. All those men next door are eating us out of winter stores waiting to see who kills him."

"I'm right here." Duncan glared at them. "I can hear and understand everything you're saying, ladies."

The both jumped back a step and stared, as if it never occurred to them that he was in his right mind and could speak.

"What's your names?" Duncan said, simply because he could think of nothing else to say to these two women who looked like round little gingerbread cookies and smelled the same.

"I'm Rachel Elizabeth," the first one who'd stepped into the room said, "and this is my older sister, Sarah J."

"Duncan McMurray, Texas Ranger, at your service." Curiosity got the better of him. "Mind telling me what you two are doing at a place like this?" He couldn't see them as whores, and they didn't fit with the mission trappings at the roadhouse.

"We're murderers on the run," Rachel whispered. "After we committed our crime, we loaded up our wagon and took off. I told Sarah J we should go north, but she thought south would be better. Warmer climate. Toledo found us lost, out of money, supplies, and luck six months ago. She offered us both a job as cooks. Apparently, she'd fired the one before, or shot him. We've heard conflicting reports. His food was so bad, half her guests and most of her hired help was sick."

"You can't arrest us and take us back, can you?" Sarah J asked, obviously finding no need to follow her sister's chatter.

"No," he said, not believing a word Rachel said. These two didn't look like they could murder a goose, much less a person. "But I can't believe you like it here."

"We don't," Rachel whispered, "but we've not enough money to leave, and where would we go? Murderers can't settle in just any place."

"Good." Sarah J smiled. "I didn't think you could

221

take us back." She looked like she might break into a dance at any moment. "Well, Ranger McMurray, if you see a crime, you can go stop it, can't you, even if you're not in Texas. That is, if you have time before you die or get killed."

Duncan saw his chance. "I'd need my gun and, of course, my clothes in order to do a proper job."

"Rachel, go get them," Sarah J said without moving. "I'll tell the ranger of the problem."

Duncan wasn't sure he could stand, much less solve any problem, but this might be his only chance to get away and he planned to give it his best effort.

Sarah J crossed her hands in front of her, looking very much like one of the mission sisters as she began. "We first thought of asking you to kill Ramon. He's no good to anyone but Toledo, and he bothers little Anna all the time, teasing her as if she were a mouse on a string. But Rachel pointed out that Toledo would just hire another guard for the kitchen rooms, and he might do more than tease little Anna."

Rachel rushed back into the room with a stack of clothes and whispered before her sister stopped talking, "We love the girl and can't stand how she's treated here. I've thought of getting the butcher knife. . . ."

"Now, Rachel," Sarah J said, "we're finished with that kind of thing."

Rachel closed her mouth and smiled sweetly. "Ramon doesn't have use of all his parts anyway, maybe he wouldn't mind if we cut off one small one."

Duncan raised his eyebrow, wondering if he should be worried about these two. For all he knew they were cutting up everyone who crossed them and cooking the bones for stew. "What do you want me to do, ladies?" he asked as the room started to spin. Forget standing, sitting up now became his challenge.

Sarah J must have sensed he had little time left before he passed out. "If we can, we'll help you escape, but if we do you have to promise to take Anna with you. The old woman will kill her in a fit of anger one of these days. She has no reason where the child is concerned. Some on the place say she's a fair boss, but in the months we've been here she beats the child several times. Just ties her to a pole and hits her with whatever is handy."

"I was already planning to take her with me," Duncan managed as the darkness flooded his mind and he leaned back against the pillow.

As if in a dream, he was aware of Rachel shoving his clothes under the bed, and then Anna ran into the room and curled up in a corner, her knees tight against her chest.

Ramon rushed in but stopped when he saw the two cooks were there. "You're not supposed to be in here!" he yelled.

"And you're not supposed to leave your post!" Sarah J yelled back. "If you say a word about us bringing this poor man water, we'll tell Toledo how you chase Anna around every time she's gone."

"I'm not hurting her. Go back to the kitchen where you two belong."

Rachel followed her sister out of the room. "I've heard," she whispered, "that a finger from a fat man's hand can sweeten the beans. You've a worthless hand. You shouldn't miss a digit or two."

Ramon glared at her. "Don't come in here again."

"Don't leave your post." Rachel smiled. "And if I were you I'd sleep with my hands inside the covers. With no feeling in that arm, you might not even miss the finger until you're eating the beans and think they taste sweeter than usual."

The door closed and the room was silent except for the crackle of a dying fire. Duncan drifted in and out of sleep, reminding himself over and over to remember that his clothes, and maybe his guns, were under the bed.

Sometime in the hours of stillness, he felt Anna curl up beside him. "I'll take you with me," he mumbled, as if he believed he might find a way out.

"I know," she answered in a soft voice, almost touching his ear.

When he awoke sometime later he tried to figure out if her answer had been real, or if he'd only been dreaming.

Duncan had no idea of the passage of days or nights. Sometimes it seemed colder; now and then he could see into the other room, which appeared to be a large kitchen, and in there it would be day. He slept on and off, not knowing if he'd been out an hour or a night. The only measure he had was Ramon bringing in wood. Once he'd said something about it being Anna's daily supply. To the best Duncan remembered, he'd delivered wood three, maybe four times.

Anna brought him soup many times, feeding him a few ounces at a time. She never spoke again, if she'd talked the first time, but he slowly talked more and more to her. He thanked her for the meals and for her care. He told her soon she'd be safe and hoped he wasn't lying.

Each time Toledo came into the room, Duncan pretended he couldn't respond to her yells or slaps, but he knew the ruse wouldn't last long. After a week, when he wasn't dead, she was bound to notice that he was improving. The wound on his leg was healing, thanks to Anna's constant care.

Anna stayed locked in the room with him for hours at a time. She didn't escape even when the door was open. The two cooks were now delivering food to both him and her as well as fresh water for bathing.

Late one night, when she'd washed his body and he'd drifted off to sleep, he awoke, more aware that she wasn't curled up beside him than of any noise. He slowly opened his eyes and saw her in the light of a single candle she always kept burning. She was taking a bath, one limb at a time, using two buckets of water.

He watched as she soaped and scrubbed one thin arm and then the other. He could see several bruises on her legs. Her back was turned to him, but he noticed the flare of her hips as she washed. When she turned to pick up her towel, her body was shadowed in the candlelight. The child was not a child. She was small and bone thin, but her breasts were fully developed.

The shock of it brought him fully awake.

Through slits in his eyelids he watched, unable to turn away. She lifted a band of thin cotton and wrapped her breasts, flattening them out against her chest. Then, using a thin cord belt, she circled her waist and looped more cotton bandaging between her legs.

Duncan tried to make his mind work as she slipped into the plain, simple clothes all children wear. Shapeless, comfortable. But Anna wasn't a child, and if he was guessing right, she was in her time of the month.

Not that he knew all that much about women, but he did know animals. He asked his father once about the workings of women, and Travis McMurray said there are things in this world a man shouldn't learn about and if he does, he's the sorrier for it.

Once she was dressed, she washed out rags in the clean water, scrubbing all blood away, and then she placed the bits of cloth near the fire to dry.

Duncan closed his eyes and tried to think. Anna wasn't a mindless child about to grow into womanhood. She was a full-grown woman pretending in order to survive and, thanks to being locked up in a room every night, she'd managed to keep her secret.

When the rags were dry, she folded them and slipped them into a tin box. She lifted a piece of paper from the lid of the box and looked at it a long time in the light, then put it back and hid the box beneath the pile of wood. She crossed to the bed and curled up beside him.

Duncan fell asleep wishing he could ask her questions, but he knew he'd frighten her if she thought he knew her secret.

෨ CHAPTER 23 ෬

Lewt rode toward town, fighting between worry over his friend and fury over Em thinking she had to come. He'd argued with her even while they'd saddled the horses, but she'd said over and over that she was in charge of the ranch while the men were gone and she'd been told by Teagen to do whatever she thought he would do if trouble came. Teagen would go after Duncan, and so would she.

Halfway to town, he pulled up beside her and tried again. "You can stay with us until we board the cattle train, and then I want you to go back to the ranch. We'll be sleeping in a stock car with the horses. That's no place for you, Em. Go back and take care of the ranch like you were hired to do and stop pretending to be someone you're not." He thought about adding that he was an expert at pretending. He'd been doing it all week.

"Once we get to Anderson Glen, I'm stopping to talk to Rose and Bethie while Sumner buys supplies." Em's voice was calm, too calm. "I'll meet you at the station. I'm going after Duncan, even if I have to step over your body to board."

"I thought we were friends," he said, fighting down swear words by the dozens. "Now just because I'm thinking of you, you're threatening to kill me."

"We *were* friends, maybe we still are, but a few kisses does not give you any power over me. You're not my father or my husband. Even if you were, I'm not sure I would listen to you on this. Duncan is in trouble and I'm as good with a gun as most and, if he's hurt, I brought medicine."

"Fair enough." He gave in. "Go with us, but when we reach the border, stay on the Texas side in camp. We'll go over, bring him back, and turn him over to you for care. How does that sound?"

She didn't answer.

He guessed she saw no need to argue ahead of time, and he doubted she'd listen when they reached the Rio any better than she'd listened when they'd left the ranch. He decided she was the most stubborn woman alive. If she ever did get married, she'd drive her husband to drink within days.

She tried to pull ahead, but he stayed right beside her.

"Don't do this, Em," he said, more to himself than her. "Stay here where it's safe."

"End of discussion," she snapped.

Anger boiled over in him. "You're right, I'm not your husband. I'm through talking. It's easy to see why no man would want to be married to you. It appears you're more man than any husband could ever be."

She shot off at full gallop, and he didn't try to keep up again. As always, the minute his words were out, he was sorry. He didn't understand. He'd spent years learning to get along with every type of person from governors to drunks, but he couldn't seem to get along with her. She was headstrong and proud and toxic. He'd probably get himself killed trying to protect her, and she hated him more often than not.

Sumner caught up to him. He had two extra McMurray horses on a lead line. The man walked with a limp, but his old body seemed molded for a horse. He rode with the ease of one born in the saddle.

They rode in silence for a few minutes, and then Lewt said, "She shouldn't come along. It's too dangerous. Can't you talk some sense into her?"

"She's a better rider and better shot than most rangers I've ridden with. I've watched her for years, that one. She's shy, afraid sometimes, but she's got spirit. She'll be fine."

"So you're not going to try to talk her into staying here?"

The old man shook his head. "It's been my experience no one can talk a McMurray into anything. You just got to ride with them or stay out of their way."

Great, Lewt thought, *the old man is playing along with the lie that she's really Emily McMurray.* In two days he'd be crossing the border with two crazy people and a ranger who had a death wish. The odds weren't good. If he had any brains left, he'd turn around and go back to the ranch himself. Maybe it wasn't too late to talk the real Emily McMurray into marrying him. Or maybe he could give Rose one more try? She didn't seem near as crazy about Boyd as Boyd seemed to think she was.

Lewt shook his head. He knew he wouldn't, couldn't turn back. For once in his life he had to play full-out against all the odds. Duncan was the best friend he'd ever had, and he wasn't prepared to lose him without a fight. Even if he hadn't known Duncan, he couldn't let Em ride into trouble alone. Much as he hated to admit it, he cared about her.

Heaven knew why. She hated him right now. She was a thousand miles away from what he wanted for a wife, and even if he did want her, she'd made it plain she didn't want him or any other man.

Lewt decided he fit right in with this group of

nuts. He was as crazy as the rest of them. "What do you think our chances are of coming out of this alive?" he asked Sumner.

"Does it matter?" the old man answered.

Lewt laughed. "No."

℘ CHAPTER 24 ℂℛ

Em walked to the little house her family owned in town while the men talked the station manager into letting them ride on a freight train at least as far as Austin. If he let them travel farther south, they could save a day's ride.

The railroads had a strict policy against riding with the animals, but a few dollars in the right palm usually got a cowboy a straw bed for the night. The main office might set policy, but the men who worked the line knew that times were hard and folks needing to get from one part of Texas to another didn't always have money. So, for the price of transporting a horse, the cowboy sometimes got to ride free, even on trains with no passenger cars.

She tapped on the door to the "little house" and was glad to find her sisters home. Mrs. Allender had decided to take an afternoon nap, so the women came back to the house while the men elected to have a drink at the saloon.

Em followed her sisters to the kitchen, where Rose poured tea and they talked quietly.

After Em explained what had happened to Duncan, Bethie cried. They'd all hated and loved him as a child, but he was family, and family to the McMurrays came first.

"There's no sense wishing Papa were here. He's not. We've got to do what we can. I'll go get him, guessing he must be injured somehow or he would have come out with the others. Rose, you and Beth will have to take turns watching over the ranch as soon as you say good-bye to our guests. Sumner tells me the men know what to do, but have Danny, the kid who's always hanging around the barn, ride with you on rounds. Sumner says he's a good shot if trouble comes up."

Beth nodded. "I'm sure Davis will go with me while he's here. He rides well and I feel comfortable with him on guard. That will relieve one hired hand to work in the barn. With Sumner gone, they'll have their hands full."

Rose stared at her sisters. She hadn't been out riding with her papa for years. The idea of spending an entire day in the saddle didn't appeal to her. "I'm not even sure I know who Danny is," she complained. "Em, don't you think we should wire Papa and ask him to come back?"

"No," Em said. "I promised I could handle whatever came up. I'll handle this. I'll bring back Duck. Papa's got his hands full taking Jamie around to the doctors. He doesn't need to worry about what's happening at home right now. We'll have

Duck back and recovered before he and Mama get home."

All three women agreed. They silently stood and hugged one another.

"I've never remembered a time when there were only two McMurrays on Whispering Mountain," Beth whispered. "It's frightening."

They held hands as they used to do as children, forming a circle. "We'll get through this." Em clung tightly to her sisters. "Remember when Rose and I had to go off to finishing school. We used to stand this way and say, 'Though apart, I'm in your heart.'"

Beth and Rose smiled. "Come back with Duck," Rose whispered. "We'll be waiting."

Em turned and walked out of the house without another word. She knew if she'd said any more, all three of them would have cried, and they were far too old to start sobbing.

At the train station, she saw Sumner loading the horses. He must have stopped by Elmo's Mercantile and given orders to have supplies delivered, because a kid stood beside him with what looked like enough supplies for a week packed in twill bags that would stand both the trip and the weather.

When Sumner saw Em, he said, "I figure we can pick up whatever I forgot when we leave the train."

Em nodded, thinking the old guy couldn't have forgotten much, because both packs looked full.

Without another word, they loaded the horses

and packs and climbed on. Lewt was the last one on, and he looked around for a moment at their quarters. He smiled, then jumped back down for a moment before tossing up a broom.

While Wyatt and Sumner tied a line for the horses, Lewt swept out a corner of the car. When the train whistle blew, they tossed their gear in the clean corner and settled in for a long ride.

Em stood and watched the land passing by, as cold and dead with winter as she felt inside. She'd known from the first that what she had with Lewt was no more than a flirtation, but she hadn't expected it to end so fast. He hadn't said a word to her for an hour, or even acted like he'd noticed she was standing five feet away from him.

She was the one who had a right to be mad. He'd tried to order her around. If she felt like it, she might laugh at how he'd reacted when she'd told the ranger that she was Emily McMurray. He'd stared at her as if he knew she was lying. It seemed not to occur to him that she might have been lying for the past four days.

To him, she was still a woman hired to work with the horses. He couldn't see her as a lady. She couldn't help but wonder if he would have kissed her like he did if he'd thought her a McMurray.

The air coming through the slits in the car walls was bitter cold, but she barely noticed. She had to forget about Lewt and what he thought of her. She had to think about Duck. Part of her had always known he'd get himself in over his head one day. They'd even talked about it once when he'd come home for a few days. As they always did when he came back to Whispering Mountain, just the two of them went riding. That day they'd gone up on the hill where their grandparents were buried along with Sage's first love and a child Em's mother had miscarried.

Duncan had climbed off his horse and lain down on the grass beside the headstones. "Promise me, Em," he'd said, "that when I die you'll go get my body and lay me to rest here."

She'd laughed. "If you'd stay home, you'd save me a trip by dying of old age right here on the ranch."

"Not me. I want to take life at a full run. I've had this hunger to do everything there is to do since I can remember, but I want to be put to rest here so I can see Whispering Mountain and know I'm home."

"Why don't you go up to the summit and spend a night? Maybe you'll do like the legend says and dream your future."

"I don't want to know. I want to be like a bird, just shot out of the sky in midflight."

Em had sat down beside him. "Not me. I want to die of old age right here."

Now, in the rattling train car, she thought about what he'd said. She loved him like a brother, but could remember only a few times when they'd talked, really talked, as adults. In many ways they were opposites, and neither understood the other.

She stared into the night. He was out there somewhere. Hurt. Alone. About to be killed by men who hated him just because he was a ranger. She had to find him or die trying.

"Cold?" Lewt asked from just behind her.

Em didn't turn around. "No," she lied.

"Would you look at me if I said I was sorry, Em? I didn't mean what I said."

"I don't want to look at you," she said, but she couldn't help but smile. There was something about Lewt that made him a hard man to hate. "And I need to make something very clear to you. Whether a man wants to marry me or not doesn't matter. I made up my mind a long time ago that I never wanted to marry. Not ever."

"Want to tell me why?" he whispered.

"No."

"Do you think, for just this quest we're on, we could be friends?"

"Fair enough." She had a feeling the peace between them wouldn't last long, but she'd try once again. Somehow this strange man had broken down fences and stepped into her life, whether she liked it or not.

"You know, you may not be cold, but I am. I'd like to stand a little closer to you, but I'm worried about having my head blown off. You wouldn't murder a friend, would you?"

"Probably not," she said. "If you'll promise not to try ordering me around. I hate that, Lewt."

"I won't even talk."

"Good," she whispered as she felt the warmth of him move very close behind her.

He kept to his word. He just stepped beside her, blocking some of the wind as his arm rested lightly at her waist.

She rolled a few inches until she pressed against his chest. Even if Sumner or Wyatt had been watching, she doubted they'd see how close they were to each other. She might not want a man in her life, but Lewt offered a kind of comfort. She liked the solidness of him. The way he smelled and the way he treated her like a woman even when she didn't want him to. She'd never let a man boss her around or control her, but a friend might be nice.

Lewt's stance was wide and seemed to steady her as the car swayed back and forth. They both watched the night as if there were answers out there waiting for the right questions to be asked.

After she'd grown warm in his arms, he leaned slightly and brushed her lips with a kiss. There had been no passion in the touch, only comfort, and she accepted it for what it was.

She turned slightly, snuggling her back against his chest as his arms circled her, pulling her close. They stood like that a long time, before he leaned and kissed her neck. "I like just having you close to me," he whispered, so low she wasn't sure he knew he'd said the words out loud. "If that's all that can be between us, Em, that's enough."

When she didn't protest, his hands began to move at her waist, spreading out over the layers of coat and clothes as if he had to feel her, had to know that she was there.

Just having him close, she thought. That would be enough. That would be all she could handle. When he was gone, she'd remember that once in her life, she'd let her guard down a bit and it hadn't been as frightening as she'd feared.

Sumner rattled his way to their side of the car, giving them time to move a few inches away from each other. "Hell of a night to be traveling in an open car," the old man said.

"It is," Lewt managed.

"I think I'll turn in. We won't get there before dawn. Once we're riding we'll be wishing for sleep, I figure."

They all moved toward the stash of supplies and spread out bedrolls. Sumner took the spot closest to the horses. He used his saddle as a pillow and, half sitting up, pulled his hat low only minutes before he began to snore.

Wyatt took the other side of the cleaned-off floor. He rolled up in his blanket and pressed his back against one of the supply bags. He didn't look comfortable, but the ranger also didn't seem like a man who complained. If Em was guessing, she'd think that this might be one of the more comfortable places he'd slept during his years with the rangers.

Lewt spread her blankets a foot from his own. When she curled up inside, he removed his heavy leather coat and placed it over her, claiming all he needed was the blanket.

She watched him stretch out flat on his back and then raise his hand in the moonlight slicing through the car sides.

Em knew what he was offering. She snuggled in the warmth of his heavy coat and laced her fingers through his. She thought she'd be too worried or too uncomfortable to sleep, but something about having this man so near comforted her. She fell asleep.

When she awoke, all three men were up and the train was pulling into the station. She scrambled to get her things together as the train stopped and the door dropped. Within minutes they were unloaded, the horses wild with fright over the steam. Everything seemed to be happening at once. Sumner strapped the bags on one of the extra horses and Wyatt disappeared to the nearest outhouse.

"Morning, beautiful." Lewt smiled as she stepped to the edge of the car, looking for a place to jump down.

She stared at him, thinking she probably looked a sight. Strands of her hair had come loose from her braid, and she wouldn't have been surprised to find straw hanging off her clothes.

He raised his hands, and she leaned forward as

he caught her and swung her down to ground. They moved to the horses in silence, but both knew that she'd forgiven him for yesterday. They were back to being friends and, she decided, just a bit more.

He lifted her saddle onto her horse and faced her. "I'm glad you're with us," he whispered. "I was wrong. You've got as much right as any of us to ride to help Duncan. Just promise me one thing. Don't take any chances unless I'm there to cover your back."

She nodded. "If you'll promise me the same thing." For this unsteady new friendship to work, he had to accept her as an equal.

He smiled as if he understood her meaning. "Agreed."

When she finished saddling her mount, he tossed her an apple. "Enjoy breakfast. We'll be ready to ride as soon as Wyatt gets back."

Five minutes later, they were headed south at breakneck speed. Wyatt led the way with Sumner just behind, then Em, then Lewt. She caught herself glancing back to make sure he could keep up, but he seemed to be having no problem. She'd taught him well.

They stopped to rest the horses about noon and again three hours later. Wyatt and Lewt passed out hardtack and canteens, but no one suggested a fire. There wasn't time.

By late afternoon Sumner had taken the lead, and they began to move slower. The old man was digging through twenty years of memory to find the trail that had once taken him into Mexico to a big place built like a stage station. He said the scarred woman sold supplies to travelers on one side and anything else on the other side. He remembered there had been whiskey and opium for those who wanted to forget what a mess they might be in and soiled doves for those looking for a few minutes to remember. Mixed in with it all, surrounding it all, were card games that lasted for days and often ended with gunfire. The woman who ran the place, Toledo by name, took no part in the gambling other than to charge outrageous prices for the drinks and food during them. She also charged the survivors for any burials.

When they stopped to water the horses, Sumner told them he'd gone down with another ranger looking for a strawberry-headed woman whose husband claimed she had been kidnapped by outlaws. They found her dealing cards, but she wasn't in any hurry to come back to Texas. Apparently the customers treated her better than her man had. She claimed he worked her harder than the plow mules during the day and then rode her half the night. She'd begged them to let her stay.

Sumner smiled his toothless smile. "We went back alone and told the farmer she was dead. He shrugged and said he'd already ordered another woman from a mail-order bride place. I've seen men who had to shoot their horses show more emotion than he did. I always wondered what happened to that girl. Who knows, she may still be there."

"But you and the other ranger did nothing about the illegal things going on down there, or the outlaws holing up there?" Em had to ask.

"It wasn't our concern. We were just there to bring the woman back, and there's no law that said we could do that if she didn't want to come."

Lewt had shown little interest in the story. "How much longer until we're there?"

"We'll reach the river by midnight and sleep there. Then we'll cross in the morning and be at the Three Forks ranch before noon."

They all looked tired as they climbed back on their horses and continued riding. Em worried that this trip might be too much for Sumner. He'd been twenty years younger when he'd crossed before, but they might never find Duncan without him.

As he'd told them they would, the little band reached the river before midnight. They camped and built a fire. Em helped make coffee and boil up a soup made from vegetables. Without more than a few words, they ate and spread their blankets out around the fire.

Lewt put the head of his bedroll so close to hers that the tops of their heads almost touched. He sat watching her unbraid her hair and comb it before braiding it once more in a smooth rope. She guessed they were both too tired to say anything, but the way he looked at her told her how he felt. He liked watching her, and the knowledge warmed her cheeks.

When she lay down, she raised her hand above her head and found his hand there waiting.

She liked the way he remembered to hold her hand and didn't kid her about it. A friend and more, she decided. A friend for a few days and then only a memory.

℘ CHAPTER 25 ℃

Duncan began to work his leg, exercising until he was sweating. If he was going to break out of this place, he had to be strong enough to overtake Ramon in seconds, before the big man could alert any other guards. From bits and pieces he'd picked up, there were a dozen men working for Toledo and they took their meals in the kitchen just beyond his locked door.

He had no idea where they were the rest of the time, but pacing seemed to help him think. The sheet wrapped around his waist was bothersome, but necessary. She'd washed every part of him, but he couldn't see himself standing nude in front of Anna, be she child or woman.

She watched him with her huge dark eyes as if she had no idea what he was doing. He thought he saw a slight reaction when he pulled his clothes from under the bed and found his guns tucked between the layers.

A few nights ago, after he knew they'd been locked in for the night, he motioned for her to sit on the floor.

She looked wary as if fearing he might be tricking her. Duncan started to take her hand, but she jerked back and he knew her fears. He lowered himself to the floor and hoped she'd follow.

She sat down slowly a few feet away, and he pulled a burned stick from the fire. With the ashes, he drew a square on the rock floor. "If this is the house, where does the sun come up?"

She watched him for a moment, then pointed to the left of the box he'd drawn.

"And where is this room inside the house?" He offered her the stick.

She drew a tiny square in the back away from the sun, and then she began adding squares to his drawing as if she understood what he was trying to figure out. A barn to the north with a corral. A road running northeast and then south just beyond the barn.

He smiled and whispered, "Horses?"

She pointed.

"Stores of supplies?"

She drew a circle to the left of their room.

For the next half hour, he whispered and she showed him on their crude map where everything was, down to the guards' stations.

"Thank you," he finally said as she handed him the stick back and began to wash the map away.

Duncan stood and forced himself to pace, working out the soreness in his leg. He listened at the door and heard nothing. The kitchen must be closed for the night. Which meant that Ramon, or maybe some other guard, was sleeping on the other side of the door.

Exhausted, he finally climbed into bed. Every night he was managing to do more, but he worried that he wasn't recovering fast enough.

Anna moved to a dark corner and removed her clothes. Every night she wore a soft gown that had been washed so many times it looked little more than a rag. She climbed onto the bed beside him, curling into her ball next to him, almost touching him. Since the night she'd cried on his chest, she hadn't come so close to him. He knew she wasn't afraid of him as she was of Ramon, but she still didn't trust him completely.

He moved so that he could whisper near her ear. "Ramon said you came here more than six years ago. He said he heard you were six or seven at the time. How old were you, Anna, when you came to stay?"

She sat up on her legs and looked at him as if no one had asked her such a question or expected her to respond. Slowly, she lifted her hands and held out all her fingers, then closed one fist and held two up on the other hand.

"You were twelve?" He found it hard to believe that even with her small build, the old woman had missed her age by five years.

She nodded.

"That would make you about eighteen now."

She shook her head.

"Nineteen?" he guessed again.

She nodded, and he thought she was brilliant to be able to pull childhood off for so long.

"Why didn't you, or did you try to run away?" He thought he remembered Ramon telling him one night that Anna had tried to run once and she'd almost died from the punishment.

She turned her back to him, then unbuttoned a few buttons of her gown. Holding it in the front, she let the garment slip free at her shoulder and showed him the thin long scars on her back from the years-ago beating. There were fresh bruises as well along her arms, as if some hand had jerked her suddenly.

Duncan got the picture. It wasn't all that hard to break a twelve-year-old; a few beatings, but as she got older, Toledo must have begun locking her in. It crossed his mind that maybe the old woman knew or suspected that Anna, though small, was fully grown. Duncan wouldn't put it past the old witch to make Ramon wait for his prize as long as possible, but Duncan had no doubt that one day she would turn her great-niece over to the man. Toledo had plans for Anna, and they were too horrible for him to imagine.

When she started to pull her gown up, he stopped her with a gentle touch. "No," he whispered. "Let me see them all. I don't ever want to forget what the old woman did to you."

She didn't move, but sat with her back perfectly straight for a few minutes, then slowly pulled button after button free until the gown fell to her waist. The thin scars, some layered on one another, ran to her waist and beyond, he guessed.

"No one should be beaten like this. No one," he whispered, more to himself than to her. He brushed his hand over the scars, wishing he could brush away the memory of the pain she must have suffered. "Anna, tell me, how did you survive?"

She looked at him over her shoulder, but she didn't say a word as she buttoned up her gown. Somewhere along the way she'd been trained too well not to talk, even to someone she trusted.

When he raised his arm, she moved into his hug. For a long while he held her, his hands spread across the damage that had been done to her so many years ago.

ᏚᎧ CHAPTER 26 ᏔᎧ

A little before dawn Em, Lewt, Sumner, and Wyatt crossed the Rio. No one said a word. They had no idea what they faced, but Wyatt swore that the gambler he'd talked to several nights ago at the border had said the roadhouse where outlaws came to drink and gamble wasn't more than a day's ride from the river.

Em believed the ranger, Wyatt Platt. He might be a man of few words, but he was proving to be a true friend to Duncan. No one else had bothered to tell them her cousin was missing. Maybe the ranger thought he'd eventually make it back, or maybe none wanted to face Duncan's father, Travis McMurray.

Once on the other side, Wyatt rode ahead scouting and they followed at a slower pace. The idea, though Em didn't think it was a particularly good one, was that if Wyatt got caught by lookouts around the ranch where the roadhouse stood, he'd say he was alone and wait for the other three to come get him.

Em thought it a better plan to storm the roadhouse firing and demand Duncan back, but Sumner reminded her that they had only a gambler's word that Duncan was there, and everyone knows what that's worth.

Lewt glared at the old man, but didn't comment.

Sumner talked them into making camp in a grove of trees an hour before dark. He said that if his memory hadn't failed him, the roadhouse was about three more miles and this would be a safe distance to camp. With the wind from the west and the low cloud cover threatening rain, they all decided to risk a small fire.

Wyatt rode in with the sunset and told them he'd

circled the place twice. He thought he saw a few men who might be guards posted around Three Forks but none on horseback patrolling the area. He didn't go in because with his years in the rangers, there was a good chance someone might recognize him.

Sumner offered to go, claiming he'd been out so many years any outlaws who knew him were long dead. Em thought of telling them she'd go into the place and act like she was looking for directions or something, but a woman traveling alone in these parts would be too rare to be normal.

"I'll go in," Lewt said from the tree line where he'd disappeared while Em and Sumner made camp.

Em turned to argue, but her words caught in her throat. Lewt Paterson stood before her, all six feet of him, dressed in a tailored white suit made of fine wool and a gold vest that reflected the firelight. As he had in the black suit he first wore, the wrangler clothes she'd given him, and the expensive western wear he'd bought in town, Lewt Paterson looked like he belonged in what he wore.

He hooked a finger into his vest pocket as if he'd done so a thousand times.

"Evening, Gambler." Wyatt laughed. "I was wondering when you'd decide to shed your skin and let your true colors fly."

Sumner stood. "You should be able to convince them you're there to play cards in that outfit, son, but can you handle the game of poker?"

"I'll manage." Lewt's slow smile had a glint of the maverick in it. "No one knows me this far south. I'm the only one of you who can walk into the place and not draw too much attention. I'll ride over tonight and see what I can find out. If Duncan is being held there, someone will know. Folks talk more at night when they're drinking than they do in the morning when they're hung over. All I got to do is play a few hands and listen."

Em wondered if Lewt could pull off such a disguise, and then she remembered how he'd once told her that the only conversation he'd had with a woman involved asking, *How much do you charge for an hour?* Apparently, the rich mole family who raised him and never taught him to ride but let him play with a knife in church also let him gamble and carry on conversations with women who sold their time by the hour.

"You'll need a gun belt," Sumner said. "I noticed all you brought with you was that rifle I lent you the other day."

"No," Lewt said. "I'll go in unarmed. A gambler with a gun is just asking to be called out if his card playing comes into question. If I'm unarmed, men are more likely to want to settle any argument with fists." He glanced at Sumner. "Before you ask, I can handle myself."

Wyatt smiled. "At least as far as *they* know, you're unarmed, right? Duncan told me once that you can halve a fly in flight from across the room with one of your thin knives."

"One of?" Em echoed. It never occurred to her that the bumbling man who could barely ride a horse might carry two or more weapons.

He met her stare. "Em, I'll be all right. It may take me all night, but I'll find out what we need to know. I'm the only logical one to ride in. If we all tried it at once, we'd be cut down."

Wyatt reached for his horse's reins. "I'll ride with you as far as I can, but once you go over that hill, you're on your own."

Lewt moved to his horse and pulled off his saddlebags.

Em walked up behind him, not sure what to say. She didn't want him to get hurt, but someone had to go in, and he did seem the only logical one.

He handed her the bags. "I'll leave my other clothes here along with everything else. Watch out to pack my other boots if you move camp. I kind of got used to those riding boots." He brushed her arm. "If something happens and I don't come back, there's enough money hidden in these bags to bribe a guard or maybe even win the auction if it comes to that. Use it however it's needed."

"Lewt, you don't have to do this. You hardly know Duncan, and I'm not sure you can pull off being a gambler." She'd worried about him every day this week, and now he thought he could handle an outlaw camp all by himself.

"Oh, believe me." Wyatt laughed. "He can pull it off."

Lewt stared into Em's eyes. "I've stepped into worse places than this one to gamble the night away."

Sumner talked with Wyatt as they moved away from Em and Lewt. She had no idea if they did it to offer them privacy or just so they could continue talking about alternate plans.

Lewt stood for a moment, watching Em as though he were trying to remember every detail of her face. "Duncan and I have been best friends for years," he said, low enough that the men couldn't hear. "I owe him my life many times over, but it was my idea to go meet his cousins, not his. I had this wild idea that I needed a rich wife, but lately, I've reconsidered. Marriage isn't for men like me. I've never had anyone to worry about me, and I don't want you worrying tonight. If something does happen to me, forget you ever knew me and go on with your life, Em."

She straightened, trying to harden, but for some reason it wasn't working tonight. "I won't. If you seem determined to go in alone and get yourself killed, I won't try to stop you, but I will not forget you."

"Good," he said. "Any chance you'd kiss me good-bye?"

She shook her head. There were too many things about him that didn't add up. The man she thought she knew was changing before her eyes.

"How about when I get back?" he teased, as if he were only taking a ride and not probably going to his death.

"If you get back," she whispered.

His smile didn't reach his eyes. "I'll think about that kiss, then. It'll help keep me awake tonight. I might surprise you and live just to come back to you, but if I do, I expect one long kiss."

He swung onto his horse and was gone before she could answer.

She watched him ride, realizing he'd made her smile when only a moment before she'd been about to lose her hard shell and cry.

Sumner walked toward her. "You really should have kissed the fool, Miss Em."

"Maybe I will when he gets back."

Wyatt laughed. "After we save Duncan, he's going to kill that gambler, so it will be too late for kissing then."

Both turned to the ranger and said "Why?" at the same time.

"Because," Wyatt answered. "Lewt Paterson done stole one of Duncan's lady cousins' hearts. I was standing not five feet from Duncan the night we rode out with Captain McNelly. He told Lewt his dad and uncles would shoot him double dead if he sent a gambler to court the girls."

Em was tired, but her mind began to put the pieces that had never made sense together. Lewt hadn't come from a rich mole family who stayed at home and counted their money. He stayed so pale because he'd been playing cards all night and sleeping all day. Of course he'd have skills with a knife; he probably fought in fights all the time in saloons. And last, what would he say to the women he met? He'd say, *How much do you charge by the hour?* No rich family. No fine education. For all she knew he'd been born in a saloon and cut his teeth on shot glasses.

Em grinned as the three of them huddled around the small fire. When all this was over, she planned to kill him herself. All through the meal of beans and crackers, she thought of ways Lewt Paterson would die, and then, when she curled up in her bedroll, she remembered one fact she'd forgotten. He hadn't courted her. He hadn't known she was one of the ladies. In fact, he still didn't know; he'd been mad because she'd passed herself off as a McMurray. He thought she was just some woman who worked with the horses.

He'd kissed her for no other reason than he wanted to.

Em revised her plan. She would kiss him when he came back. She'd give him a kiss he'd never forget, and *then* she'd kill him.

ℬ CHAPTER 27 ℭℛ

L ewt Paterson walked into the roadhouse called Three Forks. The place might have been a ranch headquarters fifty years ago, but this owner had found selling supplies and sin far more profitable than cattle or crops. The original house looked like it had been added on to several times without any consideration given to the architecture.

He'd seen worse, but it had been a long time since he'd played cards in a place like this. Most of the men looked like they hadn't had a bath in months, and the girls working the room for drinks and opportunities didn't look much better. The floor was filthy and needed a good fight to mop it up. From the looks of it, men had given up even trying to hit the spittoon. The place reminded him of a saloon in Fort Worth that was so bad they didn't clean up from a gunfight until the body got to smelling worse than the floor.

The gambling hall at Three Forks was big, several tables in play and a roulette wheel just inside the door. There was no stage or music. Men who came here came to drink and gamble. Along the back wall was a long bar and a wide door that opened into what looked like a café. Thirty or forty men were in the place, and most, including the two guards at the door, looked like they were long past drunk.

There were no social drinkers here, and he guessed the card games were not played for sport either.

Lewt turned slowly, noticing everything as he stretched and complained to the bartender about how it had taken him forever to ride in from Texas.

He counted six exits, but except for the double doors at the front, all looked like they went farther into the building. One was probably the women's quarters, and from the number of men walking in and out, the girls were doing a good business tonight. Men usually paid for an hour but needed only five or ten minutes. He heard a girl laugh once and say she worked a fortyhour day one night.

Another door, up a few steps of stairs, was probably where the rooms were rented for the night. A sign over the opening said, BED—ONE DOLLAR, BATH—TWO BITS, SEE BARTENDER. Two small doors were near the back of the bar. One might be the direction to the outhouse; another probably served as a pass-through to a kitchen.

Lewt almost missed a catwalk near the top of the high ceiling. It ran half the way around the saloon, a plain balcony fashioned to blend into the ceiling beams. One old woman, dressed in rags, stood watching like hell's guardian angel. Lewt had a feeling she missed little, from men cheating to bartenders pocketing cash. She reminded him of a buzzard on a perch.

"First drink's on the house," the bartender said in

English as he shoved a whiskey in Lewt's direction. "I'm guessing you came to gamble."

"That's right." Lewt took a swallow of the terrible whiskey. "I heard there's money to be made here for an honest man who likes to bet."

"Keep it honest and you'll stay alive. Most of this crowd wouldn't hesitate to fire first and ask questions later." The bartender pointed with his head. "Slip that man in the chair by the door a few dollars and he'll sit you at a good table. There's no charge to play other than the money you lose, but we collect for the food and drinks when we deliver. That way we don't have anyone go broke owing a tab."

"Food any good?" Lewt asked, to pass the time. He wanted to get a good feel of the place before he sat down at a table. "I don't see any samples sitting out on the bar."

"Best we've had in years. Made to order until six, then you take what's left in the oven. What would make you happy?"

"What you got?"

"Thick steaks. We got our Texas beef cheap. Any dessert they bring you, don't turn it down. This late the menu's light, but the food's great."

"Sounds good. I think I'll play awhile, then have a meal."

The bartender nodded. "You're like most. Can't wait to lose. Be sure and save enough for a meal because once you're broke, you're out the door. Toledo's got a dozen guards to make sure all's square with the house when you leave."

Lewt laid ten dollars on the bar. "This should cover dinner in an hour and breakfast at dawn."

The bartender took the money. "I'll hand you your change when you leave."

Lewt paid one of the guards for a chair and sat down to a table of cutthroats who looked like they'd committed every crime on the books and were bored with talking about it. He knew better than to make small talk. They were here to play.

Lewt was good at cards, but tonight he was careful never to win a big pot. He had a feeling the poor losers and the big winners both went out of this place feetfirst.

When the bartender brought his steak, it gave Lewt a chance to sit out a few hands and listen to the talk around him. He moved to a little table in the middle of the place so he could hear several conversations.

Lewt spotted a few other men he knew to be professional gamblers. They were men he'd seen in the rougher saloons before he worked his way up. They looked much the worse for wear. Gambling, for the most part, was a young man's game and an old man's pastime. Somewhere in the middle, a gambler would be smart to step out and take a few years to breathe fresh air.

Lewt had that all planned. Or at least he thought he had. A week ago he thought he'd marry a rich wife, settle down, and take his winnings to build a business and become part of the day world. No more all-night games, no more sleeping in the back of saloons with one eye open so he would wake up with his winnings still in his pocket. He'd planned to have a house, a real house with his name on the deed, and an office he could go to, and a wife who'd have supper ready every evening. He wanted to walk with her on his arm to church every Sunday morning and vote in the elections.

Except nothing had worked out like he'd planned. The only woman on Whispering Mountain he'd been attracted to was a long-legged mean-talking girl. He smiled and added in his mind, who had to hold his hand when it got dark. He hadn't thought her even pretty, but she had a way of growing on a man. When he kissed her, the whole world seem to stop, and if he could get her to look at him he swore she had the bluest eyes in all of Texas.

One of the saloon girls circled by, letting the sleeve of her dress, dipped in cheap perfume, drift along his arms. "Want some company later?" she asked.

"Yes," he said, thinking of Em. Even when she refused to talk to him, she was company to him. Maybe because he wasn't trying to impress her and she wasn't flirting with him. He and Em settled comfortably into silence when they were together. Even though their days riding the hills of Whispering Mountain had been hard work, he missed them. He missed her.

When the saloon girl circled back by to ask for the time he'd prefer later, he added quickly, "I have a game that may take me the night. How about waiting awhile?" He noticed that the girl looked exhausted.

"All right," she pouted, "but tomorrow is going to be busy, what with the auction and all the men riding in from miles around. So if you're interested, you'd better decide when."

Lewt forced himself not to look up from his food, but he shoved a chair out for her. She'd just told him more information than he'd gotten in an hour of sifting through every conversation around him.

She took the offered seat and ordered a drink, knowing that if she sat at his table, he'd be charged for her drinks.

"I don't like the idea of you being too busy. Are you sure it's going to be packed tomorrow? There's times I like to spend a while with a lady like yourself and not be hurried by someone waiting outside her door."

The girl shrugged, and half her dress slipped almost to her waist. Her revealed breast wasn't particularly big or pretty, but she'd gotten him to look and that had been her purpose. She leaned back and crossed her legs as she downed her drink. "The old witch who runs the joint has a Texas Ranger trapped somewhere around the place. She claims he's a murderer, and no one here argues with her. Everyone on the wrong side of the law has a relative or friend who was killed by the rangers. The witch, Toledo by name, is holding an auction to see who wants to be his executioner. She calls it 'helping him get home,' but we all know whoever takes the ranger won't be sending him nowhere but to the grave.

"Those who have the money are planning to bid. Those who don't will bet on how the ranger meets his end. The favorite way is hanging or maybe firing squad, but a few are placing money on the more unusual ways."

"Doesn't sound like a bet I'd want in on." Lewt motioned the bartender to bring the girl another drink. She'd earned it.

He wanted to ask more questions, but he had a feeling her lips were just as loose talking to the guards as to him. The last thing he wanted was to draw attention. "Good food," he said. "I wasn't expecting it to be."

The girl smiled as she took her new drink. "That it is. Toledo found two women wandering around down here about six months back. They said they were murderers on the run. We all thought they were touched in the head. Appears they're sisters. Walking proof craziness runs in families. Toledo offered them a job in the kitchen 'cause the food was so bad the pigs wouldn't eat it." She raised her empty glass and continued. "The sisters were so good, she fired the worthless cook she had and kept them on. Pays them a good salary but charges them for board. They'll probably never make enough to get out of here, and even if they did, where would they go?"

Lewt smiled as he finished off his meal. "Aren't you afraid they'll murder you one day? After all, women don't usually kill, but once they pick it up, it's something they tend to make a habit of."

"No. Even if they thought of it, Toledo keeps a guard in the kitchen."

"Why?"

The girl shrugged. "I don't know. None of us have been allowed in there for a week. We take our meals at a table behind the bar. The guards are the only ones allowed to eat in the kitchen, and they take full advantage. Every last one of them is getting fat, and the rest of us feel like all we ever get is the leftovers."

Lewt didn't have to ask more. He knew where Duncan was. In this country, Toledo would have wanted him close. In the barn, it would be too easy for someone to steal or kill him. And if she had him here, it made sense there would be a guard near.

"I better get back to the game, honey, but when I finish, I'll book some time with you if I have enough money left. Until then, why don't you have a bottle on me and rest a spell?"

"Sounds good," she said. "I might just call it a night. I'm in room three, so just come on in if you're interested in a little fun later. If I don't wake up, leave the money."

"I'll do that," he said, thinking that after kissing Em he never wanted to sleep with a woman who didn't ask or care what his name was. In fact, even if all he ever did was kiss Em, that would be far better than sleeping the rest of his life with someone like this.

He gave her money enough to buy a bottle and watched the girl go to the bar, pick up a full bottle, and disappear down the hallway to her room. He knew he wouldn't see her for hours, and when he did she'd be too hung over to remember him or anything they'd talked about.

Lewt stood and returned to the game. He played through the night, losing a little more than he won. He watched everything around him.

The old lady on the walk above disappeared about ten and never returned. The guards became far less interested in their jobs once she'd vanished. A few ordered drink after drink. About two in the morning one of the guards pulled a saloon girl into his chair by the door and satisfied his lust with her. He looked like he might have a heart attack, and she looked bored. Few in the bar bothered to notice.

Lewt had watched such acts all his life and was surprised when he heard a man call it *making love*. Nothing about it seemed to involve even mild caring. Lewt wasn't like some men who treated women like objects to own, or worse, like pets to keep around just to play with, but he'd never really thought of a woman as standing on equal footing.

He'd heard a few men talk about their wives or mothers as angels, but he'd seen little of that in his life. More than anything, women were a mystery to him. A mystery he hadn't had time or opportunity to study.

Or, maybe he hadn't wanted to until now. Until he met Em. Lewt wished he had a few nights or months to think about it, but right now he had to play poker and keep his eyes sharp. Duncan was close, he could feel it. Getting his friend out of this mess might cost him his life if he didn't play every card right. Yet as the hours passed he couldn't ban Em from the back of his mind.

By three there were more men asleep or passed out in the bar than awake. Lewt stood, stretched, and headed out the back door to the outhouse. No one seemed to even notice he'd left.

Once outside he circled around to the well as if just wanting a drink, then walked to the nearest entrance. He didn't go in but peeked in the window. Sure enough, he'd found the kitchen.

One guard appeared to be leaning against a bolted door. He looked sound asleep.

Lewt walked back to where he'd tied his horse and disappeared into the night without making a sound.

Less than thirty minutes later he was waking everyone up at the camp, and none seemed too happy about it.

Wyatt rolled awake with a gun in his hand.

Sumner seemed to crawl from sleep one limb at a time, and Em sat up rubbing her eyes like a child.

Lewt stared hard at her, needing to erase all he'd seen tonight. Needing the purity and plainness of her with her braid and work clothes and no makeup or frills.

"We've got to go in tonight," he said as the others gathered around the dying campfire. "I think I know where he is, but it'll take two to go in and get him and another two to stand guard, one with the horses, one on a rise about a hundred yards away from the house. It'll provide cover and an easy getaway into trees."

Sumner nodded, knowing his job would be as one of the two lookouts. "Does it have a clear view of the entrances?"

Lewt nodded. "From the rise a shooter can see the back entrance and, more important, the open area to the barn and corral where all the horses are kept."

"We have to get in and out before the cooks get up to start breakfast." Lewt fought the adrenaline already rumbling through his veins. He'd never thought of himself as brave, and now, somehow, he had to lead the charge. "So I'm guessing we have until a little before dawn to get Duncan out. This doesn't look like the kind of place where anyone gets up early."

Showing little sign that he'd been asleep, Wyatt stood and picked up his rifle. "From now until the first hint of sunrise it'll be darkest. I'm not sure they'll be able to follow us if we get a quarter-mile start, and Sumner and I scouted out a few routes besides the main trail that will get us home."

Lewt nodded, and they all stepped into action.

Sumner and Em scrambled, collecting their things. Wyatt had left his horse saddled, but he helped Lewt load the packs. He saddled one of the extra horses they'd brought and walked the pack horse into the trees, saying they'd come back for the animal later.

"Any word how hurt he is?" Wyatt's voice was low as he stood beside Lewt. "Do you think he'll be able to ride? If we have to take him out by wagon, we'll have to fight all the way to the border."

"No, but the old woman is planning to have the auction tomorrow. I figure he's as good as he's ever going to get, and tomorrow night will be too late."

Wyatt agreed. "Sumner won't admit it, but his hand shakes a bit. How about I go in with you while Sumner and the girl cover us? The old man will do best with the horses. She can cover us from the rise. That will keep her out of the fight as much as possible, and with luck she won't have to fire a shot."

"Sounds good. You tell Em."

"Not on your life. You're the one who can cuddle up to her. She gives me looks like she'd shoot me if I burped."

Lewt knew it was a waste of time to argue. He moved over to Em and put his hands around her waist to help her up, but he didn't lift. "Em," he whispered just behind her ear. "I want you to stay close to Sumner." He could feel her stiffen, preparing to argue with him, so he hurried on. "If it comes to a shoot-out, I need to know you're close to him and can take care of you both. I'll get Duncan. If he's hurt I may have to carry him, and I don't think you could do that. Wyatt's a fighter. He'll blast away and be fine if we're attacked. I won't worry about Sumner if I know you're keeping an eye on him."

He could feel her debating and knew she'd as soon fire up at him as go along. She'd come to save Duncan, not hold the horses or provide cover if something went wrong.

He kissed the spot just below her ear, hoping a change of subject might settle her. "When this is over, I'm coming for that kiss. It may be the only one you give me, so I plan to make it last."

Moving his hand around her, he brushed the side of her breast, hoping to distract her. She felt so soft beneath her shirt that he almost forgot his own name, and he realized his plan was backfiring.

"I'll watch Sumner," she whispered as she shot into the saddle without his help. "I'll also be close enough to cover your lying, nogood hide. Now, Mr. Gambler, I'll thank you to keep your hands off me."

Her words were so cold they shocked him. He fought down an oath and climbed on his horse. As they rode through the night he tried to figure out how a woman could run so hot one minute and so cold the next. She could cut him to the bone with her words and make him feel on fire with her kiss.

He didn't know if she was crazy, or if she'd driven him over the edge.

By the time they were within sight of Three Forks, Lewt decided he should marry her and keep some other poor soul from going mad. Any man who married her would need armor to survive a year.

ℰℴ CHAPTER 28 ℭℛ

Duncan didn't know what time it was, but the candle had burned low, telling him Ramon would unlock the door soon. The guard would send Anna out to the kitchen to start the fires and stare at Duncan for a while.

They no longer talked. Duncan couldn't pretend not to hate the huge man with his ugly face and worthless arm that swung at his side when he constantly shifted, like some huge animal looking for footing.

Standing slowly, Duncan tried not to make a sound. He dressed, watching Anna sleep in the candle's glow. He had to get her out of here. It meant more to him than his own life. He'd watched her carefully. Though she never spoke, there was an intelligence about her that surprised him. Everyone treated her like a slow-minded child, but he noticed method to her actions.

He stepped away from her, faced the door, and began practicing pulling his Colt from leather. He wanted to shoot Ramon the moment he opened the door, but that would draw too much attention. If he could somehow get the big man down, dead or unconscious, maybe he'd have a few minutes of time to slip out before anyone noticed. He also had to keep Anna near, for there would be no time to look for her.

When he moved the chair behind the door, he glanced at the bed and saw her staring at him. Fear danced in her dark eyes along with the firelight.

"It's time," he whispered.

She nodded once, understanding.

He motioned toward her clothes, but she didn't move. Crossing the room, he held out his hand and waited.

Slowly, she laid her hand in his and let him tug her toward her stack of clothes.

He bent down and whispered, "We're leaving today, Anna. You have to be dressed by the time the door is unlocked. Get ready. Take what is important to you. You will not be coming back here."

She began to pack the few things she owned. A change of clothes. A hairbrush. A small bag that looked large enough to hold a few coins. Then, with him standing close watching her, she slipped out of her nightgown, rewrapped her breasts and put on her clothes.

She might be less than five feet tall and have the angel face of a child, but she was definitely a woman. Duncan guessed it might have been proper manners to turn his gaze elsewhere, but he couldn't have looked away if a gun had been at his head. One way or the other, their time in this room was over and he wanted to see the only lovely thing he'd seen since he'd been hurt and brought here.

When she finished dressing, she looked up and smiled. It crossed his mind that she was aware of the gift she'd just given him.

He smiled down at her. "Ready?"

She strapped the bag over her back like a pack and nodded.

He explained his plan to her and they got in place and waited. Most mornings Ramon came after dawn. Duncan could hear the women in the kitchen when he opened the door. But twice, the big guy must have not been able to sleep so he'd unlocked the door while all the house beyond seemed silent. He'd said he was checking on Duncan, but he always stayed to talk.

Duncan suspected he'd broken in early to bother Anna because after he said a few words, he'd always close the door so no one would hear and try to touch her. Once Duncan was well enough to watch, the big man slowed his game. Maybe he worried that Duncan might tell the old lady, or maybe he thought Duncan might try to help the girl.

"I've touched her a few times," he'd brag when he was too out of breath to chase her any longer. "And soon, I'll handle her good and proper. When

I'm through with her she'll be lucky if she can walk from my bed, much less run. After she's mine, I'll touch her whenever I feel like it."

Duncan stared at Anna and knew Ramon's predictions would never come true. She'd escape today, or die. Either way, she'd be free of him.

They needed to be ready early. If Ramon didn't unlock the door before the candle that never lasted the night went out, Duncan planned to make some noise that would draw Ramon in early. He had to knock the man out and get away before anyone woke.

About the time Duncan thought Ramon wouldn't be coming in early, he heard a shuffling sound from the other side of the door and the bolt slid sideways.

Anna stood at her post five feet in front of the door. She'd combed her wild hair and, for once, stood tall as if she knew she was the bait for the trap.

Duncan hoped Ramon would see her first. She'd be close enough to catch and he'd head toward her without looking toward the empty bed. Once the big man stepped one foot in, Duncan would slam the chair into his head and hopefully knock him out.

If he didn't go down, Duncan planned to fight while Anna would run and close the door. He had no doubt Ramon had a powerful punch with his one good arm, but Duncan knew he could and would take the man to the floor.

It wasn't much of a plan, but it was all he could think of.

The door swung open.

Ramon walked in, staring straight ahead at Anna. "Well, there you are waiting for me this morning like I told you to be."

Anna took a step toward him, making sure he looked nowhere but at her. Ramon raised his good hand, reaching for her, almost touching her. "I'm going to be easy on you this morning, girl, if you don't fight me. All I want to do is feel if you've grown any and maybe touch your legs a bit. We'll—"

Duncan swung the chair hard, then pulled his Colt and delivered another blow before Ramon hit the floor, out cold.

Duncan glanced up at Anna, expecting to see her smiling, but her big black eyes were filled with terror as she stared at the open door behind him. He was confused for a moment before he heard a familiar low voice.

"Well, that was easy," Wyatt said. "I thought I'd have to kill the bull and carry you out."

Duncan straightened. "'Bout time you got here." He couldn't hold back a smile. The one ranger who never gave up hadn't given up on him.

Wyatt grinned, then dropped to his knee and began tying Ramon's good hand to his useless one. "Don't look like you needed me, partner."

"I'll need you to get out." He moved toward Anna. "We're taking her with us."

"It's too dangerous," Wyatt said as he gagged Ramon.

"We're taking her," Duncan answered, knowing there would be no more discussion. He took Anna's hand, fearing she'd freeze with fright.

The door bumped again and Lewt stepped in almost casually. "Hello," he said, and tipped his hat at Anna. "Mind if I join the escape?"

Duncan laughed. "What are you doing here?"

"I came to help. It seems the only people they welcome here are gamblers. So I rode in first and figured out where you were. We couldn't very well go knocking on doors in a place like this." He watched Duncan favor his leg. "How are you feeling? Can you ride?"

"I'm weak as a kitten, but I can make it. Doesn't look like I have much of a choice. My stay here is over. It's ride or stay around here having them fight over who kills me."

Lewt helped Wyatt lift Ramon onto the bed and tie his head to the bedpost. If he wiggled too much, he'd choke himself.

"Is he alive?" Duncan asked as he collected his gun and hat.

Wyatt raised an eyebrow. "Do you care?"

"Nope," Duncan answered, remembering how the big man had let Toledo hurt Anna. "I don't care at all as long as he doesn't wake anyone up."

"We need to move fast," Wyatt said, as he pulled his gun and crossed to the door. "Lewt unbuckled any saddles still on horses, and I opened the corral to other stock. Hopefully by the time they figure out we've gone, we'll be too far ahead to catch. The hard part will be making it to our horses without being noticed."

Duncan motioned for Anna to stay close, and they stepped out into the kitchen. Halfway across the floor, they heard a rattling at the back door.

They all froze, as if making a sound would draw more attention than being seen.

Sarah J, the taller of the two cooks, came in first. She glanced across the room and saw them in the shadowy light.

Rachel Elizabeth bumped into her sister, then turned and looked at them. Her eyes widened, but to her credit, she didn't say a word.

"We'd best get the coffee on first," Sarah J said as she stared at Duncan. "The first of the guards will be in directly."

"I'll do it," Rachel whispered. "I believe the second door nearest to the pot leads to the gambling room directly. This time of a morning it's dead as a graveyard in there."

Wyatt and Duncan prepared to fight, but Lewt pulled them backward to the door leading to the bar. He and Duncan both nodded their thanks to the women, who still stood blocking the kitchen door.

In single file, they slipped into the saloon. Ducking low in case one of the drunks might look up, Lewt moved behind the bar, careful not to awaken the bartender sleeping in a nearby chair.

Duncan thought he heard one of the little Irish murderers yelling for someone to wipe his feet good before stepping foot in the kitchen. They were giving them seconds, but it might be all they needed to get away.

The gambler led them down a hallway to a door with a three painted on it, and they vanished into a saloon girl's room.

Lewt picked up an empty bottle as he crossed the room and opened a window.

"Friend of yours?" Wyatt asked as he followed.

"Just met her," Lewt said, "but she invited me in so I thought we'd stop for a visit before we leave."

"Friendly type," Wyatt said, as he climbed through the window with both guns drawn. "Wish I had time to stay awhile. I have a fondness for blondes."

Duncan lifted Anna through, then started out the window. "In case I forget to say this, Lewt, thanks for coming after me. You didn't have to put your life at risk."

Lewt grinned as he left a twenty on the table by the sleeping girl. "Sure I did. Who else can I beat at poker so easily?"

Duncan limped out into the blackness of night. A moment later, Lewt was behind him, holding him up just in case he needed support. They moved around to the side of the house, where Sumner waited beside the horses. He helped Duncan climb into the saddle, then lifted the girl up behind him. She held on so tightly he could barely breathe.

They walked their horses twenty yards before they heard men shouting, and then a moment later, three shots rang in rapid fire as if a signal.

"They've found Ramon," Duncan whispered.

"I knew this was too easy," Wyatt said, taking command. "Duncan, you and the girl ride hard toward the river. Sumner, you and Lewt cover them. I'll hang back a little and try to slow anyone down who got into the saddle fast."

As they kicked their mounts and began to run, shots came from the house. A moment later the thunder was answered from a rise just beyond the barn.

"Who's covering us?" Duncan shouted.

"Em," Sumner answered.

"You've got to be kidding."

"Don't worry, she'll be along. I told her to hold the men in the building for five minutes, then get the hell out of there before someone manages to sneak up to her on foot. She knows where to meet up."

"Em?" He had no idea how his cousin got here, but she was a good shot. If she was firing, even in the dark, men running for their horses better be ducking. "You shouldn't have brought her!" he yelled, angry at Sumner.

"We couldn't stop her," the retired ranger yelled back. "Take it up with her, not me."

Duncan and the girl were out of range before the sleepy guards could find rifles and try once more. Every shot they fired from the house was answered from the direction of the barn.

He glanced back and saw Wyatt slow, fire a few rounds, then kick his horse to catch up to them. Duncan wasn't sure if he'd stopped anyone in close pursuit or was simply firing a warning for anyone who thought of following.

When they reached the first bend in the road, Sumner turned them off toward a stand of trees. They wouldn't be able to travel as fast as they might on the road, but they'd have cover. With luck the guards would pass by in the dark once they did follow and be miles down the road before they noticed they were trailing no one.

Lewt slowed and circled Duncan. "I'm going back for Em. Wyatt and Sumner will see you to the river and beyond."

Duncan wanted to yell no, but in truth if he had been able and hadn't had Anna to worry about, he would have already been heading toward her. "Be careful," he said.

"We'll meet you on the other side of the river."

Duncan saluted and prayed his friend spoke true.

Lewt took off at full speed just as Wyatt caught up to Duncan. "Where's the gambler going?" he asked as they moved slowly into the trees.

"He's going after Em and he doesn't even know her."

Wyatt laughed. "He knows her better than you think."

They were on the move now. There was no time for questions.

ℰℭ **CHAPTER 29** ℭℛ

Lewt made a wide circle around the ranch until he found the dilapidated barn. Chaos stormed across Three Forks, with guns cracking the silent night and shouts following. Men were trying to catch horses half crazy from the noise.

He'd seen the blink of fire from Em's last shot and knew where she was, but she'd stopped firing. With luck, she'd be riding past him any moment on her way north. Em had to be gone from this place before the men below could get organized. She'd done her part; she'd held the guards inside the house for more than five minutes. He knew he'd be wise to vanish also, but he couldn't leave until he knew she was safe.

He climbed along the ridge, careful to stay out of sight of anyone below. As soon as they figured out the direction of the firing, someone would climb the ridge and look for signs of the shooter. He and Em needed to be long gone by then.

Lewt found no sign of her at the top.

Men in the corrals were saddling horses and starting out toward the border after Duncan and the others. The first light of daybreak colored the sky like prairie fire in the distance. If Em was going to get away, she needed to be coming his direction soon.

He circled the ridge. Nothing.

He rode near where she must have climbed to watch the house, but there was no movement. Hope made him believe she'd already gotten away, but logic called his hope a liar.

Walking his horse carefully down the back of the ridge, rocky and overgrown, he thought he heard someone crying.

Panic slammed into his chest. Had Em been hurt?

He slid down the incline and moved toward the sound of someone softly crying as if her heart were broken.

In the shadows of a boulder, he saw her kneeling beside a horse on the ground. Relief let him take a breath before he whispered, "Em, are you all right?"

She stood slowly, shaking her head. "A bullet must have ricocheted off one of the rocks. It hit my horse. He's dead. I thought I left him in a safe place, but he's dead."

Lewt touched her shoulder lightly. "Em, we've got to get out of here." He could do nothing about the beautiful animal now, and if he didn't hurry, he and Em might suffer the same fate. Men must be climbing the rise now looking for a shooter.

"I know," she answered, "but I don't want to just leave him."

"Em, we have to go." He pulled her a few feet, but she kept shaking her head.

"No," she whispered. "I can't just walk away. Papa told me to watch over the horses."

Lewt leaned down and lifted her over his shoulder. "We have to go," he repeated, angry at her for caring more about the horse than herself and angry at himself for caring more about her than saving his own skin. "We'll both be dead if I don't get you out of here. You may not be able to leave the horse and I may not be able to leave you, but unlike you, I can carry the object of my apparent obsession out of here." He tossed her onto his horse and climbed up behind her. They had to be out of sight before full daylight.

Em didn't argue or say a word. She must have known what had to be done, but she couldn't make herself leave one of her beloved horses.

They rode east for a long while, then doubled back to head north. The night had been still, but the morning broke with wind whipping the dust around them with a vengeance. It erased their tracks within minutes and blurred the sky with dust devils.

Lewt kept one arm around her waist as he led the horse in the shadows and out of the wind as much as possible. They were making slow progress, but at least they would be impossible to track.

He knew Duncan and the others were flying toward the border. They would be waiting for them on the other side of the river. Lewt didn't know much about this land, but he figured if he went a few hours east before turning north, he'd eventually reach the river, cross, and wander west to find where they'd camped on their way south. No one would look for them to be traveling east. It might cost them a day's ride, but if it saved their lives it would be time well spent.

Only the Rio Grande twisted, making it hard to judge how far he'd gone. They reached the river while it was still light, and he decided to wait until after dark to cross. Lewt didn't discuss his plan with Em. She hadn't said a word for hours. He didn't know if she was in shock or mourning over the horse. He didn't care. She was with him, and that was all that mattered right now.

He stopped near a rock formation that offered a canopy from the afternoon sun, and the small cave sheltered them from the wind. While he took care of his horse, she brushed rocks away and spread his bedroll in the cool darkness of the cave. Then, without a word, she lay down and was asleep before he returned.

They'd both gone two days or more without sleep and he guessed they were too tired to talk. He lay down beside Em and pulled her almost roughly against him, then put the rifle down beside them within easy reach. For a while, he tried to stay awake, but as the sun set, he fell asleep holding her tightly.

There was something primal about the way he

held her. As if by his saving her today she was his, if only for a while. She'd needed him, and her need filled a hollow in him.

Deep in the night he woke and felt her beside him. Without much thought, he moved his hands over her, first in comfort, then with interest. This woman felt so right, like he'd always thought a woman should feel. Not all soft and fluffy, but lean and strong, running the length of him as a perfect mate should.

He thought of the few women he'd been with over the years. None of them had felt right. They'd been yielding in his arms, hungry and in a hurry. Nothing like her. The others had talked of love and passion, something Em might never speak of, but he didn't care. He'd rather be with her than with any woman he'd ever seen, simply because she felt right next to him.

He asked no questions about the way he needed her close. He didn't know if he felt like she belonged to him or if he belonged to her, but somehow over their days together a bond had threaded itself between them. Nothing else mattered. She'd probably come nearer to killing him than accepting him now that she knew he was a gambler, and he was angry with her for lying to Wyatt and thinking she had to put herself in danger for Duncan just because she'd told some McMurray she'd take care of his ranch while he was gone.

But right now, none of that mattered.

Lewt buried his face against her hair and breathed her in as he slid his hand from her waist along the side of her leg to her knee. Gently, he lifted her leg and laid it over his. "Sleep," he whispered. "Sleep next to me. Sleep so close to me we share breath."

She shifted slightly without waking. Her back straightened and he felt her breasts press against his chest. His hand moved over her once more, loving the feel of her against him. His fingers slid down her back, pressing just enough to mold her to him, then moving lower over her hips as if he had every right to caress her so boldly.

He felt her as he'd never felt a woman, with admiration and curiosity and caring. He wanted to know her this way, but not with her asleep. He wanted her to feel his touch, to crave it, to beg him for more, and he had a feeling she never would.

Gently he leaned her head back on his arm and kissed her throat. "Grow used to me," he whispered against her damp skin. "Grow so used to me that you crave me near." Pulling loose the buttons at her collar, he tasted her skin once more. All night, while he'd gambled, he'd thought of her, and a need for her grew inside him. Not the kind of need a man has for a woman, any woman, but the kind of need only one woman can satisfy.

She moaned softly and he froze, afraid he'd awakened her, but she rocked against him, settling back into deep sleep.

His hands brushed one last time over her back. "Until the next time," he whispered as he pulled her blouse wide and kissed the pale skin just above her camisole. "Get accustomed to me, Em, because I plan on holding you like this again."

He rested his hand on the roundness of her hip, took a deep breath against her throat, and let sleep blanket him.

When he awoke, she was gone. For a moment in the blackness of the half cave he panicked, and then he heard her whispering softly from a few feet away. Her words were loving and kind and he smiled, liking the change in her. Maybe he'd tamed a bit of the wildness in her last night.

It took him several seconds to realize she was talking to the horse and not to him.

He stood, mad at himself for bothering to hope. "Em?" he whispered, as his eyes adjusted enough for him to see her outline next to a horse.

"Over here," she said. "Come slow or you'll spook the horse."

"I've been on good terms with that mount for days. I don't think—" Lewt stopped in midsentence as he made out the markings of the animal she was reaching out to pet.

It wasn't his horse.

"Where . . ." he whispered.

"I don't know how she found us, but she's a McMurray horse. I'd know the midnight-gray color anywhere. I'm guessing she's Duncan's." She smoothed her hand over the horse's neck. "You're Shadow," she said to the horse. "Born to run with the rangers and black as night."

Lewt took the last few steps carefully. The horse jerked her head up once, as if taking a look at the gambler as well. "It's Duncan's horse," Lewt managed. "Or at least I think it is. To tell the truth, I didn't look all that much at horses a week ago when I was in the barn watching Duncan and the other rangers get ready to ride."

"They are all very different, just like people. Only this one Duncan trained himself. I remember my uncle Travis shipping a yearling down to Austin as soon as she was weaned. I heard him say that Duncan planned to take over her care. He said Duncan would be the only one who fed her or trained her. There are a few horses that will only have one rider, one master, and this is one of those horses. I guess that's why Wyatt told us he swam the river to set her free. He knew it was better to let the horse go wild than try to break her."

"That doesn't tell me how she found us."

Em laughed. "She didn't find us. She found your horse. We'd never be able to rope her and lead her over the river, but she'll probably follow us."

Lewt frowned. "You're saying the horses know each other? That's a little hard to believe."

"Herds travel together. They're from the same herd."

Lewt shook his head, not believing a word she

said. The horse had probably just wandered by and decided to graze with his mount. This Shadow might be Duncan's horse, but Lewt thought it coincidence that they'd found her, nothing more. He decided to change the subject. "Are you up to crossing the river? We might just make it before daylight."

"I'm ready."

"Good." He picked up the blanket. "I wish I had those clothes I left with the supplies. You didn't happen to bring my boots, did you?"

"No," she answered. "But I'd think you'd be more comfortable in your own style of clothes. After all, you *are* a gambler." Her last words had an edge to them.

He didn't try to deny it. "You found out, did you?"

"Wyatt told us all about how you weren't supposed to come to Whispering Mountain and how Duncan would be furious if he knew you were on the train he sent."

"I don't care about how Duncan feels. My little plan didn't work, so he should be happy. I don't belong with the ladies. This past week proved that. If I'd had to listen to one more round of singing or eat one more sandwich cut in little squares, I'd have gone mad. You're probably mad at me too. You not only think I insulted the ladies, but the horses as well. Gamblers just aren't invited to dinners or even late suppers with the likes of the McMurrays."

She poked him in the chest with her finger. "Stop ranting. We don't have time. I'll take my time telling you what I think of you, Lewt Paterson, when we get across the river."

He could tell she was angry. For all he knew the only reason she was waiting was that she wanted a witness when she shot him. True, he had lied to her, tried to enlist her help to marry a rich woman, and pretended to be something he wasn't, but maybe she'd take into account that he'd saved Duncan's life, not to mention hers. The way his luck was running lately, she wouldn't think of that until the graveside service.

Lewt saddled their horse. They walked toward the water. The midnight-gray horse followed from a distance.

Before they waded in, they pulled off boots, jackets, and vests, bundled them into a blanket, and piled it on the saddle in hopes of keeping some of their clothes dry.

When the water was waist deep, he said, "Hang on to the horse; he'll get you across."

"I know how to cross a river, Gambler," she said. "You just make sure you don't sink. All those lies you've told must weigh heavy on your soul."

"Not really," he admitted, then tried to act like he felt bad about it. She probably didn't want to hear that lying was part of his job. Men wanted to gamble with someone they thought was similar to themselves. One of the few people Lewt was honest with, at least until lately, was Duncan.

Three steps later, Lewt slipped on a rock and went under. When he pulled himself up, he saw she'd done the same.

"You all right, darling?" he yelled, as he moved closer to her side of the horse.

"I'm fine," she said, as she spit out water. "And don't call me darling. In fact, don't talk to me at all."

Em was dripping wet, but before he could laugh at her, he noticed how her blouse hugged her chest, leaving little to the imagination. Heat warmed his blood to the point that he no longer noticed the cold water.

If he didn't know better, he'd think she was intentionally trying to drive him crazy. "Em," he managed, having no idea how he planned to finish the sentence.

She must have thought he was about to try lecturing her again because she answered, "Why don't you take your own advice and hang on to the horse? He seems to be the only one of us who isn't drowning."

When he laughed, he caught her smiling for just a second.

The current caught them and he had to concentrate on staying alive so she could torture him more. Neither had time to glance back to see if the midnight horse followed them.

ᔥ CHAPTER 30 ᔥ

When they reached the Texas side of the Rio, Em felt as if her arms might drop off. The current seemed far worse than it had two nights ago when they'd crossed over, and the water too deep to stand up in most places.

She glanced at Lewt, and he didn't look much better than she felt. They sloshed their way to a stand of cottonwoods much weathered by the wind and floods, then followed a stream farther inland. When they were far enough away from the river not to be seen by anyone on the other side, they dropped their gear in a small area circled by trees.

As she'd taught him, Lewt took care of the horse first before seeing to his own comfort. The midnight mare wouldn't let him very close, but his mount seemed to welcome the weight of the saddle being removed. The horses needed a rest, and now that they were on U.S. soil there didn't seem to be the urgency.

She guessed they were miles from where they'd all camped before crossing over. Part of her wanted to push on, but the practical side of her knew they needed time to rest and dry out.

Once she'd found dry matches in the tin in her coat pocket, Em built a fire in a small sandy clearing between three of the ancient trees. Firewood was not a problem, with downed branches and limbs circling the place along with driftwood twisted into branches during the last flood. Surprisingly, the clothes they'd wrapped in the bedroll on top of the saddle had stayed mostly dry. The sleeve of her jacket was dripping wet, and Lewt's white coat, which had been on the bottom of the pile, was soaked. His vest was dry and their boots were fine. All in all, the crossing had been successful.

The wind blew in the branches above them, but the day had warmed considerably. Though winter had stolen most of the leaves, the branches blended light and shade over the area, making the sand look like a patchwork quilt done in shades of gray. Em removed her blouse and hung it on a low branch near enough to the fire to help the heavy cotton dry. After an hour of fighting the current and no food, she felt weak, barely able to function.

When Lewt returned from taking care of the horse, she ordered him to take off his shirt. "We really should remove our trousers," she said. "They'll chap our legs if wet, but with the fire they could be dry in half an hour."

"What if someone comes along?" Lewt asked, sounding very much like an old-maid aunt. "You're already standing there half naked."

She looked down. Her camisole was almost dry, but it still clung to her skin. On the ranch she'd often stripped to her undergarments and swum in the water on hot summer days. All of the girls had, even though their father raged about it.

Only now, she wasn't with her family. She was with Lewt, who was definitely staring. She reached for her coat.

Lewt frowned. "Don't. The sleeve of that is wet." He picked up his vest and offered it reluctantly. "Here, take this."

She wrapped the colorful vest around her and buttoned it up. She'd never seen anything quite like it. Soft, finely made with gold buttons.

Lewt stepped behind her and pulled a strap, making the back come together and tightening the vest around her.

When she looked at him, he smiled. "You look a hell of a lot better in that than I do. Now, take off those trousers."

"Only if you do the same," she challenged, realizing that despite everything, she still liked and trusted him. She'd never dreamed she could feel so free with a man, but there was something about Lewt. Maybe the way he tried so hard and dreamed so high. He'd risk his life for Duncan and for her.

He never took his eyes off her as he unbuckled his belt, pulled off his trousers, and hung them on a cottonwood branch near the fire.

She warmed, very much aware that he was watching as she unbuttoned her pants and pulled her long legs free. She wore no long johns beneath, but her cotton bloomers went almost to her knees.

"You look adorable," he said, as he handed her the bedroll.

"You look hairy," she answered, as she spread the blanket close to the fire where they could use one of the low branches to lean against. She began twisting her hair free from its braid.

"Oh, but you've seen me before. You had my trousers off the first day, remember," he said, still watching her. "This is my first look at you."

He frowned when she tugged her knees al-most to her chin and shook her hair in the warm air to dry. A mass of waves tumbled almost to her waist.

"If anyone comes by, I'll probably die of embarrassment." She motioned him away. "Go over to the other side so I can't see you."

He ignored her order and sat down beside her. Apparently he didn't think his hairy legs looked all that bad. "You've got sunshine hair, you know."

She wasn't distracted. "Doesn't it bother you to have hair all over your legs like that?" She seriously considered them the ugliest thing she'd ever seen. Oh, they looked strong, and scarred in a few places, but the hair bothered her.

"My chest is hairy too," he commented. "Want to see?"

"No." She laughed.

"All right, I'll just have to let my shirt dry on me."

"Please do." She pulled the edge of the blanket over her legs. Maybe he'd stop staring if she covered up more.

He leaned against the low branch brushing the ground in spots and crossed his arms.

"You going to stare at me until our clothes dry?"

"I was thinking about taking a nap, if you'll stand guard." He passed her the rifle. "Wake me if you hear anything." He lowered his hat over his eyes and went to sleep.

The warmth of the fire made her wish she'd had the nap idea first, but one of them had to stay awake. The last thing she wanted was someone finding them here like this. So she watched through the trees for any sign of people and listened to the birds around them.

The day passed from morning into noon and still Lewt slept. Finally, she realized the clothes had to be dry, but she wasn't sure how to wake him. She didn't want to yell at him from three feet away, and touching him didn't seem proper.

Em laughed. She was sitting next to him in her underwear and his vest. She'd already gone way beyond proper.

Finally, she crawled over to him and lifted his hat. His brown hair that he always kept combed back and neat was a mess. His face that had been so pale when he'd arrived at Whispering Mountain now looked tanned and rugged, with the beginnings of a beard darkening his chin. She thought she could see a bit of the boy in the man as he slept, and she wondered what had molded him into a gambler.

On impulse, she leaned forward and kissed him.

For a moment, he didn't respond, and then she felt him smile against her lips and come awake. He pulled her to him as he returned her kiss. Em knew she should pull away, but the moment seemed magic. Time out of time.

She kissed him as he held her in the cradle of his arm. When he deepened the kiss, she went with him, knowing that this was a moment in her life worth saving, treasuring. When she remembered this moment years from now, she'd wonder if it really happened or if she'd just dreamed it.

His hand moved along her body so gently she barely felt it, but every sense followed his touch. She opened her mouth to him and the touch settled over her, stronger, bolder.

When he broke the kiss, she leaned her head back and let him brush his lips along her neck, warming her skin wherever he paused to taste, to kiss. His hand moved over the vest and pushed beneath her breast, shoving the mound up slightly so he could kiss the skin just above the material.

She started to say something but couldn't seem to think of words. He stopped her attempt by returning to her mouth and kissing her until she forgot even trying to make an effort to speak. What he was doing to her was beyond what she thought could happen, and it felt so much better than anything she'd ever known.

She felt boneless in his arms. She felt worshipped, cherished. He held her tightly with one arm as he raised his head and stared down into her eyes. Silently, he studied her as his hand moved over the vest until it rested, spread over her breast, and then he tightened his grip ever so slightly and she arched her back with the jolt of pleasure that shot through her body.

His slow smile warmed her from inside as his hand relaxed, then pressed slightly once more over the peak of her breast. When his fingers tightened again, she rode a wave of fire streaming through her. He smiled, knowing he was learning what brought her joy.

He whispered softly against her ear as his hand moved down to her waist, and for a while he felt each breath she took with the rise and fall of his hand. While she calmed, he kissed first her ear, then gently down her throat. "Hush now, my Em," he whispered when he returned to her ear. "Relax. Don't be afraid of me. I would never hurt you."

Then he moved back to brush her mouth feather light as his hand crossed tenderly back to her breast. This time she felt the warmth of his fingers through the thin material of the vest. He was touching her with a boldness that surprised her. She leaned into his palm, wanting his caress, wanting the pleasure of it.

When her mouth opened to sigh, he kissed her again, deep and endless, and all the while his hand held a firm grip over her breast.

Wave after wave of passion washed over her

tired body. He trailed his fingers along her legs and kissed her throat all the way down to where the buttons held the vest together. When he stopped kissing her long enough to look into her eyes, she watched him smile, and she knew he was loving this moment as dearly as she did.

She kissed him back, enjoying the way his arm tightened around her when she explored his mouth. But she didn't touch him. She didn't know how. And he didn't venture further, though she doubted she would have stopped him. What few clothes she had on, stayed on.

Finally, when she was exhausted and cuddling in his arms, he whispered as his fingers moved lazily down her throat, "Don't say a word, Em. Not one word. We have to go, but I want to hold you longer in my thoughts."

She understood. Slowly, with several last kisses, she left his arms and dressed. She was aware of him doing the same. They collected their belongings and started out again, the afternoon sun burning away newly made memories.

Neither said a word, but now and then his hand would brush across her leg in a familiar way of one who knows his touch will be welcomed, or his arm would press against the side of her breast and she knew they were both remembering.

When they stopped to water the horses, he stepped in front of her, cupped the back of her head gently, and kissed her so sweetly she wanted to cry. Only their lips touched, but the memory of the way he'd held her returned almost as if they were back by the fire.

The next time they stopped, the sun was setting and they saw the campsite they'd camped at just before they'd crossed into Mexico.

He circled his arm about her waist and pulled her back against him. "What we had back there was real, Em. Not pretend, or lies, or the way we thought we should be. It was the most beautiful hour I've lived. No matter what happens after we ride into camp, the way I feel about you, the way I want to hold you, won't change but like you did by the fire, you'll have to come to me. I'll not come to you. When, or if, we go further has to be up to you."

He moved his hand along her leg, more in comfort than passion. "I know something or someone must have frightened you once, and I want no part of frightening you again. If you want me to touch you, you have to come to me. I'll be waiting." He moved her hair aside and kissed her neck.

She didn't know if she'd ever be as brave as she'd been today. By the river, hidden in the trees, it seemed another world. In a few minutes she'd step back into the real world, where proper ladies didn't do what they'd done. "How long?" she asked, knowing she needed time to think about all that had happened. "How long will you wait?"

He kissed her cheek and guided the horse toward camp. "Forever," he answered. "Forever."

ᏚᎧ CHAPTER 31 ᏨᏒ

As they rode in Lewt watched Duncan, Wyatt, and Sumner all stand, rifles in hand. He saw no sign of the girl Duncan had called Anna and wondered if she'd decided to remain behind.

"Relax, Rangers. It's just me." Lewt laughed, glad to see that they'd all made it back.

Duncan limped a little as he rushed to meet them. He was within ten feet of Lewt's horse when Em jumped down and ran into his arms.

Lewt watched her. He knew that she must know Duncan—after all, her father worked on his family ranch—but he hadn't quite expected her to be so friendly.

"Duck!" she yelled, as he swung her around laughing. "You're all right."

Lewt wore the exhaustion of the day as he climbed down and walked toward them. The contentment he'd felt holding Em shifted to a memory. They were back in the real world, where he was a gambler and she worked with horses, no longer two lonely people who'd found each other for a few short hours in time.

When the ranger finally set her down, Lewt complained, "Watch out, Em, you'll break his neck." He tried to smile, but the effort hurt. "You two act like you're in love."

"I do love him," Em shouted. "Though now and then over the years I've hated him too. Mama used to say that a wolf pup would have been easier to housebreak than him."

Duncan kept his arm around her. "I'm glad you came, Em, but if you ever do something so foolish again, I swear I'll give you that spanking you're long overdue for. You should be back at the ranch, not here."

Lewt wasn't sure he liked any of this. What kind of woman let him touch her and hold her like he'd been doing a few hours ago, then turned around and ran into another man's arms?

She laughed, looking only at Duncan. "That will be the day, Duck. Rose and I have already planned terrible torture for you for sending houseguests and not even showing up to help entertain them."

Duncan looked at Lewt. "I didn't send this one," he said.

Lewt didn't miss the edge in Duncan's tone. The ranger didn't give up on mad easily.

"I know, but he was the pick of the litter, as it turned out. He was the only one willing to come save your hide. One had his mother to think about first, and the other complained that since he didn't even know you, he could hardly abandon his ranch on a wild mission across the border. Only Lewt rode with us."

The look in Duncan's eyes didn't soften.

Lewt raised his hand. "Now before you start

beating me to a pulp, Duncan, I got to tell you, none of your cousins liked me. You were right, I didn't fit in. I could barely keep up with the dinner conversation, and the group sing-alongs almost drove me to drink."

Duncan raised an eyebrow.

Lewt continued, "I didn't spend much time with the ladies. In fact, I chose to ride with Em and let her spend the day trying to work me to death rather than sit around with your cousins. No offense. They're all three beautiful ladies, but they weren't for me."

Duncan scratched his head. "Let me get this straight. You got on that train planning to court one of my cousins but ended up not spending time with *any* of them?"

Lewt smiled, thinking he'd finally gotten his point across. "Right. They were sweet ladies, but not one was interested in me. Rose was polite, Beth was sweet, and Emily silent most of the time. I would have been smart to stay in Austin and let Freeport the Fourth take the train. Only, trust me on this, those very proper cousins of yours would have hated him. He couldn't hold his liquor or his tongue."

Duncan looked at Em. "Want to explain what this gambler is talking about, Emily?" he asked. "One of you didn't hit him in the head real hard, did you, because my former friend here seemed to think he hasn't spent any time with you and Sumner tells me the two of you have been together for a week."

"She's not Emily . . ." Lewt froze, his finger pointed at Em. As if lightning had struck him full force, the truth hit him. The times he'd seen Em, Rose, and Beth putting their heads together talking. The way Sumner treated her as if she were the boss. The way she stood up to Wyatt and demanded to come along. She'd said her papa taught her to know horses. Papa was the name the girls called Teagen McMurray.

As the truth hit him, so did the knowledge that he'd been fooled completely—no, tricked. Hell, he'd been conned. He'd forgotten the first rule of reading people. Always look for what they don't say.

Em stood between the two men even now and didn't say a word. She didn't have to. They'd both figured it out. Duck realized his cousins had tricked Lewt, and Lewt realized he'd been fooled by women way out of his league where manipulation was concerned.

Duncan ignored Em and turned to Lewt. "I could use a drink before I kill you. How about you?"

Lewt nodded once. He followed his friend to the camp without glancing at Emily. She'd lied. For more than a week she'd only been pretending. Pretending to be someone she wasn't. Pretending she was his friend. Pretending more, far more.

He should be furious with her. If he had any pride, he would turn around and yell at her. Tell her what he thought. She must have had some great laughs with her sisters talking about how he told her he was planning to marry a rich wife. He'd even been dupe enough to ask for her help.

No wonder she was always around the house. She had no family in the hills to go home to. She was living right under the same roof, and he was too dumb to know it. She'd played him as no one else had ever played him. And when they were alone, she played him for a fool.

Today, in the shadow of the trees, he'd thought he was falling in love with her. Falling in love for the first time.

Lewt swore under his breath. "Falling in love for the last time. Damn dumb thing to do."

He didn't hate her, he hated himself for being so blind. He could have made love to her today, but he hadn't; he wanted to wait because she was so special. More special than the McMurray girls with their small talk and their lace napkins. His Em was so much more, so much deeper, so much more worth the loving.

Only his Em wasn't what she appeared to be. She wasn't his Em, she was Emily McMurray, a rich pampered brat who thought she could play with a man. How she must have laughed at him.

Lewt accepted the bottle from Duncan and downed a third of it.

Duncan laughed. "Slow down there, partner," he said. "I've never known you to drink like that."

Lewt noticed Em—correction, Emily—step into the circle of light from the fire. Her slender body moved with such grace, even now, that knowing what he knew about her, his hand itched to touch her.

He forced himself to turn away and face Duncan as he downed another drink. "I'm thinking about becoming the town drunk as soon as I can find a town with an opening." He glared at Em. "You were right, Duncan, I should never have gone to Whispering Mountain. Men like me don't belong there. While I'm still sober enough, I wish to say I'm deeply sorry to have tricked my way into your plan to marry off your cousins and I wish you more success next time. From my point of view, you'll need it."

Duncan took the bottle. "I'd be mad at you, but you seem to have been beat up enough. Don't feel alone, though; the girls have been playing tricks on me for as long as I can remember. Maybe this time I'll let you live for what you did back there for me. Besides, you look like a man bent on killing himself."

He started to offer Lewt the bottle, then thought better of it. "How about we call it even? You got me out of that hell, and apparently you sent yourself into a whole different kind of one."

They heard a horse ride out, and all turned.

"Where's Wyatt going?" Lewt asked.

"He's running patrol down by the water. It's

unlikely, but Toledo might send a few of her guards to find us. I really doubt it, though. I wasn't worth that much to her. My guess is she'll cut her losses, and tomorrow it'll be business as usual around Three Forks."

"Where is the girl?" Lewt asked. "Didn't she make the trip with you?"

Duncan nodded. "She's over there curled up asleep in the dark. It seems she likes me all right, but she's afraid of Sumner and Wyatt. She watches them as if she thinks they might attack her at any moment. So after supper, I finally sat with her and got her to sleep. It's really sad to think that the only time she feels safe is when she's locked in a room."

"What are you going to do with her?"

Duncan shook his head. "If she has people, I can't get her to talk and tell me where they might be. My guess is she doesn't have anyone, or she wouldn't have been with the witch. She's so young, she'll need folks to take her in and take care of her."

"Duncan." Wyatt's voice echoed through the night air. He'd ridden out on a horse a few minutes before, but now he dismounted and walked back toward the fire.

Both men looked up as Wyatt's shadow continued to come closer, as if he didn't want to yell.

"You need to come with me." Wyatt pointed with his head. "I found a horse out here."

Lewt grinned. "We found your Shadow, but she

wouldn't come within fifty feet of us. I guess she followed us over."

Duncan ran to Lewt's horse and took off. "Thanks," he yelled back at Lewt.

Lewt managed a smile. "Got any coffee?" he asked Sumner as he warmed by the fire.

"Yep," Sumner said. "And there's stew in the pot. We figured you two would be in sometime tonight, so we left it warming."

Em didn't look at Lewt as she helped herself to the stew. She'd been so quiet he'd almost forgotten she was there.

Lewt watched her out of the corner of his eye. He was starving, but he wasn't going to ask her to pass him a bowl or get anywhere close to the pot until she moved away. He didn't want to be in the same state with her, much less around the same campfire. The sisters would probably put their heads together and have a great laugh when she got back home and told them what a fool she'd made out of the gambler.

He's spent his life reading people. It didn't seem possible that those three could have fooled him. Thinking back, he knew the signs were there, he'd just been too distracted to notice.

The night seemed suddenly very quiet. The fire crackled and now and then an owl hooted from somewhere beyond the light. Sumner banged around the camp collecting cups and tossing out bedrolls. When Em moved away, Lewt filled his bowl and sat as far away from her as he could manage and still be in the light of the fire. He ate without tasting the food.

Finally, the old man seemed to have had enough of the silence. Sumner stood halfway between them and cleared his throat. "I've watched you two for a week," he said, without looking at either one of them. "It surprised the hell out of me, but you seemed to get along. Now, the way I see it is, neither one of you has enough friends to lose one over a minor lie. Lewt, you lied to get introduced to a McMurray, and Miss Em, you lied so you wouldn't have to meet him. In my book that means the lies cancel each other out."

"Nobody asked for your opinion," Lewt said.

"It's none of your business," Em added, as she began scraping the dishes clean.

Sumner swore and moved toward his horse. "Think I'll ride out and talk to that devil of a horse Duck rides. He's better company than you two."

Before either of them could say anything, he was gone.

Lewt stood staring at the fire for a long while, and then he rummaged through the packs and found the clothes he'd bought when he'd gone to Anderson Glen with Em. He began stripping off the remains of his wrinkled muddy suit as he remembered how they'd had fun eating in the café. She'd been pretending to be a man then—and not doing a very good job of it, as he remembered.

He wasn't surprised when he heard Em's sharp voice. "You're not going to undress in front of the fire, are you?"

"Why not? No one's here and you've seen me before."

She turned her back. "That doesn't mean I want to see you again."

"Well, as soon as I can get out of here, lady, you'll never have to see me again, so you might as well take a last look." He stripped down to his skin and grabbed the warm work shirt. "I can't believe I was just a game to you ladies. What did you do, decide which one of you was going to play me? Tell me, did the short straw get me, or was it more like a vote to see who had to play the charade?"

Em turned her head toward him, squealed, and turned back around.

Lewt smiled. "Now you know, darling, what I look like all over."

"I already knew," she shot back. "I saw you sleeping in the bath."

He pulled on his heavy twill trousers. "I don't care."

She faced him as he buckled his belt and reached for his coat. "I'm not the only one who lied here, Paterson, so get off that high horse. Your whole life story was a lie."

"You're right, Miss Emily. I lied to try to make a dream come true. I wanted the normal life everyone else seems to have. But you, you lied for the fun of it. Just a little trick you played at my expense. Tell me, did Boyd and Davis know? Were they in on the game? Sumner must have been and all the other hands. And sweet-little-always-sewing Emily or whatever her name is, did she just go along, or did you pay her?"

Em frowned. "We paid her, but she's a friend; she would have helped just because I asked her to. Her real name is Tamela. Everyone always said we looked alike in school, and she was between husbands at the moment, so she thought it would be fun."

"I don't give a damn," he yelled.

"Don't you dare swear at me." She moved a few feet closer.

"Why? Hasn't anyone ever yelled at the rich little Miss Emily McMurray before? I find that hard to believe, as irritating as you are most of the time."

She raised her hand to slap him, and he caught her wrist in midair. For a blink he saw fear flash in her eyes, and he realized she thought he might hit her.

He dropped her hand and stepped away, all the anger knocked out of him without a blow. If he ever got through hating himself, he decided he'd hate her for a while. All the years he was growing up he'd always thought of himself as worthless; everyone including his parents treated him so. With one look she'd told him what she thought of him. She agreed with the majority. She thought he might be the kind of man who hurt women, the lowest kind of man.

He turned his back, closed his eyes, and wished that they could go back to the cottonwoods, where there was no world but the trees. Her lie had taken that memory from him. He hadn't held his Em, he'd held Emily McMurray.

When he opened his eyes, he was looking down the barrel of a gun.

"Don't make any fast moves, mister," a voice with an Irish favoring whispered. "I don't want to have to fire this thing. It might bring back the other men."

Lewt stood perfectly still. Even in the poor light he recognized the two cooks he'd seen in the kitchen of Three Forks. The tall one held a rifle so old he doubted it would fire, but he didn't want to test it. Part of him wanted to yell at the cook to just shoot him. It might be better than letting Em kill him a slice at a time with her looks.

"You was one of the men who took Anna, weren't you?" The shorter cook moved forward. "Sarah J, I think we've found the right camp."

Lewt doubted if there were many campfires around this part of the country, but if these two could find them it wouldn't be long before Toledo's men came riding in. "What are you doing here?" Surely the old witch hadn't sent the cooks to kill the men who took Duncan.

"When you left, all hell broke loose. Toledo sent everyone but us out to track you down. Then she went into a rage like I never seen in my life. She kept yelling, 'I got to get her back. I got to get her back.' It took me and Sarah J a while to figure out that she didn't care nothing about the ranger, it was the girl she thought she had to have back."

Em moved up, and to Lewt's surprise the woman lowered her gun, as if seeing a woman by his side somehow made Lewt not so frightening.

"We have coffee," Em said, as if she hadn't noticed the rifle. "You're welcome to some and the fire."

It crossed Lewt's mind that since Em hated him, she might not think it all that unusual for these women to threaten to kill him. With his luck, over coffee they'd form a lynch mob.

When the ladies sat down as if they were at a tea party, Em began, "Duncan told Lewt the girl, Anna, was mistreated by your boss. It's my understanding that he didn't take her against her will."

"That's no lie," Rachel whispered. "I've seen dogs treated better than that child. We even asked him, if he lived long enough and tried to escape, to take her with him."

Em continued, "Why would this old woman want her if she only beats her and locks her away?"

Both women shook their heads, but Rachel spoke for them both. "We don't know, miss. We decided to take our chances and leave when all the trouble started. We hitched our two mules to our wagon, stole all the food and money we could find lying around, and headed here. A few hours ago we got to the river and found Toledo's guards camped about three miles downriver."

Sarah J smiled and interrupted. "Rachel offered them some of the fresh bread we brought and told them Toledo, in her rage, had fired us. For a few coins they helped us cross the river. Then we followed the water's edge, hoping to find a road or a camp that would let us travel with them or at least point us in the right direction."

"Are Toledo's men coming after us?" Lewt asked from where he stood in the shadows.

All three women looked up at him as if he were bothering them.

"Not tonight," Rachel predicted. "They sent a rider back to Three Forks to ask Toledo what they should do. She's got them all afraid to think for themselves. From what I gathered, they don't think you've crossed yet, but they don't have enough men to patrol the river. The old witch's orders were for them to catch you before you crossed. They'll have to get new orders before they come this way, and that will take another day."

Sarah J giggled, interrupting again. "After learning we were fired, I think they're worried about their jobs. We didn't tell them, but from what we heard the old woman screaming, she plans to go to hell and back to get that girl. The guards are all hired hands with no love or loyalty to Toledo. They may not see a profit in that."

"And," Rachel said, with a nod toward her sister,

"that Ramon is right behind her. He wants what he considers soon to be his." She shook her head at Lewt, looking very much like a schoolteacher talking to a wayward student. "Why did you leave that man alive? If I'd just had a few more minutes before they found him, he would have been leaking blood."

Lewt was starting to believe the story about the cooks being murderers.

Duncan, Sumner, and Wyatt returned. After the surprise of guests at their campfire, they asked a dozen questions. The two little ladies seemed pleased to be the center of attention.

As the fire aged, Anna woke and stepped into the light. She looked very much the frightened child, but Duncan and the ladies had talked of her being older than she appeared. The cooks seemed to think that maybe she'd been beaten so many times she was simple in the mind.

She let the two cooks hug her and make a fuss over her being free, but when she settled down to eat more stew, she sat next to Duncan.

Lewt studied them. Duncan was protective of her and kind, but not like a lover or even a friend. More like a father, even though they were not that many years different in age. Anna was good at playing a child. Lewt had seen women do it in saloons now and then. One girl swore she was just sixteen until she was well into her thirties.

As the others talked of what to do, Lewt watched

Em, or Emily, and wondered if she'd ever sit within touching distance of him again.

Finally, when everyone had turned in except Wyatt, who took the first watch, Lewt lay on his bedroll knowing that he'd not sleep. Despite all the arguing, he wanted Em near, but she'd spread her blanket on the other side of the fire.

After an hour of staring at the stars, Lewt got up and took over the watch. If he couldn't sleep, he might as well let Wyatt.

He walked the edges of the camp with a rifle in his hand. The fire was low, and the place looked peaceful. The two cooks were sleeping in their wagon. Wyatt and Sumner used their saddles as pillows and slept facing out, away from the fire, so they'd see anything coming in a blink. Duncan and the girl were near the trees, their bedrolls almost touching. Em slept alone, close to the dying embers.

After a while, Lewt walked over and sat on a log a foot from her bedroll. Without giving it much thought, he reached down and closed his fingers around her hand.

She didn't open her eyes, but he felt her hand close around his and he thought he saw a slight smile on her sleeping face.

It was enough to make him believe in possibilities.

He decided that what they'd had beneath the cottonwoods was real, and if it was real, maybe they could build on that and forgive each other the beginning.

ဆ CHAPTER 32 ၆ေ

At dawn Duncan had everyone up and ready to travel. He'd talked possibilities over with the group and come up with only one logical answer. They'd all have to stay together until Austin. The wagon would double the amount of time it would take, but the cooks couldn't ride a horse, even if they had an extra few, and he couldn't leave them behind. If Toledo's men crossed the border, they'd have little trouble tracking the wagon and the women would be killed.

Duncan frowned, thinking that for a man who always traveled light, he was collecting far too much baggage. The men could all take care of themselves, but Duncan couldn't forget that they were in this mess because of him. Anna was always in his shadow, looking for him to protect her. Emily might be a fine horsewoman and a great shot, but she would be no match for the cutthroats who worked for Toledo. The two cooks didn't even seem to know what direction to go.

Wyatt offered to ride ahead and get help, but if trouble came it would be soon and Duncan might need his friend's gun. The hardened ranger didn't seem to know how to talk to any of the women, so he stayed out of their way as much as possible.

To make matters worse, if things could get worse,

Lewt and Emily weren't speaking to each other. Sumner thought the two murdering cooks should be tied up until he could find out more about them. Em refused to ride in the wagon, where she'd be safer if they were attacked, and Wyatt looked at him now and then as if he thought Duncan had completely lost his mind.

So, with his band in tow, Duncan set out to Austin, hoping to get there as fast as possible. Within an hour it became obvious that if they wanted to keep the mules on the road, someone who knew how to drive a wagon was going to have to relieve the cooks.

Duncan tried not to swear as he climbed on the bench beside the cooks and took the first shift as their driver. His hope that they might not talk evaporated in seconds.

"Well, Ranger, tell us, will it go worse for us now that we're not only murderers, but thieves as well?" Sarah J looked thoughtful. "I told Sister not to take the money we found in Toledo's desk, but she thought we might need it."

"And," Rachel interrupted as usual, "once we started taking things, each got easier, and before long we were loading up the wagon while Toledo was busy planning how to kill you and everyone who helped you."

Sarah J agreed. "It's a slippery slope to becoming a criminal. Murder, stealing, lying. Once you start, there doesn't seem a place to stop. First we took the bread, and then, of course, we had to take the butter and jam, and then I thought of the pans we'd need to make more and Rachel remembered the bowls and spoons."

Duncan had no idea what to advise them. These two were a lawyer's nightmare. He had a feeling that if he talked to them long, other crimes might pop up along with recipes. "Mind telling me who you ladies think you killed? You know, the first crime you committed that sent you on the run?"

Sarah J glanced at her sister. "Our husbands," she finally said. "We fed them mushrooms in the gravy."

Duncan smiled. "Ladies, that's not murder, that was an accident. I'm sure you didn't know they were poison."

Both shook their heads slowly as if easing into a new lie.

"You did know they were poison?" he tried again.

They both nodded.

He didn't ask more, but he decided he'd probably turn down any dinner invitations.

Rachel looked like she might cry. "They rode off after supper and we never saw them again."

Duncan had to ask, "You found no bodies?"

"No, but we know they're out there. Both complained about not feeling well, and after they left, we fed the rest of the meal to the dog. He died before morning."

"We killed them," Rachel whispered, "dog and all."

The day passed. When Duncan drove, he tried not to talk too much to the cooks. Lewt, however, seemed to enjoy visiting with the women when he took his turn driving the wagon. The gambler liked people, all kinds of people, or at least he pretended to.

Duncan preferred traveling with Sumner. He caught up on all that had happened at the ranch. The old man never gossiped, but he did relay facts when one of the McMurrays asked. By the end of the day, Duncan felt sorry for Lewt. The gambler was a good man, honest as anyone in his profession can be. He didn't deserve the trick his cousins had played.

Duncan wasn't sure, and he couldn't tell by the way they acted, but he guessed Lewt had feelings for Emily. Em, on the other hand, had never liked any man who wasn't related to her, and most of the time she wasn't too fond of relatives either. When she was little he thought of her as the silent one because she didn't talk enough for anyone to notice her. Once she started talking, it was mostly to pester him. They were opposites in almost every way, except one. They both loved horses and riding free across Whispering Mountain.

By midafternoon clouds began to form to the west. The choices were to camp out in the open or try to make a run for a mission almost ten miles away.

They ran, with the cooks' screams carrying on the wind. The road was well traveled by now, but Duncan knew that five minutes after the rain started, it would be a river of mud. If they didn't make the mission, the wagon would be stuck.

He laughed. Even if Toledo heard the screams she'd have to be flying to catch them, and once they were in the mission, she'd never find them. The missions of Texas had long been a place where rangers could rest or vanish for a time if they needed to.

They reached the mission door just as the downpour hit. Duncan pulled the wagon as close as he could to the chapel and helped the cooks in, then went back to carry Anna through the rain. As always, she didn't say a word, but clung to him.

When he set her down inside the thick walls of the mission, her eyes were huge, not so much with fright, but with wonder.

"It's all right," he whispered, pushing the hair out of her eyes. She was back to looking very much like a child again. "The priest likes rangers. He'll put us up for the night and make sure the gates are locked. There are nuns here too. They work with the school. You'll be safe among them."

Anna nodded slightly, but he wasn't sure she believed him. She stayed right beside him as they were served soup and hot tea. He watched her closely as she seemed to study every detail around her.

Duncan told everyone the story that his family believed—that their grandmother and grandfather met at this very mission. He'd been a teacher without a job who stopped here to help teach reading to the Apache. She'd been the daughter of a chief. "The story goes"—Duncan smiled at Em—"that our grandfather fell in love when he touched her hand beneath the book."

"They were barely twenty when they married and settled at Whispering Mountain." Em picked up the story. "They had kids and started the ranch, but the strange thing is, my grandfather on my papa's side died thirteen years after he married at another mission called Goliad."

Duncan glanced at the cooks, who looked as if they'd lost the thread of the conversation. "Goliad wasn't much of a battle compared to the Alamo. The men were shot by firing squad, but they died for Texas. Some say it made the rest of Texas so mad that Houston's men yelled, 'Remember the Alamo' and 'Remember Goliad' as they overtook Santa Ana's camp a few months later."

As the others talked on, Duncan thought of his adopted grandfather. All Andrew McMurray ever wanted was his family and his ranch, yet he'd given it all up to stand and fight for Texas. All Duncan wanted was the adventure, the fight, but he knew with all the men gone from Whispering Mountain, he might have to go home and stay for a while. He'd have to give up his freedom for the ranch.

Strange how one man's dream is another's prison.

He finally realized why his cousins had never married. There hadn't been time. The little ranch Andrew and Autumn McMurray started had grown so huge it threatened to consume the family. Duncan didn't want to think about his responsibility.

As thunder stormed outside and rain pounded, the priest showed the women to their rooms in the hallway called the Sisters' Wing. The rooms were all small, meant for one person. When Anna saw that she had a lock on the inside of her door, she smiled for the first time.

Duncan stepped inside and set her tiny bundle of clothes down. "Will you be all right in here?"

She nodded, looking around the simple room as if it were grand.

"I'll tap on your door when it's almost time to leave."

He left her there, almost sad that she didn't need him tonight. Moving along a winding veranda, he finally crossed a courtyard and joined the men bunking in the shed. It was cold, but dry.

"Where's your shadow?" Sumner asked when Duncan reached the circle of their lantern.

"I've been replaced by a lock."

"She's safe tonight," Wyatt said, "but I don't think it would be a bad idea that we post a guard. I'm not sure one lock at the gate will keep anyone out who wants to kill us."

They all agreed.

Duncan knew he wouldn't sleep until they were back in Austin—or even better, he thought, back at Whispering Mountain. Anna would be safe there while they looked for her relatives.

ᔓ CHAPTER 33 ᔕ

Lewt took the first watch. He'd been restless all day. Em was never out of his sight, but he felt like she was moving farther and farther away from him. He tried to think of something to say to her, but the angry words they'd yelled at each other in camp the night before still hung in the air.

She wasn't avoiding him so much as ignoring him. It was as if he'd disappeared in her vision. Maybe in her memory as well.

He thought of going to her, but he didn't want to frighten her. That, and the fact that she might shoot him outright if he stepped over the invisible line that stood between them like a ten-foot wall. The days at the ranch seemed a million years away, and the afternoon they'd shared under the cottonwoods seemed more like a dream.

Lewt walked the grounds for a while, then settled in a passageway where he could see both the front gate and the back wall of the mission. The rain had turned into a drizzle, tapping off the buildings into the mud like the sound of a hundred clocks ticking at once.

He leaned against the wall, feeling like his life was this passage and he had no idea which way to go. He'd saved a great deal of money during the ten years he'd been at the top of his game as a gambler. If he quit and bought some business, he'd always be that gambler who tried to go legitimate. No one would truly trust him.

Something caught the corner of his eye. Someone silently moving through the dark hallway where the women were being housed.

Lewt lifted his rifle and waited. Reason told him anyone meaning harm would come from the outside, not the inside. So he waited.

A tall woman dressed in a straight white gown moved out into the watery moonlight. Her hair was so light it looked almost white, and she moved with a grace he'd recognize anywhere.

Em.

He lowered his rifle but didn't say a word. They'd developed a habit of not speaking since the fight, and he wasn't sure how she'd react if he yelled. Besides, what could he say? *Hello* didn't seem right for someone who'd been so close, and *Give me another chance* sounded too much like begging.

She moved with her head down, following the brick walkway worn smooth over a hundred years.

He'd seen her hair down so rarely, he hadn't really thought about how beautiful it could be. Unlike when she'd pulled the braids, tonight her hair hung straight without a single wave. It flowed behind her almost like a veil.

She was within five feet of him when she looked up and saw him. He heard her sharp intake of breath, but she didn't move. She just stood staring at him.

Lewt knew he should say something. Maybe that he was sorry for being in the way and intruding on her silent walk. Maybe he could make an attempt to say that he was sorry for what he said. Maybe he should just remain silent. The less they talked, the less he'd have to apologize for later.

She studied him without any expression. After a long minute, she moved closer.

"I don't want to talk to you," he finally said, guessing that she'd only begin listing all the things she hated about him, as she had last night.

"Neither do I," she answered.

She took another step and leaned forward, her face an inch away from his. Then, without warning, she pressed her lips to his. When he didn't move, she dug her fingers into his hair and pulled his head closer. Her kiss was simple, closed mouth, almost punishing.

Lewt wasn't sure what she wanted, or, more accurately, what she wanted him to do.

She leaned closer, almost touching him, and began brushing her cheek against his. When her mouth touched his again, it was softer.

He was sure he was losing his mind. His body seemed to mutiny. He kissed her back.

Surprisingly, it seemed to be exactly what she

wanted. She leaned against his chest, pushing his back into the wall, and wrapped her arm around his neck. The kiss caught fire. All the anger between them stood down, and passion took its place.

He felt like he'd been starving for days and she offered him exactly what he needed to survive. He moved his hands over the soft cotton of the plain gown and felt the wonder of her beneath it.

She didn't touch him, but she sighed with pleasure as he touched her. When he broke the kiss, he turned her around and pulled her to him. Her head leaned against his shoulder as his hands moved over her body. He could feel her breathing. Tonight there were no hesitant brushes or light touches. The need to hold her was too great. He covered both of her breasts in his tight grip as he bit lightly into the curve of her neck. She cried out softly, then sighed as he continued moving his hands over her gown, getting to know the graceful body he'd watched so often.

She'd come to him. He laughed with pure joy against the soft skin below her ear. She'd come to him just as he'd told her she'd have to.

When he could wait no longer, he twisted her to face him once more and kissed her.

Her breathing was rapid and deep when he gripped her shoulders and pushed gently, putting her back against the wall and them both into shadows.

She was here with him . . . wanting him, and nothing else mattered at this moment.

Slowly, he began unbuttoning her gown. He could feel her trembling as he moved from button to button, pulling each free and taking the time to push the material aside.

"Em," he whispered. "My Em."

When he shoved his hand inside and touched her flesh, she drew in a breath and held it as he moved over her bare skin. She was perfection. Her gown was open to the waist, but the shadows prevented him from seeing the heaven he felt.

"Breathe," he whispered against her ear.

She let out her breath in a rush and began to gulp for air. He placed his hand on her abdomen to feel each breath rise and fall. "I love to feel you breathe," he whispered, "almost as much as I love taking your breath away."

He raised her arms above her head with one hand as the other slid down her rib cage. "Breathe," he whispered, "while I feel you." Spreading his hand wide, he moved over her as he kissed her face lightly. When she let out a sigh of pleasure, he covered her mouth and kissed her deeper than he'd ever kissed a woman. Her arms lowered to his shoulders as her body seemed to melt into his.

There was no hesitance in his touch, only passion. He'd wanted her all day, dreamed of her all night, and now she'd come to him. He wouldn't pretend his hunger for her was any less. Shoving the gown off her shoulders, he let it settle on her hips as he caressed her.

When he ended a long kiss, he didn't remove his hands from her. She was warm now to his touch. He kissed her face and throat gently until her breathing slowed, then moved his hand up to the valley between her breasts. His fingers were slowly passing over each breast when he decided to kiss her again. He cupped her face with his free hand and opened her mouth with his thumb, then began another long endless kiss.

Her arms tightened about his neck as his hands moved behind her, shoving the gown lower as he cupped her hips. He pulled her against the length of him without breaking the kiss. The day without touching her had left him hungry. He wanted to be gentle, to move slow, to be sure of his footing before he jumped into passion, but the taste of her, the feel of her, drove all rational thought away, leaving him exposed and open.

She wanted this too, he thought. She'd come to him. She was returning his kiss. If only for a moment in the shadows, she was his Em again and she wanted him.

When the kiss finally ended, they were both exhausted from wave after wave of passion. He pulled away, knelt, and lifted her gown slowly from the floor. He was so close, his breath warmed her skin as the material moved up her body. Slowly, he buttoned her gown, then kissed her forehead as if he hadn't just been roaming his hands all over her and loving every moment of it.

For a long while, he just held her, moving his fingers in her hair, kissing her lightly now and then on the cheek, pulling her briefly into a hug. Neither said a word. She swayed slightly into his embrace and pressed against him so closely he could feel her heart beat next to his.

A thousand questions came to his mind, but for now just holding her seemed enough. He brushed his hand lazily over her hip and heard her soft sigh. She was his mate, he thought. A perfect match, if only in the shadows.

When Lewt heard footsteps, he turned and lifted his rifle. Someone was coming from the direction of the shed. He stepped out of the shadows and waited.

"You awake?" Wyatt's low voice asked as he materialized out of the night.

Lewt glanced over his shoulder. Em had vanished. He thought he saw her nightgown caught in the blink of moonlight, but he couldn't be sure. "I'm awake," he said, wishing he could return to the dream he'd just experienced.

"No," he whispered to himself. It was real. Em had been in his arms.

"Did you say something?" Wyatt asked as he stared out into the night sky.

"Only that it's time to turn in." Lewt headed into the darkness. "Good night. See you at dawn."

A few minutes later he spread out on the hay and relived every moment he'd spent with Em. He could still feel her skin on his fingertips and smell the honeysuckle fragrance of her hair.

If she was mad at him and had decided to use this as a way to punish him, it was working. He'd be dead from the need for her in no time.

At dawn the men ate breakfast with the priest, then saddled the horses while the women took their meal of simple porridge and honey bread.

They were ready to leave when the women finally came out into the morning sun. Anna moved to Duncan's side and let him help her into the wagon. The cooks kept up a steady stream of conversation, even though none of the men paid much attention.

Lewt watched Em and wasn't surprised she didn't look at him. She was back to ignoring him. He told himself it didn't matter as long as she came to him at night, but he realized he wanted her . . . all of her.

Lewt rode point, scouting far enough ahead to make sure trouble didn't surprise them. The land was growing rocky with bends and turns in the road. He knew they were in Texas and should feel safe, but the feeling of being hunted still hadn't washed out of his system. He felt like he did sometimes when he walked the streets after midnight, only now it was daylight and he couldn't just tell himself to stay in the streetlight glow to be safe.

Duncan interrupted his thoughts by riding up beside him.

"Another day and we should be far enough that we won't have to worry about Toledo," Duncan said, as if talking to himself. "No matter how much she wants the girl, she's not likely to stray too far into Texas."

"Does she have the right?" Lewt asked.

"No. Anna can make her own way now. If I hadn't ended up at Three Forks, I have a feeling Ramon and Anna would have been married within the year. The way I see it, the girl's life stopped when she was shipped to Three Forks. She's small, but she's full grown—in her body, anyway. In her mind she may always be a little kid."

"So we can't just drop her off at the nearest street corner. What do we do with her?" Lewt didn't want to think about what would happen if she wasn't protected.

"Take her to Whispering Mountain, I guess." Duncan didn't sound too sure.

Lewt smiled. "Well, while you're planning, what do we do with the two little cooks? Send them to jail? Let them go? No jury will find them guilty if they can't find the bodies."

Duncan didn't look like he liked dealing with a problem he couldn't shoot to get rid of. "I don't know. I've asked them for details. You know, did they hate their husbands, were they worth killing? They seem to talk about everything else. Without proof of a murder, they can't be arrested. For all I know their husbands just had enough of their chatter, ate supper one night, and then decided to ride off."

"So take them home with you. Rose could use some help. Near as I could see, she does the lion's share of the cooking."

Duncan looked at him. "I'm not sure I like you knowing all about my family. It doesn't set right."

Lewt laughed. "You've got a gang of bad guys chasing you with a leader who wants you dead, two cooks who confess to being murderers, a woman/child who won't get two feet from you, and you're worried about me? Duck, you've lost what little brains you had."

Duncan laughed. "You have a point. But stay away from my cousins. Much as I like you as a friend, I don't want you in the family."

Before Lewt could say anything, Duncan kicked his horse and circled back to Wyatt riding trail.

Lewt slowed, letting the wagon and Em catch up to him. Sumner was driving the rig and didn't look too happy about the chatter around him. For once, the cooks were riding in the back of the wagon, and Anna sat beside the driver. She didn't appear happy about it. Her back was straight as a rod, and she held herself as far away from Sumner as she could manage.

"Everything all right?" Lewt asked.

Sumner nodded. "Watch this."

He pulled off his gloves and laid them on the seat between him and the girl.

A few moments later Anna picked them up and slipped them on her small hands. Then Sumner handed her the reins.

"She's not sure of herself, but she's a good driver." He motioned her to ease up on the lines. "I tried this a few times yesterday. It's the only time she's not shaking with fear." He turned away from Lewt and instructed her in a low tone.

Lewt moved around the wagon and pulled up even with Em's horse. "Did you see that?" he asked.

"I did," she answered, without looking at him.

"Any chance we're about to have a normal conversation?"

"No."

He fought the urge to circle his arm around her, pull her onto his horse, and kiss her soundly, but with his luck she'd fight and kick and they'd both end up on the ground. He would have liked to tell her how wonderful last night had been, but she didn't look to be in a listening mood.

An hour later Lewt was still trying to think of something to say to reach her when they heard horses riding in fast.

"Get off the road!" Duncan shouted. "We've got company coming."

Sumner didn't take the reins but directed Anna where to go. They moved onto a rocky side and down an incline to where the ground sloped into almost waisthigh grass. Beyond the grass were trees growing along a gully.

As the wagon disappeared from the road, Duncan reached Lewt and Em. "Looks like men coming up fast about a mile away. I'm guessing six, maybe seven. We have little chance of outrunning them with the wagon, and if we stand and fight, we're outnumbered."

Lewt and Em nodded as Wyatt joined the group.

"How about I face them?" Lewt said. "They saw me at the ranch, but they don't know I'm involved with you. I could talk to them, act like I haven't seen anything. Maybe head them off in the wrong direction."

"I don't know." Duncan shook his head.

Lewt smiled his slow easy smile. "Look at it this way, all I'm doing is bluffing and we both know I'm an expert at that."

Duncan finally agreed. "It's not much of a plan, but it might work. Em and I will take cover between you and the wagon. If they head toward it, we'll open fire, so make sure you stay out of the way."

Wyatt headed down the rocky incline. "I'll stand with Sumner at the bottom of this gully. Any man who makes it past you and Miss Em will be walking straight into our fire."

They all moved into action. Duncan and Em climbed the rise to watch and be ready. Wyatt brushed any tracks away where the wagon had left the road, and Lewt unsaddled his horse in the grass on the far side of the road. He brushed the animal down with the saddle blanket, hoping no one would notice the sweat where the saddle had been. There was no time to build a fire, but he tossed a few things around to make it look like he'd been there for a while.

He'd just sat down on his bedroll and pulled out a deck of cards when he heard the men coming.

Lewt glanced back in the direction Em had gone. He scanned the ridge, but he saw no sign of her. The need to see her was an ache inside him. He touched two fingers to his hat in a salute, hoping she could see him.

As the riders came into sight, Lewt stood and began rolling up the bedroll he'd just tossed on the ground.

The band slowed. They were dirty and muddy and looked madder than hell. Lewt recognized the leader as one of the guards from when he'd gambled the night away. The man looked more animal than human on a good day, and this wasn't a good day.

"Morning," Lewt said, as if the men were in their Sunday-go-to-meeting best. He counted seven men. One man behind the leader pulled his gun, but the rest just slowed their horses and stared.

"If you've come by to rob me, you're out of luck. I left all my money back at Three Forks. I'll play you a round for any food you can spare, though. It's a long way to Austin."

The leader raised his hand to signal the other outlaw to lower his gun. "I remember you," he said.

"Where's your vest with all the colors braided with gold?"

"I don't wear it when I travel," Lewt said with a smile. "Sun bounces off it."

The leader laughed as one of the men behind him mumbled something Lewt couldn't catch.

"My friend says one of the girls claims you spent the rest of the night in her bed, then shot out the window like a coward when you heard shooting."

Lewt stood tall, facing them straight on. "Look, I'm a gambler, not a gunfighter. I don't even carry a gun, so of course I took off as soon as the shooting started. I want to live to gamble again. I paid for my time with the rather drunk lady with my last twenty."

Lewt was doing what he always did when being confronted. He was blending as much truth into the lie as possible.

It worked. The leader of Toledo's band believed him.

"How long have you been here, Gambler?"

Lewt shrugged. "I had too much to drink last night. To be honest, I'm surprised I got my bedroll on the ground before I fell asleep." Lewt scratched his head. "If I was guessing, I'd say I've been here since about midnight."

"Did you see anyone pass?"

Lewt shook his head. "Who you looking for?"

"A man traveling with a child almost grown. He'll be limping, but he's a dead man if we catch him.

He kidnapped the child. One man who thought he saw them ride away said he had two, maybe three men with him."

Lewt shook his head. "Nobody like that has passed by here."

Lewt was an expert at reading people, and he could tell the leader didn't believe him but hadn't quite found the lie in his story.

"Why don't you saddle up, Gambler, and ride along with us for a while? We're headed in the same direction."

"Thanks for the offer, but . . ."

The leader smiled and added, "I insist."

Lewt had no choice. If he made too much fuss, it would make the leader even more suspicious. Maybe if he rode along he could draw the group away from the others. So, much as he hated the odds, he saddled up and went along.

If he'd had any sense, he would have been worried or at the very least plotting his escape, but all Lewt could think about was that he wished he'd seen Em one more time before he left. He wanted to see those Texas blue eyes looking at him, and somehow that seemed to matter as much as his life at the moment.

ᔧ CHAPTER 34 ᘐ

Em watched from the ridge as Lewt joined the band of guards they'd been running from. She wasn't close enough to hear what was being said, but she could tell by Lewt's slow movements that he wasn't happy about going with the outlaws. There were no guns pointed at him, which was a good sign.

When the men surrounded him, she knew he was, at the very least, an unwilling guest of the outlaws.

"What do we do?" she whispered to Duncan a few feet away.

"Nothing," Duck answered, as he swore under his breath. "It would take all four of us to even have a chance in a fight, and that would mean leaving the cooks and Anna without anyone to protect them. Whatever happens to Lewt, he's alone from here on out."

Em didn't like the plan at all, but she could see Duncan's point. They crawled down off the ledge they'd been watching from and rode back to the gully, where Sumner and Wyatt waited with the others.

For a few minutes she listened to the men talk, guessing how much trouble Lewt was in, wondering what they could do about it.

Finally, she could stand it no longer. "We have to do something," she said.

Sumner met her gaze and nodded, but Duncan kept his head low. "I've known Lewt Paterson for years. He grew up in saloons. If anyone can handle those men, he can. I've seen him, unarmed, talk his way out of being shot. I say we give him a few days. He knows where we're heading. He'll catch up with us in Austin."

All the other men seemed to agree with Duncan, but Em couldn't see the logic. Lewt had risked his life to save them, and now they weren't going to do a thing.

"You're all cowards." She fought down a scream. "I'm going after him, and I swear I'll shoot any one of you who tries to stop me."

To her surprise, Duck smiled, then Sumner, and finally Wyatt.

"Have you three lost your minds?" she asked, feeling sick that they might call her bluff.

"No, Em, we just wanted to see how much this gambler meant to you. Sumner told me, but I didn't believe you could care for any man as much as you do a horse. It appears I was wrong."

"Nonsense," she argued. "I just know he's your friend."

"He's more than that to you," Duncan answered directly.

"Maybe he is, but don't tell him. I'd rather he be the last to know."

Wyatt laughed. "That right there is why I never considered marrying. There is no logic to women.

Seems to me if you care for him, Miss Em, you should tell him and ease him out of his misery."

"That's not the way it works," Sumner said. "First a woman keeps a man guessing until he puts a ring on her finger, and then she goes to work at driving him slowly mad. I've rarely seen a man married over ten years who wasn't completely insane. Once a woman gets them mixed up, she just leads them around and points to what she wants done."

Duncan moved to his horse. "Why don't we debate this later? Right now we need to get the women back to the mission and start looking for Lewt. We'll lose four or five hours, but we can make it up. A few of those outlaws looked like they hadn't been in the saddle for months and had grown fat on beer and the sisters' cooking. They'll be needing to stop often and long. If I know Lewt, he'll put out a deck and try to extend each stop with a little game."

"We've got better horses and better riders. We'll catch up to them and then we'll figure out what to do." Wyatt grinned at Em. "But I can tell you right now, when we find him, I ain't the one who'll be kissing on that gambler."

Em had no more time to talk. She simply made a face at the ranger as Sumner turned the wagon around and they doubled back to the mission.

Duncan told her to stay close to the wagon while he and Wyatt lagged behind to make sure the outlaws hadn't decided to double back. "If you hear gunfire," he whispered to Em, "ride hard toward the mission."

"Aren't you going to tell Sumner the same?"

He laughed. "Sumner knows. He's been in a few fights before, but for you, cousin, this will be your first. Up to now, you've been a virgin."

Em didn't miss the glint in his eyes. He was teasing her, but she wasn't sure exactly about what.

Duncan was born for this life. He loved the adventure, the fight. She simply hoped they all lived to tell the story.

He tipped his hat and yelled, "I'll catch up to you before you reach the mission doors."

She rode with her rifle across her legs, ready if needed, but her thoughts were on Lewt. She'd told herself that last night had been more dream than reality. She'd found him alone and wanted to kiss him one more time. His life would never blend with hers, but she needed the memory of this one man. He'd touched her body and soul deeper than anyone else ever had. He'd made her feel desirable and wanted beyond all reason. Even when she knew what he was, she still longed for the touch of his hand and the taste of his kisses.

Before she faced Lewt again, Em knew she had to make up her mind about how she felt about him. She thought she knew how he felt about her. He hated her for making a fool of him. For lying to him and letting him share his secrets about wanting to marry rich without telling him who she was. She also knew he wanted her. Not just a woman or a wife, but her.

It took them more than two hours to get the wagon back to the mission. Her cousin rode in at full speed just as the priest closed the gate. She saw no sign of Wyatt and guessed he was somewhere up ahead scouting things out.

Duncan spent thirty minutes convincing Anna that she would be safe there without him. Finally, he put a second lock at her door and a tiny hole so she could look out before she unlocked either bolt.

With Sumner and the two cooks promising to stand guard over her, Anna finally turned loose of Duncan's hand.

Em hugged Sumner.

"I should be going with you," he whispered. "I need to look out for you."

Em smiled. For the first time she saw that the old man liked her. "I'll be all right with Wyatt and Duck. You're needed here."

He looked at the two cooks and frowned, as if worried he might be the one facing true danger. "You take care of yourself," Sumner warned, "just as I plan to. Bring that wild cousin of yours back in one piece along with that gambler. He's starting to grow on me even if he'll probably never be much of a horseman."

She smiled. "He's growing on me too."

Duncan and Em left the mission at a run. They rode McMurray horses bred for strength and distance. It was time to put them to the test.

An hour later they reached the spot where she'd last seen Lewt playing cards on his bedroll and talking with the outlaws as if he were just passing time. Wyatt was waiting for them. He'd ridden ahead and knew the direction so they didn't have to worry about tracking, which was a good thing because a winter rain began to fall. Not a soft dribble of a rain, but large plops that erased the trail of a road completely.

It was afternoon when Duck called a halt. Without a word, they moved into the shelter of the trees and climbed down to let the horses rest.

"The trail's gone," Wyatt said. "We've gone beyond where I saw them turn off. They could have veered off to the east or west by a few hundred feet and we couldn't see them in this rain. We've no way of tracking them now. We'd be better off to stay here for a while. With any luck they're holed up somewhere just ahead of us."

Em stared out into the sheets of rain curtaining her view. Lewt was out there somewhere alone, and there was no way for her to get to him.

"When this rain stops, we'll ride on. We have to give it another try." Duncan's words didn't sound like he held much hope.

As she often did when she rode the range, Em ignored the cold. She felt wet to the bone, but she wouldn't complain. Her thoughts were on Lewt and finding him. In the rumble of the winter storm, she thought of Lewt's arms around her and how he'd said he'd wait forever for her to come to him.

As soon as the rain stopped they raced across the land, each studying the afternoon shadows, each hoping for one sign. A campfire. A shot to kill game. The reflection of a rifle off the aging sun.

Nothing. Finally, it was too dark to continue. They camped in a dry spot beneath an old elm. Em curled up in her blanket and thought of Lewt holding her hand and wondered if he was close, thinking about the same thing. Wyatt offered her jerky and a biscuit, but she was too tired to eat.

Before dawn the next morning they were back in the saddle, three shadows moving beside a muddy road. If the gang stopped for the night and didn't leave until morning, they'd be leaving a trail in the mud now.

If they were following the right road, Em thought.

If they were even going in the right direction.

If Lewt was still alive and with the band. She feared that the outlaws might think him worthless and kill him, or worse, discover that he was lying and torture him for information.

The sun was high when Wyatt found a camp by a swollen stream. Seven or eight horses, he guessed. The same number of men. From the remains of a fire, it looked like they had stopped long enough to rest the horses, cook rabbits, and maybe warm themselves. The ground was still wet enough to follow their tracks across the campsite.

Em stood very still as Wyatt read the tracks. "There's blood," he said, "but it looks like it's from the rabbits. This could be our men, or a dozen others traveling. Whoever stopped here did so after the rain. I'm guessing they left one, maybe two hours ago. They must feel pretty certain they're not being followed if they stopped to cook."

"Wyatt," Duncan called from twenty feet away. "Look at this."

They all moved to a muddy spot behind a rock. No footprints stomped across the spot, but someone had drawn a circle and inside written *WM.*

"What's it mean?" Wyatt asked.

"Whispering Mountain," both Duncan and Em said at once.

Wyatt picked up a playing card tucked just beneath the rock. "Maybe it's Lewt telling us not to follow but to meet him back at the ranch."

"Or maybe he wanted to leave a symbol that would mean nothing to the men he was with, but would let us know he'd been in this camp."

"We should still try to follow." Thunder threatened again as if calling her a liar.

Wyatt shook his head. "From the looks of it, they crossed into the stream here. We have no idea which way."

Em wouldn't give up. "Why don't we separate until the rain starts? I'll do upstream; Duck, you go downstream. Wyatt, you cross and ride north like they've been going. With luck, before it starts raining we'll pick up some hint of a trail."

"Once it starts raining there will be no trail to follow. We all agree to come back here even if we find something." Wyatt didn't look like he liked the plan, but like the others he didn't want to stop hunting. "If it doesn't rain, we turn back in one hour no matter what." He looked straight at Em. "If you find something, anything, don't get too close, just turn around and come back here."

She nodded.

"Em, watch for the place where horses have come out of the stream." Duncan turned his horse downstream. "That's the only clue we'll need to pick up the trail."

"I know what to look for," she snapped. Both of them were treating her like a child on a rabbit hunt.

Duck laughed. "That's my Em. Nobody could ever tell you anything."

She was already heading upstream and didn't answer. The stream was shallow, not more than three or four feet in the center, but wide enough that two or three horses could easily ride abreast.

Now and then she felt the splash of water but blamed it on a branch she'd brushed or her horse splashing. She didn't, couldn't feel the rain, for if she did it would mean that she would have to stop, and Em had no intention of stopping. Her horse fought the current, so after a few hundred feet, she rode the edge of the stream, not caring that she left a trail. No one was following her.

The trees grew denser, with dead moss hanging off their branches that reminded her of huge spiderwebs wide enough to swallow her if she wasn't careful. In places, thanks to the rain, the water splashed over its banks. Twice, her horse stumbled, tossing her into the water, but she didn't stop. She had only an hour to find the trail, and if she didn't, she'd have to turn around and pray that Wyatt or Duck had found something.

In a bend in the river, she slowed, searching both banks for any sign. Her horse was tired and she knew the outlaws' mounts would have been also. They couldn't stay in the water much longer or they'd be traveling on foot.

Her teeth were chattering, but she didn't care. She wouldn't stop. In the stillness just before she rounded the corner, she thought she heard voices. Em walked her horse onto the bank and listened, then moved slowly forward.

After only a dozen steps, Em froze. Men not thirty feet beyond the trees lining the stream were talking. Yelling almost. Laughing. Swearing.

She looped her horse's reins over a branch and moved as silently as she could toward the noise.

Ten feet into the brush and trees, she saw the men she'd been looking for circled around a campfire. For a moment, she couldn't believe her eyes. Lewt was in the middle of them playing cards.

She counted them, unsure if there had been six or seven tracks in the mud. She counted five men around the fire besides Lewt. One on the ground looking more like he'd passed out than fallen asleep. Frantically, she watched the trees. Were they all present, or was one missing?

Again and again her gaze traveled to Lewt as if her eyes were hungry for just the sight of him.

All day in her mind she'd pictured him suffering, maybe even dying. It had never occurred to her that he might just be playing cards with the outlaws. She didn't know whether to feel angry or relieved. She'd found him. He was surrounded, and worse, he appeared to be one of them. The man was a chameleon. Change his clothes, change his company. It didn't matter. He blended in.

A twig snapped from a few feet behind her and Em felt something slam against her head a moment before the world went black.

ℬ CHAPTER 35 ℭ

Lewt watched one of the men walk into camp carrying Em over one shoulder like she was no more than a deer he'd killed for supper. He felt his own heart stop and it didn't start up again until he heard her moan in pain.

She was alive.

"Look what I found," the troll of a man shouted. He had wide shoulders and trunk legs but not the height that should have gone with the rest of his body. As the world's shortest giant stomped into camp with his trophy, Lewt watched silently with the others. He knew if he tipped his hand now, his life as well as hers would be worthless.

The self-appointed leader of the group, a big sloppy man named Binns, moved closer. "Where'd you find her?"

"Down near the water. She was watching us," the troll said as he dropped her near the fire. "I wouldn't have hit her so hard if I'd known she was a woman. Dressed like that, I thought she was a man."

"Where's her horse?"

"I must have spooked him 'cause he took off downstream."

The leader swore as he jerked Em's chin up to have a look at her. "Never seen her before. Kill her."

Lewt took a step, but the troll widened his stance and shoved the leader. "How come you get to say what we do with her? I'm the one who found her. I've about had enough of you thinking you're the boss around here."

The leader's anger was barely in check. "She looks half dead from you bashing her head in. What do you care if we finish her off? Kill her. We'll need to be moving on as soon as it's dark, so toss her body in the stream. She'll float down a few miles and turn into someone else's problem."

The troll of a man must have known he couldn't win, so he tried bargaining. "How about I play with her while it's raining, then I'll kill her before we leave? I couldn't tell much with that coat she's got on, but she might be something worth a look."

Lewt saw his chance. "I got a better idea. Why don't we play cards for her? We're all too broke to play for money, and playing for something makes a more interesting game." He stepped up and fanned the cards as he studied the troll. "It'd be an interesting way to pass the time. I say she's worth a hundred toward the pot. You win, you have her and extra money."

The leader frowned. "Why would we risk our money to play for a half-dead girl when back at Three Forks we get all we want for free? Toledo don't care long as we don't hold up the cash flow."

All the men seemed to agree. Lewt had already figured out that between them they had very little cash. That was probably how Toledo kept them working for her. She gave them room, board, and women, but no money. A man with money might think of leaving. A man with empty pockets would stay and work his shift.

"I don't get free women," Lewt said. "And I don't have a hundred dollars, but I've got my vest. That should stand me for twenty in the game."

The troll was interested. He must think he had nothing to lose. "String the girl up so we can all see her. I'll play this fool a few rounds. If I win your twenty, I'll have me a new vest and I'll still have my fun with her. If you win a little off of me, I'll let you have a turn if there's time after I'm finished."

One of the guards pulled Em to the nearest tree, raised her arms above her head, and tied her up, leaving her hanging like about-to-be-butchered meat.

"I need to make sure she's alive." Lewt walked toward her. "I don't want to waste my time playing for a dead woman."

The troll laughed. "It don't make all that much difference to me one way or the other long as she's still warm."

While the others laughed, Lewt moved his fingers along the side of Em's throat and felt for a pulse. It pounded strong and fast in his palm even as blood dripped from a cut at her hairline.

"Let's get on with the game!" someone yelled, and the men circled a stump that had already acted as Lewt's table. They'd been passing around bottles since they'd stopped to rest, and the whiskey had begun to take effect. None of the others wanted to play, but they all wanted to watch.

Lewt leaned close to Em, praying she was conscious enough to hear him. "When I say run, turn and run into the trees and keep running. Do you understand? No matter what, don't stop."

He thought he felt her nod slightly, but she didn't open her eyes.

"She's barely breathing," he shouted. "If she dies before the game is played, all bets are off."

"Then let's get to it," the troll yelled. "I'll look mighty good in that fancy vest of yours."

Lewt moved away from her, forcing himself not to look back. If he did, if he saw her hanging there, hurt and helpless, it would be his undoing. He moved to the center of the circle and began the most important card game of his life.

The rain poured above them, and now and then it managed to filter through the trees and sputter in the fire.

Lewt laughed and kidded with the men, but he counted every minute. Finally, after several rounds of play, he saw Em's feet shift beneath her and take her weight off her bound wrists. He knew she was awake.

He won one hand, then lost one, but slowly his twenty pieces of twigs that served as chips began to multiply and the troll's dwindled. The man seemed to be enjoying the attention from his peers and wasn't too concerned about losing a little. After all, it wasn't real money, and the tall, thin woman wearing the clothes of a man didn't really appeal to him. He even told everyone that since he'd knocked her senseless, she probably couldn't play the way he liked to play.

By the time he'd lost most of his sticks, he was bragging that he liked his women best when they were yelling and screaming even if he had to break a few bones to get their attention. The others teased him that the only women he could catch in the saloon were the new girls, and he only caught them once.

Lewt didn't say anything; he hoped Em wasn't listening to any of the rough talk. She was frightened enough of men.

Unfortunately, he knew she probably was, because he'd seen her shift a few times, balancing her weight, turning her wrists so blood would circulate.

Finally, the last guard, a morbid outlaw who did nothing but complain, woke from his sleep. The big man stood, his worthless arm swinging at his side. "What is everyone doing?" he yelled. "We need to be on the road. If we don't bring that girl of Toledo's back, I'll see to it you all are hunted down and murdered in your sleep."

Lewt thought he recognized the man as the guard who'd been in front of Duncan's prison. The thought crossed his mind that the cooks were right; he should have left the man dripping blood and not just tied him to the bed.

The crowd was drunk enough to argue, and the leader of the band, Binns, appeared to have had enough of the bossy slob they called Ramon. The two men faced one another and began poking and shoving.

As the shouting escalated and fists began to fly, Lewt slipped a thin knife from his belt and in one quick shot sent it flying toward Em.

The rope above her hands sliced in half.

"Run," he shouted, knowing that she might make it free, but he'd be trapped. It didn't matter.

Before Em's arms dropped in front of her, she was moving into the brush, heading for the water. When she broke from the trees, she realized how hard it was raining. Her one hope was to hit the water and let it take her downstream.

Downstream. Back to Duck and Wyatt. Back to life.

As she jumped into the current, one thought filled her. She was heading away from Lewt.

Underwater, she jerked the wet ropes off her wrists and began to swim. Long, powerful strokes like her papa had taught her the first year she'd come to Whispering Mountain.

Teagen McMurray would yell, "Half our land is framed by water, so my daughters need to swim." Then he'd pick her up and tell her to gulp in air just before she hit the water.

She'd learned the lessons well, and now they might save her life.

When she finally broke the surface and tried to breathe in the rain, she heard shouts, but they seemed far behind her. She cupped her mouth, gulped air, and floated in the center of the stream, where the water pushed her along. Away to freedom. Away from Lewt.

ℬ CHAPTER 36 ℭ

Duncan was spitting mad. He'd told Emily to return in one hour, and they'd waited for her half an hour before they'd decided to head upstream and find her. "Surely she can tell time," he mumbled, simply because he didn't want to allow himself to think of the other reasons she might be late.

He watched along the left side and Wyatt searched the right bank as they pushed through the rain and shallow water. They needed to rest the horses. Hell, he thought, he needed to rest, maybe drink the last of the coffee, but what was he doing? Looking for his cousin. She'd never followed orders; he didn't know why he expected it now. When she'd been little, her mother was constantly insisting that Em wear a dress to school. Half the time she was taking it off and switching into trousers and a shirt on the way home. The only person she listened to was Teagen, and everyone listened to him. It was hard not to. The man came into the world at full volume and worked on getting louder.

After several minutes, Duncan spotted her horse near the stream. He'd been running.

Wyatt caught the reins. "You think she fell off?"

Duncan swore, deciding it would become an incurable habit if he stayed around her long.

"Maybe. More likely she decided to walk the bank a little farther. Tie the horse; we'll pick him up on our way back. Right now we have to find her." Silently he hoped it would be faceup and not facedown in the water.

They rushed on.

"She couldn't have gone much farther," Wyatt finally said as they neared a bend in the stream.

"Of course she could. She's probably forgotten all about the time." Duncan was into his rant. "At least I'm not worried she's kidnapped. Who'd want to take her? If anyone ever thought of kidnapping a McMurray for ransom, she'd be the last one picked. She's bullheaded. She never listens. She's never going to marry and settle down, not her; she's got to have control of everything and everyone."

Wyatt jerked his horse toward the center of the stream. "She's in the water!" he yelled, a second before he dove off his mount.

Duncan grabbed the horse as he watched Wyatt pull Em up. For a moment she kicked and fought as if she thought him a stream monster, and then when she finally opened her eyes and looked at him, she stilled.

"Lewt's in trouble." She pointed to the bend. "Hurry. They're going to kill him."

Wyatt carried her to the bank and set her down. "Stay here. We'll get him."

She looked like she might argue, but she was gulping air and slinging her wet hair. The ranger swung up on his horse and joined Duncan, already heading upstream.

Em buried her head on her knees and began to shake. She had no idea if it was the cold or the fear or the exhaustion. All she knew was that she wanted to help Lewt. With no horse or gun she had little chance. So she waited in the rain, feeling more broken and alone than she ever had in her life.

Gunfire rattled in the storm like the echo of thunder. Em knew she should move back in the trees for shelter, but she couldn't unfold her arms from around her knees. All at once she was six years old again and frightened of everything. She knew she was by the stream in the middle of a thunderstorm, but in her mind she went all the way back to the small room over a bookstore in Chicago.

The room seemed always cold and damp. Her mother slept on the bed with them most nights, but now and then they'd hear her father climbing the stairs and her mother would lift them onto the floor beside an old wardrobe. Rose was younger, she never woke, but Emily did. She always did.

She'd lie there knowing she had to be still. She'd face the wall and try not to listen as her father hurt her mother. Her mother never cried out, not even when he finished and sometimes slapped her while he called her names, but after he left she cried sometimes until dawn.

In the days he was rarely there, and when he was, Em remembered that the smell of whiskey circled around him. He never spoke to her or Rose except to order them to leave. When they'd return to the kitchen or bookstore, their mother would be crying.

When he died, Em hadn't even thought to cry. She'd just helped her mother pack. By then Bethie was born. Em remembered the days of trains and boats and finally the stage. The trip seemed endless, but it didn't matter. They were heading away from the man who'd hurt her mother.

When they finally got to Texas, they found Teagen McMurray, her papa. He was a big, strong, powerful man who took care of them all, and once he put his arms around her mother, Em never saw her cry again. But somehow the ink of Chicago nights had blotted her soul. Until Lewt, she'd never let a man close enough to hurt her.

Until now, she hadn't cried. She cried so hard her body shook. She cried so hard not even the rain could wash her tears away.

When she finally ran out of tears, she raised her head and realized that it had stopped raining. The air was still cold, with a wind rumbling in the trees. Clouds hid the sun, making it seem more like twilight than day.

Like shadows floating on the water, she saw three men riding toward her. Their heads were down, hats low, but she recognized them. Duncan. Wyatt. Lewt.

Em slowly stood, watching them, almost afraid they were ghosts leaving a battle.

None of them said a word when they reached her. Lewt leaned down from his saddle and lifted her up in front of him. Em wasn't sure she could speak. She just felt the solidness of his chest and let him hold her tight as they moved on down the stream.

A hundred questions came to mind, but she let them wait. Somehow, he was alive, and that was enough for now.

When they reached the camp they'd used the night before, they stopped. Duncan took care of the horses, Wyatt built a huge fire that warmed the whole clearing, and Lewt doctored the cut along her forehead as best he could.

A warm feeling of being safe washed over Em's tired body as she leaned her chin on Lewt's knee and closed her eyes.

"They found your horse," he said simply, as if there were nothing else important in the world to tell her.

Em opened one eye and looked at him. She'd left him at an outlaw camp about to die, and all he could think of to say was that they'd found the horse. She considered yelling at him, but she didn't have the energy. "What happened?" she asked, as Wyatt and Duncan stretched out on their bedrolls around the fire.

"I lived," Lewt said with a smile, as if he were amazed.

"He wouldn't have if we'd been a few minutes later," Wyatt added.

"But I thought they'd shoot you immediately after I ran."

Lewt grinned. "They wanted to, but to my surprise, they got in an argument over who got to kill me. The big guy with only one arm that worked seemed to think he had the right, but the stump of a man who found you claimed he was the one cheated. They tied me up to argue about the time Wyatt and Duncan hit the camp firing at everything that moved. I pulled a knife from my boot, cut myself loose, and took cover until the firing stopped."

Em turned to stare at Wyatt. "Did you kill them all?"

Wyatt shook his head.

Lewt answered, "Your date to the party, the short guy, took a bullet to the head. It wasn't a pretty sight. What little brains he had departed. The big slob of a man who claimed he was little Anna's future husband had three slugs in him, and both these rangers say they only shot him once, so I'm thinking one of the other guards put a bullet in him while he had the chance. There were several wounded, but apparently two rangers were too much for them. The gang surrendered."

"We didn't want to mess with paperwork at the station, so we made a deal. They bury the dead, get the wounded to a doc, and all promise not to go back to Toledo's place." Duncan smiled. "Surprisingly, they all agreed to get out of Texas as fast as possible, heading any direction but south."

Lewt laughed. "You didn't give them much choice. You said you'd shoot them on sight if you ever saw them again."

Em looked at Lewt. "I thought I lost you," she whispered.

Wyatt didn't seem to realize they might be having a private conversation, and he butted in. "No chance of that, Miss Em. Gamblers are like bindweed: No matter what you do, you can't get rid of it. Besides, in a gunfight, no one thinks to shoot the gambler."

"Don't you think it's time you turned in?" Lewt frowned at Wyatt.

"Sure," Wyatt said, and rolled into his blanket.

Duncan stared at them. "Lewt, don't you think you'd better turn in too? There's a good spot on the other side of the fire."

Lewt looked up at Em's cousin. "I'm sleeping right here next to Em, if she agrees. I almost lost her today. I'm not moving away now, and if you have a problem with that, I'd better hear about it now."

Duncan looked like he might argue, but he backed down and moved to the other side of the fire.

"Besides"—Lewt laughed as he looked at her—"I won her in the poker game. She's mine for tonight anyway."

Duncan's back straightened, and he looked at them.

Em laughed. "He's kidding, Duck. But just for tonight, I think I'd like to sleep in his arms. That's all."

Duncan didn't look happy, but he nodded once and stretched out on his bedroll.

Em snuggled her back against Lewt's chest and sighed.

Lewt whispered into her ear, "I wasn't kidding, darling, and that's not all."

She smiled as he spread the blanket over them both, then without hesitating began to move his hands over her. When he reached her shirt, he unbuttoned the buttons to her waist and pulled the material away.

Lewt was silent, aware that others were close, but he wasn't shy.

He caressed her breasts for a long while until the campfire grew low and they heard both the rangers snoring softly in their sleep. Then Lewt rolled her to her back and moved over her.

"I want you, Em, more than I've ever wanted a woman in my life." His words brushed against her face as he kissed her softly. "But not like this. Not until we are alone and in a feather bed." He brushed her ear with the tip of his tongue. "And believe me, darling, whatever it takes, you'll come to me again when we're alone."

He lowered his body, pressing against her breasts with his chest. His hips made her fully aware of just how much he wanted her. His kiss turned hungry for a moment, and then as if forcing himself with his last bit of control, he moved away.

Em took a deep breath and felt his hand spread out over her middle.

"I know there's not a chance in heaven or hell that a woman like you would marry a man like me, but when you come to me again, you'll be coming to my bed. This need I have for you is too great to play halfway games. I'll be your lover or I'll be your friend." He kissed her cheek. "I'll be whatever you want me to be."

She closed her eyes and tried to understand what he was talking about. Finally, she whispered, "Will you hold me tonight? All night?"

"I will," he whispered, and pulled her against him.

His arms wrapped around her, holding her tight. Slowly, a breath at a time, she fell asleep, wondering if Lewt could ever understand that maybe she wanted him to be everything.

ஐ CHAPTER 37 ௸

They arrived back at the mission about noon the next day. The priest offered them all a bath, and the cooks had been busy in the kitchen. A meal was waiting for them when they were clean and dry.

Though Sumner asked questions, Wyatt and

Duncan gave only the barest of details. To them, they'd done what they rode out to do and it was finished. The old man seemed to understand. He was cut from the same cloth.

Em finished eating and went to her tiny room in the nuns' quarters. The mission smelled of incense and memories two hundred years in the making. Its thick walls closed out the world and all sounds. She slipped into the simple white gown they'd given her when she'd first arrived and curled up beneath a warm blanket. Within seconds she was asleep. The sound sleep of those too tired to even dream.

It was dawn the next morning when she woke. Sometime during the night her mind had let everything settle in her thoughts, and in the stillness, Em saw the world more clearly than ever before.

Ten minutes later, she found Lewt at breakfast. He smiled at her, but not his usual bold smile. There was an uncertainty in his gaze, as if maybe he'd stepped over the line. They weren't two people alone now; they were surrounded not only with others, but with who they were.

"Morning," he said, without adding a *darling* to it as she thought he might.

"Morning," she answered, very much aware that the cooks were watching. "Where is everyone?"

"We're loading up the supplies," Sarah J said, as if she thought she was part of their conversation.

"Sumner says we're heading out in an hour, and I don't plan to be hungry on the train. Rachel made some of her wonderful bread for the priest and the sisters, but I made a few meals for the road."

Em looked at Lewt, hoping he'd fill in the details.

He pulled out her chair and poured her a cup of coffee before he spoke. "If we move fast, you can make the night train into Austin and from there to Anderson Glen by dawn tomorrow though we'll probably have to ride on one of the freight runs."

"We're heading home." She almost jumped out of her chair. "I can't wait. I've never missed anything as much as I miss home."

"Sumner and Wyatt are getting the wagon in better shape to make the trip. Duncan's saying good-bye to Anna, and I was assigned to pound on your door if you didn't appear soon."

A dozen questions came to mind, but they'd have to wait. If she planned to be ready when they pulled out, she had to hurry.

Lewt stood as she jumped up and caught her chair as she knocked it back in her haste. "We're going home." The other three didn't look as excited as she felt.

Em ran to her room and packed her few things as fast as she could. She wanted to have time to check all the horses before they started out and to say good-bye to the priest and nuns she'd met.

When she glanced out her window into the courtyard, she saw Duncan standing beside Anna.

She'd removed her little-girl shift and was wearing one of the habits the sisters had given her, but her wild hair was still free.

Em turned away, not wanting to eavesdrop.

It appeared all were safe and they were heading home. By tomorrow she could be riding across the ranch and they'd all sit around at dinner and talk of all that had happened.

℘ CHAPTER 38 ℘

Duncan stood in front of Anna, fighting the urge to touch her. For a week she'd slept beside him, nursed his wound, bathed him. They'd shared hours of being together, locked in together, but he'd never learned to talk to her.

"Are you sure you want to stay here?" Duncan asked.

She nodded.

"Well, I'd rather you come to Whispering Mountain with me. My cousins would take good care of you, and you'd be safe there also. But I can't very well order you to come with me. Appears to me you've probably had enough of people telling you what to do. The priest told me you took right to the order of nuns here, even been going to prayers with them."

Anna took his hand in hers but didn't say a word.

"I guess you got a right to make up your own

mind. I've left money with the priest in case you change it. He said he'd see you had traveling clothes and he'd take you over to a rail station himself."

Duncan shoved his hat back on his head, wishing he could persuade her to go with him. Nobody around here knew what she'd been through. Nobody knew how strong she was. Maybe, he told himself, nobody including him knew what she wanted. "If you come to Austin, the ranger station will know where I'm at. If you make it to Anderson Glen, somebody at Elmo's Mercantile will bring you out to the ranch. I wrote everything down and left it with the priest in case you forget.

"Any chance you want to talk to me, Anna? I thought I heard your voice once, but maybe it was a dream."

She shook her head, then stood on her tiptoes and kissed his cheek.

"I guess that means we're friends." He smiled. "Mind if I stop by now and then and check on you?"

Anna smiled.

She was tiny, he thought, but beautiful. Maybe the most beautiful creature he'd ever known. She might be nineteen, but he had the feeling she was just newborn.

"I'll take that as a yes." He tipped his hat and turned to leave, but she caught his hand.

Without looking at him, she slipped a piece of paper into his hand and ran back to the nuns working on fencing in what looked like a garden.

Duncan turned the worn paper in his hand. It looked like a corner of an envelope yellowed with age and smudged. He couldn't make out the name at the top, but the address was a number on Lantern West in New Orleans.

He flipped the scrap over, and in a child's block writing someone had penciled *Anna Margaret Barrister.*

Duncan smiled. He had her name and a clue. Anna wasn't giving up on life and hiding out in a mission; she was giving him the key and waiting for him to return with an answer.

"I'll be back," he whispered. "I promise, if you have family left, I'll find out."

When he walked through the kitchen, he began his investigation. "Ladies," he said to the cooks, "do either of you remember Toledo ever getting mail from New Orleans?"

Rachel shook her head, but Sarah J spoke up. "She goes to Mexico City every June or July, and once I seen her bring back a box of mail. Mostly things she ordered that we couldn't get, but once I remember I saw a package from New Orleans tucked between the sewing notions and mail-order catalogs. She saw it about the same time I did and jerked it up. Headed straight for her office, and when she came out an hour later that package was nowhere in sight. One of the girls told me later that Toledo must be touched in the head because she built a fire in the fireplace in her office. No one in their right mind would do such a thing that time of year."

Duncan thanked them and headed out to load up. He had his first clue and now a belief that Toledo might be corresponding with someone. It would take time, maybe years, but he'd solve the puzzle.

His gaze found Anna working with the nuns. She'd wait, he thought, for as long as it took. She'd kept a scrap of paper hidden for years. She'd never lost hope. She wouldn't lose it now.

"Ready to load up?" Duncan yelled at Sumner.

The old man nodded, then moved closer. "You sure we should take those two cooks to Whispering Mountain? They could murder us in our sleep, you know."

Duncan grinned. "Well, we can't just turn them loose on the world. Who knows what would happen? I'll stop at the Austin office and see if they can't look up their crime. In the meantime, we can't put them in jail just because they say they're murderers and I wouldn't feel right letting them go, so the only thing I can think of is to keep my eye on them."

Sumner followed his logic. "They ever say who they killed?"

"Nope, but you can work on getting me a few names when we get home."

The old man didn't look happy about it, but he nodded.

Duncan thought he heard Sumner mumble

something about first gamblers and now murderers. Houseguests sure weren't what they used to be.

The two cooks came out with a basket of food and climbed into the wagon. Em followed, talking with the priest. Lewt and Wyatt were already mounted.

Duncan grinned. Now that everything had calmed down, he was ready for another mission, but he knew his cousins would insist on him resting up and healing. They'd also try to fatten him up.

Maybe he could take a few weeks off and stay home.

℘ CHAPTER 39 ℭ

Lewt rode ahead of the wagon. The nearest town would take most of the day to get to, but once they were on the train they'd be in Austin in a few hours. He felt like he'd been away for a year. His room at the small hotel he'd found a few years ago would be waiting, his clothes in the wardrobe, his papers and books scattered across the desk.

He'd always found a kind of quiet peace in his room. The landlady wasn't the type to rent to gamblers, but he'd caught her when money was lean and she'd agreed he could stay as long as he entered from the side door after hours so as not to disturb her respectable lodgers. The only meal she served was breakfast, and he rarely got up for that. When he did, he made sure he wore his most conservative suit and talked little. When someone asked him what line of work he was in, he simply said banking. No one ever asked more. Though banking was solid, the inquisitive person assumed any further discussion would be either boring or over their heads.

Lewt realized that for the first time ever, he wasn't in any hurry to get back to his room—or his life, for that matter. He'd spent a week almost dying daily, it seemed, and the realization that he'd miss it surprised him. Or maybe it was the knowledge that he'd be saying good-bye to Em at the train station in Austin. He had a feeling she thought they'd all be going farther north, but for him, the trip had ended.

Suddenly, he wished he could slow down the small caravan. If they missed the train they'd have to stay the night at the train station and he'd have one more night away. One more night with Em near.

"Glad to be getting back?" Duncan asked as he pulled up next to Lewt.

"Not really," he answered honestly.

"Want to travel on up to Whispering Mountain with us? I could lend you a horse to ride back to Austin. You seem to have taken to riding lately."

Lewt knew it would only prolong the inevitable. "No," he finally answered. "I think it's time for me to go back to work."

For the rest of the day, he watched Em as they moved closer and closer to the end of their time together. He decided he didn't mind that she wore men's clothes; he'd felt what was beneath and could imagine how she looked all long and lean and nude. There was no time for them to be alone, not even for a few minutes. In what seemed like a moment, she'd become a memory even though she was still standing in front of him.

When they reached the train, he grew silent, already missing her.

As they pulled away from the station, he stood on the back platform and watched the sun set as the train rushed toward Austin. He'd told Em she'd have to come to him, but she wasn't coming. She was talking to Duncan and Sumner in the next car, or having dinner with the cooks, or checking on the horses, but she wasn't coming to him.

The night grew dark, and he felt it on the inside as well as on the outside.

He thought of all they'd shared during the days together and how close they'd held one another that last night on the way back to the mission. If he'd known it would be their last time together, would he have done anything different? Would he have made love to her? Would he have pulled away and held her less so the pain of losing her now wouldn't hurt so badly?

When the door opened, Lewt let hope flood his thoughts for a moment before he realized it was only Duncan coming out to smoke his nightly cigar.

"Wish you'd consider going on home with us,"

Duncan said. "At the least, you'd be a great help with the cooks and all their loot."

"No thanks. I don't belong there. You were right."

Duncan raised an eyebrow. "Still friends?"

Lewt offered his hand. "Still friends. I'll take your money at cards or join in any fight with you, Duck."

"Good to know. I don't know when I'll be back to Austin, but I'll look you up." Duncan slid the door open. "Coming in?"

"No. I think I'll stay out here awhile."

When the door opened and closed, he expected to be alone. Em's voice startled him. "Mind if I join you?"

He tried his best to smile. "Anytime, pretty lady," he said, realizing how much he meant the compliment. Somehow she'd become the most beautiful woman he'd ever known. Maybe she always had been; he just hadn't seen her.

"Duck says you're not planning to stay with us all the way." She sounded angry, or maybe hurt.

"That's right. It's better to make a clean break."

She lifted her chin. "That the way you want it?"

"It's the way it has to be, Em."

She nodded, a jerky nod he thought looked adorable. He wanted to touch her so badly the ache went all the way to his heart, but he wouldn't reach for her.

She moved to his side of the window so no

one from inside the car could see them. "I want something," she whispered.

"Name it." Lewt didn't care what it was; if it was in his power to get it for her, he would.

"I want to touch you. I want to remember not just how you touched me, but I want to know you better."

She lifted her hands and began at his face, like a blind person feeling her way.

He closed his eyes, trying to memorize the sensations running through him.

She kissed his eyes and dug her fingers into his hair, then moved her hands over his shirt. When he didn't move, or say a word, she unbuttoned the shirt and pushed her hands inside, letting her fingers spread out over his chest.

"You're right. You are hairy, but it's softer than I thought it would be."

He smiled. "We shouldn't be doing this here."

"I know," she giggled. "I'm not afraid of you, not at all. You've told me not to be, over and over, and you've shown me what loving is like, but I had to let you know. I'm not afraid of you."

She kissed him then.

He didn't pull her near. He wasn't sure he'd be able to let go if he did. He just stood there taking her sweet good-bye. A gift of passion. A gift of longing he'd carry with him the rest of his life.

The whistle blew and the lights of Austin came into view. Em pulled away, and he buttoned his shirt before he went back inside.

The group collected their luggage and stood on the platform as Duncan went to get tickets for the north train. Lewt helped the cooks with their stolen goods. He thought of leaving, but he wanted to watch Em for a few more minutes.

Duncan returned with the news that they'd missed the train. Sumner had wired his father that all were safe, and Travis had sent a carriage and word that if they missed the train he'd be expecting them.

"Come with us to my father's house for a drink," Duncan said as they loaded up. "I'd like him to meet you."

Lewt had heard about the famous Texas Ranger Travis McMurray for years. "I'd be honored."

Duncan went inside to hurry the women along. Lewt smiled. In the past week he felt like he'd been near death a half dozen times. He'd fallen in love with a woman far too good for the likes of him, and now, most unbelievable of all, he'd been invited to the home of Travis McMurray. He might still have the dust of the gutter on his shoes, but he was definitely moving up in the world.

An hour later Lewt was standing in the study of one of the most powerful men in Austin. Duncan was relating the story of how Lewt played cards for Em, then risked his life to get her out. They'd all had a few drinks.

Travis didn't say much. He just watched and

smiled now and then at his oldest son. He might be a powerful lawyer, statesman, and judge, but he was first a father.

When the stories slowed, Travis suggested the men join Emily and his wife for a late supper.

Lewt wished he could disappear into the shadows. They were all nice, all friendly, but he knew he didn't belong in a place like this. Wyatt and Sumner had been smart to duck out when they arrived. They were probably where he should be, at the saloon having a steak and telling stories. Lewt didn't seem to be able to even add to the conversation.

When they stepped into a small dining room, Em crossed the floor, ignored Lewt completely, and kissed her uncle on the cheek. "Uncle, are you still sworn in as a judge?"

"Yes," he said. "After what you've been through, Emily, are you thinking about making out a will?"

"No." She looked nervous suddenly, but she lifted her chin. "I want you to make this man marry me."

To Lewt's shock, she pointed at him.

Travis laughed, and Duncan choked on his drink.

"Does this man want to marry you, Emily?"

"Yes, he told me he did."

Lewt couldn't get words out. He couldn't breathe. Even after two weeks she was still bossing him around and probably trying to get him killed.

Em continued, "He told me the first day I met him that he wanted to marry one of Duncan's cousins, and it didn't matter much which one as long as she was rich."

Lewt closed his eyes. Travis McMurray, one of the toughest rangers ever to ride, would shoot him right in front of everyone and clean up the blood before he sat down to supper.

When he opened his eyes, Travis and Duncan were standing within strangling distance of him. "Did you say that, Lewt?" Duncan asked.

He saw no point in denying it. What were the chances they'd believe anything he said? "I did, but . . ." He couldn't think of a bluff.

"He said he wanted a wife and a home and a family. I can be the first part, buy the second part, and we can work on the third part."

"Do you want to marry Emily?" Travis's voice had lowered to deadly calm. "I know you're a gambler, son, but you might want to think about taking this bet."

"I do, but not because she's rich or a McMurray. If she has any sense she won't want to marry me."

"I'm confused." Duncan looked from Emily to Lewt. "Do you two want to marry or not?"

"I'm not . . ."

Em stepped between her uncle and Lewt. "I want him, Uncle Travis. Can I have him or not?"

Travis scratched his head and looked to his wife for advice, but she was laughing too hard to help. "Both of you follow me," he said as he headed back to his study. "Not you, Duncan," he added, as if he had eyes in the back of his head and knew his son was following.

He shoved Lewt and Emily into the front parlor and told them to talk while he drew up the papers. If they both agreed, when he got back he'd marry them. Then he looked at Emily and said simply, "If he doesn't agree, Em, you can't have him and that's final. I know your papa gives you and the girls everything you want, but I draw the line at this."

Lewt heard the door slam, and suddenly the room was silent. He looked into her Texas sky-blue eyes and said, "You don't have to do this, Em. Just because I saved your life or I touched you doesn't mean you have to marry me."

She moved to him, close enough to touch. "I touched you too, so we're even. I figured something out while you were trying to walk away from me. I've been afraid of men all my life because of one bad man who hurt my mother when I couldn't do anything to help. I let one bad man color all men, even though I've been surrounded by good men for years. Then I met you. A good man, not because you saved my life, or put up with me when you knew I was afraid, or listened even when I didn't make sense. You're one good man because you love me just the way I am."

"What makes you think I love you?" They were words he thought he'd never say.

"I know you do because you always let me come to you."

Lewt smiled. "And that show you just put on in front of your relatives? What was that for?"

She moved a few inches closer. "That was to let you know I'm coming right to you, right now, and if you don't want me, you'd better start running."

He couldn't help himself; he kissed her. He'd meant it to be one kiss, but turning down anything when Em was offering was impossible. She was a headstrong, bossy, beautiful woman, and if she wanted his love, he figured he'd been saving it up for a long time.

When Travis opened the door, they were deep into the best kiss Lewt had ever dreamed of.

"I guess that answers my question," Travis said. "I'll get the pens and the witnesses."

Two hours and a wedding later Lewt let her in the side door of the small hotel and up the back stairs to his room. She stood straight and tall, but he knew she was nervous.

"Ever been married before?" he asked.

"No," she answered, looking around at his things.

"Me either." He watched her, still not believing she was his wife. "Have any idea what we're supposed to do?"

"No," she lied.

"Me either." He set her bag down on the table by his few books and papers. "Want to play some cards?"

She finally looked up at him. "Really?"

"Really." He pulled a deck from the desk.

"I don't have any money." She giggled, knowing that he was trying to make this easy on her.

"Last time I played for you, I used my clothes."

She started to relax. "You mean you bet your shirt against mine, your boots against mine, and so on."

He nodded. "Last one standing with any clothes on wins."

"All right." She surprised him.

He dealt the first hand. She asked for two cards, then folded, losing her boot.

On the second and third hand, she lost her other boot and her belt.

"Are you sure you know how to play this game, darling?" Lewt saw her concentrating on the cards, but she didn't win.

She folded the next hand, giving up her blouse.

The next round she lost her trousers, then her socks.

By the next hand, when she pulled off her camisole, Lewt couldn't take his eyes off her long enough to see if he'd won the round.

When the seventh hand was played, she stood and pulled the string on her underwear, and he thought he'd have to give up breathing, for there seemed to be no air in the room. The most beautiful woman in the world stood before him, and she was smiling.

Without a word, she walked across the room and crawled into bed, then turned to him and said, "Blow out the lamp, dear, and come to bed."

Lewt blew the lamp out and undressed in the dark.

Half of him wanted to run for the bed and the other half wanted to run for the door. This woman, his wife, was giving him a heart attack. His chest was pounding and his hands couldn't seem to remember how to undo his trousers.

"Don't be afraid," she whispered. "I promise not to hurt you."

Suddenly, he smiled and walked slowly to the other side of the bed. "I never saw anyone lose seven straight hands," he whispered as he slid under the covers. "You even folded on the three aces I dealt you."

"Did I?" She giggled as her hand brushed timidly across his chest.

"If I didn't know better, I'd think you wanted to undress in front of me."

"No, that wasn't my plan, but you didn't seem to mind." She reached for his hand and pulled it to her.

"What was your plan?"

She laughed. "I just didn't want to see those hairy legs, so the only choice was to go first."

He laughed, finally relaxing. "I'd think as much as you love animals, you'd like my legs."

"I'd just as soon never see them." She tickled her fingers across his chest.

"Fair enough." He pulled her close, loving the way she felt with no clothes between them. "I'll watch you undress every night. I'll even help, and then I'll turn off the light and undress in the dark."

He kissed her then for a long while as his hands moved over her body. When he pulled away from her mouth, he moved to her ear and whispered, "I love you, Emily McMurray Paterson. Live with me, sleep with me, all the days of our life."

She cuddled against him, learning his body as he already knew hers. "And what will we tell our children and grandchildren when they ask how we met?"

He leaned down and kissed the tip of her breast, knowing it would take her breath away. "We'll tell them that I won you in a poker game."

She was laughing when he kissed her again, and they both knew it was time for the talking to stop and the loving to begin.

EPILOGUE

Four days later, Mr. and Mrs. Lewton Paterson picked up horses Duncan had sent down from Whispering Mountain. They rode across the countryside alone. They camped under the stars wrapped in each other's arms and talked for hours about nothing and everything.

Lewt found he knew nothing of loving, but he was always gentle. Each night she came to him willing and ready, and he learned more of her and how to please.

When they'd finished making love, she'd lie next to him and sigh as he moved his hands over her body for a long while, as if he couldn't get enough of the feel of her. Then he'd hold her hand in his and she'd go to sleep on his chest.

"I love you," she'd whisper just before she drifted off.

She'd feel his hand move over her one more time, then settle on her hip. "I love you too, darling," he'd whisper. "Forever."

A week later, when they finally reached the ranch, everyone around turned out to the party. The two cooks proved to be a wonder. They even made a wedding cake four layers high.

Lewt danced with his bride until they were both exhausted. While he poured her a punch he thought had been spiked, he said, "Everyone is smiling at us."

"Maybe they've never seen me so happy," she whispered.

"Maybe they don't know I'm a gambler who stole your heart."

"Oh, they all know you were a gambler. They also know you risked your life for me and you stood by Duncan when he was in trouble." She kissed his cheek, and they heard several people laugh. "They don't care what you were, Lewt, they only care about what you are."

"And what am I?" he said, thinking that he had no job and no hint of one.

"Don't you know, Lewt Paterson, you're a good man." She smiled. "You're the man I love."

He kissed her full on the mouth and didn't care if folks laughed. "No, darling, I'm the luckiest man alive."

They danced another dance and talked with people who'd grown up with Emily, but Lewt's thoughts were on getting her back to the cabin where they were staying and watching her undress before he turned off the light.

When he looked into her beautiful blue eyes, he knew she was thinking the same thing.

He'd gambled with his life and won her heart.

Center Point Publishing
600 Brooks Road ● PO Box 1
Thorndike ME 04986-0001 USA

(207) 568-3717

US & Canada:
1 800 929-9108
www.centerpointlargeprint.com